T0129188

SUBMARINE LOST!

Also by Daniel Lloyd Little and available at iUniverse:

Unheard, Unseen...
Conflict in the North

SUBMARINE LOST!

Daniel Lloyd Little

SUBMARINE LOST!

This is a work of fiction. All of the characters, names, incidents, organizations, and dialogue in this novel are either the products of the author's imagination or are used fictitiously.

iUniverse books may be ordered through booksellers or by contacting:

iUniverse
1663 Liberty Drive
Bloomington, IN 47403
www.iuniverse.com
1-800-Authors (1-800-288-4677)

ISBN: 978-1-5320-1040-8 (sc)
ISBN: 978-1-5320-1041-5 (e)

Library of Congress Control Number: 2016918172

Print information available on the last page.

iUniverse rev. date: 11/15/2016

This novel is dedicated to the men and women of Canada's Armed Forces and the Canadian Security Intelligence Service. As a writer, I have a deep appreciation for the freedoms I enjoy to express my thoughts without fear of reprisal. Thank you to the veterans, to those currently serving, and especially to those who paid the ultimate price, so this great country could remain the bastion of freedom it is today.

Beijing, China

The polluted air hung over Beijing like a dirty brown blanket. Gazing out at it from his office window, an old, but distinguished looking man, remembered how in years past his countrymen had ridiculed the capitalist Americans about the polluted air in their filthy, choking cities. Now, the same thing had happened here, to the city he loved ... only far worse. What should have been a beautiful and bright early spring day, was instead dark and dull. The party members kept telling him that this was the price of progress as China took her rightful place in the world economy. Some progress, he murmured under his breath.

The man longed for the evening walks he used to enjoy in the small park just across the street. That had been before the air quality became so bad, he could still taste it in his mouth an hour after returning to the air-conditioned building. The Chinese President shook his head while straightening his tie and adjusting the simple suit he wore. Perhaps the price was too high ...

"...that is why we have him in Russia."

"I am sorry," he apologized, turning from the window to face the Vice President who had been briefing him. His mind returned to their conversation. "Of course, it makes sense to have him there. If anything goes wrong, the Russians will be blamed."

The ongoing operation was complicated and dangerous, he realized, but the results would propel his country to ... to what? It

1

was far too late to question that now, he realized. The President of China turned back to the window and the view of the city he so loved. "Keep me informed," he ordered, dismissing the Vice President with a wave of his hand.

* * *

Yelizovo Tank Factory, Kamchatka Peninsula, Russia

DAMN!

Instead of coming out as a scream, the word only echoed around inside the young man's head, unable to escape through the bloody mess that was his mouth. Nothing he had gone through in the previous month's survival training in Canada's north had prepared him for this. Intense pain smothered his entire body, as though it was attempting to snuff out the last trace of sanity remaining in his tortured mind.

The room's smell however, still managed to cut through the agony he endured; a pungent combination of sweat, urine, and blood. The nauseating stench of stale tobacco wafted from the mouth hovering inches from his face. Words also emanated from it and he had to force himself to concentrate on each one as wave after wave of pain threatened to render him unconscious. He knew that would not happen, for he had quickly learned that his torturer would ensure there would be no release from the pain that once again threatened to cause him to vomit.

The submariner sat slumped over to the right against the restraints binding him to an old wooden chair. Now, only his torso was bound to the chair's back, barely holding his body erect. There was no longer any need to bind his arms and legs. What strength he had remaining would not be enough to stand on his own, let alone try to escape.

Ugly welts covered most of his body, accented here and there by open wounds, regular blows ensuring they wouldn't heal. His short brown hair, matted with blood, sweat, and he didn't want to think what else, covered some of the bruises on his head while his face was an unrecognizable map of bruises, cuts and dried blood.

"And so my young friend, you see now there is no hope for you."

Although the putrid breath he could feel on his face told him otherwise, the voice seemed to be coming from far away. It carried a distinct Russian accent, and after five days of beatings, Darren was beginning to think the voice might just be right about there being no hope.

"No one is going to break door down and save your sorry hide ... no one!" The final two words were spoken with a strong note of finality.

Had he been able to speak, Chief Petty Officer Darren Cole would have tried to come back with a smart retort. His face, swollen almost beyond recognition, and his mouth full of blood prevented any noise from escaping. The best he could manage through tattered lips was a pathetic grunt. The expectation that he should be dead by now, or at the very least, passed out from the torture he had just endured, kept creeping through the numbing pain.

The figure towering over him began to smile. At least that's what he appeared to be trying to do. Through his one remaining good eye—the other had long ago swollen shut—Darren saw the man's face contort before an evil grin slowly spread over his scarred, ugly mug.

The scarring that covered so much of the man's face had obviously been caused by burn injuries, and as he had done before in an effort to focus his mind on anything else but the pain he was enduring, Darren tried again to imagine what might have caused them. How much had it hurt? It did not appear as though his torturer had received any form of plastic surgery to correct the damage. Once again, he played what had become a game in his mind, creating possible fire scenarios as a coping mechanism to try and think of anything besides his own pain. He imagined the Russian may have been a firefighter who had been injured while fighting a particularly bad fire, but quickly dismissed the thought.

Firefighters are heroes, and this man is no hero. No, more likely the result of a hit on a tank he was riding in; perhaps in Afghanistan when the Russians had tried, and failed, to control that bitter little country. It had been during one of the games in his mind that Cole had decided to name the man 'Ugly Russian'.

"What's the matter, kid? Cat got your tongue?"

The man's lean, muscular body convulsed in laughter at what he thought was a very funny comment. He was probably in his fifties, Cole surmised, and clearly wise when it came to the science of inflicting pain without killing his victim.

The ugly face, so close now, laughed again. The sinister sound filled the room, and Darren's head, where it seemed to bounce mercilessly from one side of his cranium to the other. Through the excruciating agony, Cole managed to raise his head. The light from what he presumed was a spotlight mounted on the wall opposite to where he sat, stung the only eye he could see out of. Trying to focus his remaining eye straight in front of him, Darren caught a blur of red on the opposite wall. Bricks? Or maybe, he imagined, it was the blood of others who had been here before him. He wondered where his nameless predecessors were now. Were they all dead? Would he soon be joining them?

"You Canadian submariners are pretty tough!" The Russian paused to let that sink in as he glared straight into the submariner's one open green eye. "Oh yes," he attempted a chuckle. "We know who you are."

Daren felt a wave of nausea wash over him. No fear there, he realized. He'd long ago thrown up the contents of his stomach on the floor where it had mixed with the blood, his blood, forming a sickening pool of … Look at all the blood; his mind interrupted the thought. If all the blood lying in pools on the concrete floor is yours, the voice inside his mind continued, you'll soon be dead. He found the thought somewhat comforting. Then he would not feel …

'YOU ASS!'

"What? Who said that?" The words barely escaped through his torn lips.

They were the first legible words Darren had managed to speak today. His torturer looked down at his battered prisoner tied to the wooden chair in the centre of the room. The Russian could have sworn a smile crossed the kid's battered mouth.

Through the stabbing pain in his body, Darren saw Heather, his wife, standing in front of him. She was giving him the disgusted expression she reserved for whenever he had said or done something really stupid. Her hands were planted firmly on her hips and she was leaning towards him. Her long brown hair fell forward and he could almost detect the scent of her favourite perfume. He tried to reach out to her but the restraints holding him firmly to the heavy wooden chair barely allowed him to breathe, let alone move. Lifting his arms proved to be more than he could manage. Darren knew what she was thinking though. What the hell was he doing? He could hear her voice inside his head, asking the same question over and over again, 'Why are you giving up?' Then the image faded away.

The Russian looked into Cole's undamaged eye and quickly turned away, recognizing what had happened. He had seen this reaction in captives before. They were the ones who usually died without revealing anything to him. This one, he knew, wasn't going to break easily, if at all. Walking around his prisoner, to an old wooden table a few feet behind the chair, he looked down at the tools of the trade he had made use of so far. They were all covered in blood and bits of dried flesh and yet ... he had not even begun extracting anything of value from this man.

Reaching down, his hand moved towards a small metal box. Flipping a catch on the container's side, he opened it to reveal a syringe encased in a sealed plastic pouch. He would have liked to shoot the entire load of murky, yellow liquid into the young man's veins. Then he would talk, for a short time anyway. But that he knew, would be admitting defeat. He prided himself on the successful use of less scientific methods, and besides, he'd seen what happened to others who had endured the chemical 'shortcut'. At least he left them alive, and sane, for future use. "Well, for the most part anyway," he muttered under his breath.

Ugly Russian ignored the black metal box and instead, grasped another tool. This one was not yet splattered with blood. It had once been a pair of pliers of sorts. Two rows of extremely sharp teeth had been neatly welded along the inside of its two curved jaws. There was no size adjustment. They started with an opening of about three inches and closed until the points lining the jaws meshed together like the teeth of a crocodile.

The instrument had never failed him. Never. He'd only had to show the device to his last prisoner to extract what he wanted to know.

* * *

SEAL Training Base Coronado, California

"WHERE IS MY DAMN BOAT?"

The shout carried clearly through the humid night air at the sprawling southern California navy base.

"What in hell's name," the voice shouted again, "is wrong with you assholes!?"

Six men, barely able to stand on wobbly legs, looked at their instructor. Half of the candidates outranked him, not that any of them would have dared mention the point. At the US Navy SEAL training base in Coronado, California, rank didn't count for the men and women attempting to join one of the world's most elite fighting units. They were considered lower than the fleas that inhabited the sand on the beaches. The man glaring at them, his body silhouetted by the floodlights behind him, looked and sounded menacing—because he was. A few of the candidates had already learned that fact the hard way. At an even six feet, Ensign Stu Cunningham was not the tallest of the men desperately trying to stand still in front of him, and at 26, he was not the oldest. He may not have been the strongest, but if one of them had possessed a physical advantage over Cunningham, it was negated by the instructor's combat skills, signified by the gold Trident crest printed on the dark blue T-shirt he wore. The shirt contrasted with his closely cropped blond hair and the SEALs steel blue eyes pierced theirs, seemingly all at once, as though his gaze alone could break them. Most would swear it could.

This was Stu's third training class since recovering from wounds received during a mission with his old SEAL Team 6 detachment. That expedition, a couple of years previously, had been to destroy rocket boosters on their way to North Korea aboard an old freighter. Everything about that operation had seemed jinxed from the start; culminating with the captain of the Korean ship taking exception to their plan and expressing that displeasure by firing his shotgun at Stu and catching him between the panels of his vest from a few yards away.

Ensign Cunningham had known his operational career with the SEALs was over when his barely conscious body had been hauled out of the Mediterranean Sea to the deck of *HMCS Corner Brook*, the Canadian submarine that had inserted the team. He was grateful though. Some men never made it back. Determined not to be pushed out of the SEALs, or worse, stuck behind a desk, he had worked long and hard to get his broken body back into shape. His superiors had been impressed—impressed enough to allow him the greatest responsibility a SEAL can have—making more SEALs.

A few months ago, during a clearance exercise, one of the candidates had burst into a room inside the training building without clearing it first. Stu had slammed him against the wall in front of the rest of the class and glared at the younger man. "You do that for real kid, and you will put the rest of these guy's lives in danger as they try to retrieve your sorry dead ass!" Then turning to face the rest of the class, he'd lifted the T-shirt he wore, exposing the scar tissue from the shotgun blast that had caught him under his arm and above the vest he had worn that day at nearly point blank range. "See this?! THIS is what can happen when you do the RIGHT thing! Imagine what will happen to your sorry butts when you screw up!"

There had been no more room clearance issues after that day.

"Now, one more time," he hollered, "where is my damn boat? Tell me you assholes did NOT lose my damn boat!"

It was Hell Week for this class at the Naval Special Warfare Training Centre in Coronado, California and the remaining potential SEALs of his class were barely able to stand after the previous few days and nights.

The men were exhausted, beaten, cold and wet. Stu knew this last remaining group of men who had managed to survive the debilitating training program so far without ringing the bell would probably all make it. At some point in the last few days they had crossed over. No longer were they six men trying to survive the most gruelling test of strength and stamina ever envisioned by man. They were a team now, and each man was working his heart out to make sure they all survived this last stage together as a team. Their goal was to earn the coveted Trident insignia which would forever set them apart from all other men and women in uniform and they were so close now, they could taste it.

Two weeks ago, one of the other instructors had overheard a candidate commenting about winning his Trident. The ten minute tirade about the difference between EARNING something and WINNING it had been witnessed by the remaining members of the class. When that same candidate had given up and rang the bell two days later, the instructor had yelled him right out the gate. He could be heard over half the base taunting the sailor that he could always come back when he was ready to EARN his damn Trident!

Stu took a deep breath and slowly exhaled. Appearing to calm down, he slowly walked up to the six men, looking over their shoulders at the water beyond before stopping in front of one of them. The man was a good three inches taller than the SEAL instructor and although the candidate could look down at the top of the ensign's head, he stared straight ahead, not wanting to antagonize his instructor any further.

"Where's my boat, Jenson?" Cunningham's voice was soft and friendly now; his blue eyes reflecting the moonlight bouncing off the waves.

"We lost it sir. We ..."

"LOST IT?" The trainee backed slightly from the unexpected blast, barely managing to catch his balance. "HOW in God's name did you lose my boat?! Do you have any idea what that boat cost the taxpayers, Jenson?!"

Through chattering teeth, the man tried to explain what had happened but before he could utter a word, Stu was on him again.

"Lost it Jenson?" The friendly voice was back now and the SEAL smiled, placing a hand on the man's shoulder. "I understand. Stupid, heavy thing just gets in the way, don't you think?"

"Err … yeah …" The utterly exhausted man spoke without thinking, and knew he was screwed before he could close his mouth.

"WHAT?" The word echoed off the surrounding hills. "YOU THINK THE TAXPAYERS …!"

A shout from behind cut him off.

"Oh hell, Stu. Give the poor, dumb shit a break! I'll buy you a new freakin' boat!"

Stu turned in the direction the shout had come from. He was blinded by the intense glare from the floodlights lining the beach, but in his peripheral vision he could just make out a form casually leaning against one of the light standards. The figure moved, staying within the glare, and started walking down the sand dune towards the SEAL. The floodlights reflected off a clean-shaven head and Stu noted the unmistakable swagger and compact, muscular shape of someone he hadn't seen in a long time.

"God damn … COOKIE! You damn Canuck! What the hell are you doing here?"

"What? A guy can't just go for a leisurely stroll along the beach around here?" Chief Petty Officer Cookie Barnes held out a huge paw.

"Class! Report to Lieutenant Kowalski! Get the hell out of here! NOW!" Stu hollered at them before warmly shaking hands with his old friend. Turning back towards the recruits who were mostly tripping and falling from exhaustion as they attempted to run, he shouted after them, "…and I STILL want my damn boat back!"

The men kept running, grateful for the stranger who had saved them from the dire consequences which would surely have followed the loss of their boat. As though reading their minds, Stu pulled out his cell phone and pressing a couple of buttons, held the device to his ear.

"Kowalski? Yeah, I just sent them over. Can you take the rest of the night? Oh, and they lost the boat in the surf." He paused before laughing. "Okay Len, but don't let them off too easy. Yeah, I'm going to

pass them anyway. At least they didn't set the damn boat on fire like …"
He laughed at the comment from the other trainer before adding,
"Thanks Kowalski! I owe you one—big time!" Slipping the phone back
into a pocket of his fatigue pants, he turned to the Canadian, "Shit,
Barnes! What brings you to California? Your boat down here on a visit?"

"Nope," the Canadian submariner replied. "I was just enjoying
some vacation and thought I'd drop in and see if the holes in you are all
plugged up," Cookie joked. "Guess so from the looks of things. They
actually trust you to train these kids?"

"Of course they do! I'm the best! All plugged and water tight! I'll
easily hold the brews you're about to buy me," the SEAL laughed,
pointing his visitor around the hill to a path leading away from the
water. Gesturing to the briefcase he had earlier noticed the submariner
carrying, Stu added, "Traveling pretty light, aren't you?"

"Wha …? Oh, yeah," Cookie replied, wishing he really was on
vacation. "I have a small bag in the rental, and I brought something to
show you."

The two men hiked over to the command building where Stu had
a quick shower before changing into fresh fatigues and signed out a
Hummer to take them into town. Less than an hour later, they were
relaxed in a booth at Alexander's Pizza enjoying a hand-tossed pie with
the works. Taking another large bite, Cookie wondered how friendly
the cook was. He had to find out what was in this pizza sauce. It was
actually better than anything he'd eaten in Halifax, let alone made
himself.

He had first met the US Navy SEAL during a temporary duty
aboard *HMCS Corner Brook*, when the boat's crew was tasked with
getting the SEAL team Stu was part of over to France. The boat's
regular cook, seeing that he was clearly outclassed in the culinary
department by the gregarious petty officer, had arranged for Cookie
to have free run of the mess and cooking space. Although Cookie and
Stu's rank and age differences would have normally precluded a close
friendship from developing, Cookie's past experiences working with the
SEALs had forged a quick bond between the two men.

"So how are you liking the west coast, Cunningham?"

"Katy Perry lied, man."

"Katy Perry?"

"Yeah, California girls are okay, but give me an east coast woman any day."

"Oh, you mean the Beach Boys."

"No, girls."

"Never mind," the Canadian muttered as he took another huge bite of pizza.

Stu took a long swig of draft, enjoying how the cool beverage felt going down his throat that had become raw from all the yelling at candidates. Then leaning forward and looking at the submariner, he asked in a low voice, "Okay, we both know you're not here on vacation. What's really going on?"

Cookie took his time chewing. If he was going to change his mind about sharing what he considered an unbelievably dangerous plan and not involve his friend, he had to do it now. Once he filled Stu in on the details, there would be no turning back. He swallowed the chunk of pizza, took a deep breath, and began. "Young Mr. Cole has gotten himself into a spot of trouble. I need your help."

Stu's mind flashed back to a morning two years earlier, when seriously wounded and certain that each breath he took would be his last, he struggled to remain conscious. As his team's boat had come alongside *HMCS Corner Brook*, the tall slab sides of the submarine had been more than the wounded SEAL could manage, and seeing his distress, Darren had kicked off his shoes, dove into the water and grabbing the ropes hanging over the side, had pulled and shoved Stu's broken and bleeding body up to the submarine's deck.

The mission to France had run into snafus right from the start when at the last minute, the *USS Jimmy Carter* had become unserviceable and was replaced by the Canadian submarine to insert his SEAL team. From that moment on, the joint US/Canadian mission had run into further snags; by far the worse being the attack on *Corner Brook* by a French SSN.

Stu had run into Darren before the mission—almost literally—when he had nearly forced the Canadian petty officer off the road at a Virginia Beach intersection. Cole had been sent to the popular vacation resort area aside the US Navy's largest base on an exercise. Hoping to spot *Carter* leaving Norfolk Naval Base as part of a joint training exercise, his mission was to report the sighting to a Canadian submarine, *HMCS Victoria*, lying in wait outside Chesapeake Bay. The events that followed had led to Cole being tasked with accompanying the SEALs on their trip to Nova Scotia where they would depart for the mission to France aboard *HMCS Corner Brook*.

After returning from the operation, the two men had become close friends and Stu had made the trip to Virginia the previous summer to be best man at Darren's wedding to Heather Carroll, daughter of the Chief of Naval Operations for the US Navy. Everyone involved had considered their wedding day to be the 'happy ending' of that mission. Now, sitting in the pizza joint, and watching Cookie devour more than his share of the pizza, Stu did not hesitate.

"Whatever you need."

"Thanks man," replied Cookie, grabbing yet another slice and pondering the events that had brought him to this point.

The previous morning, Admiral Brent O'Hanlon had called Cookie to his office at MARLANT headquarters in Halifax, Nova Scotia. The chief petty officer assumed it was to receive his orders sending him back to the west coast after his rather long TDY aboard *HMCS Corner Brook*. When the submariner had walked into O'Hanlon's office, expecting a coffee and exchange of sea stories, he had stopped short upon seeing the look of concern deeply etched in the admiral's face.

"What is it, sir?"

"It's Cole," Brent had replied, slumping down in his chair; his grey eyes examining a spot on the floor to avoid looking up. "He's in trouble, Cookie. Bad trouble."

Brent had gone on to explain how Darren had been assigned to a survival course at 5th Canadian Division Support Base Gagetown up in New Brunswick. Submariners were being sent for the training whenever they could be fit in as the *Victorias* were now being deployed on more 'creative' ops and it was imperative that their crews be able to handle situations that might arise if the situation required them to go ashore. As part of the training, Cole had gone out with a small unit on an exercise in the Canadian north.

"North, as in Arctic north?" Cookie had asked.

"Yes."

"Are they missing?"

"Not all of them."

The admiral's expression had softened and for a brief moment, Cookie thought he'd seen tears welling up in the man's eyes. "They found the army unit. They were all dead." O'Hanlon paused, running a hand through his grey hair. He was clearly having difficulty with what was coming next. "Cole wasn't with them."

"Bad weather?"

"They were shot, Cookie."

"Shit ..."

"There's a huge SAROP running, but it's mostly for show. The Rangers have scoured the area and they report it appears as though something—a ship or submarine—had dropped off and picked up some people. The ice is pretty thin up there this year," the admiral continued, "so there's a lot more marine traffic than usual."

The two men had sat quietly for a moment; each of them examining their thoughts and emotions. Cookie had finally broken the silence. "You wouldn't have called me here unless you had more information than that, sir."

Brent smiled for the first time since Cookie had walked into the office and brought out a large manila envelope from a drawer in his desk, handing it over to the submariner. Sliding out the contents, Cookie had noted an Air Canada ticket amongst a pile of papers and what appeared to be a few satellite photos.

"You flyin' somewhere, sir?"

"No," the admiral had replied. "You are. Today. Your flight leaves in three hours. You have a stayover tonight in TO and you'll be in California tomorrow."

"California?"

After arriving in California late the next afternoon, Chief Petty Officer 2nd Class 'Cookie' Barnes had rented a car and driven directly to the SEAL training base. Getting through the main gate had been quick as the sentry recognized Barnes's name on the submariner's ID card from the day's classified entry list and had waved the sailor through. Odd lookin' bubblehead, the guard had thought, noting Cookie's physique and thinking the guy kept in pretty good shape for his age. He looked more like some of the older SEALs on the base.

Now, after glancing around to ensure no one else in the pizza shop was within earshot, Cookie shared with Stu what he knew about the exercise Darren and the group of soldiers from Gagetown had been on, leading up to how they had all been found dead except for the submariner.

"What makes you think Cole is still alive?"

"The Rangers found signs of someone coming ashore. The ice is pretty much non-existent up there this year."

"A sub?"

"We think so," Cookie replied. "Our people checked your satellite folders back thirty-six hours and there were no surface craft transiting that area.

Stu knew better than to ask what 'people', or how they had managed to get the 'bird's' files. "So, what's the plan?" Stu stretched his legs and scooped up the last slice of pizza, bringing a hurt look to the submariner's face.

"Well, our sources said they've heard rumblings of a Canadian being held in Russia."

"Russia?" Stu repeated, around a mouth full of pizza, nearly choking on the food.

"Yeah, I know; doesn't make any sense. Your guys had a track on an *Akula* up in the Arctic around the same time as Cole went missing. It apparently gave them the slip."

"Damn bubbleheads must be getting lazy."

"Not necessarily," Cookie answered, taking a long drink from his mug. "We have reports that it was probably *K-335*, a *Mark II Akula*. She was used to test equipment and quieting methods for their new *Graney* class and she's a first rate boat."

"You seem to have some mighty good intelligence goin' on there, Barnes."

The Canadian winked and reached for the briefcase he had carefully set down on the seat next to him. The SEAL had noticed he had not let the case out of his sight since their meeting back on the base. Unlocking it, Cookie slid out a photograph, handing it over to Stu who immediately recognized it as a satellite image from a spy bird. Seeing TACSAT-4 in the ID section printed on the photo, he realized that someone must be calling in a lot of favours to get their hands on this stuff. The image showed part of an industrial area in what appeared to be a small city, although he could not be sure as the photo did not extend much outside of a few blocks.

"What am I looking at?"

"See that building?" Cookie jabbed a toothpick he'd taken from the small jar on the table at the image.

"Looks like a warehouse. Maybe a factory?"

"An abandoned tank factory. That's where they were holding him as of twenty-four hours ago." Cookie reached into the briefcase and took out another photo. "This one is of the surrounding area."

The SEAL reached for the glossy sheet of paper and nearly dropped it as his eyes focused on the image. "You have got to be kidding!" Stu sputtered; an incredulous look on his face.

"I wish I was," the submariner answered quietly.

Ensign Stewart Cunningham carefully looked over the image. Someone had written descriptions and directions on parts of the photo, identifying the building as being located in the city of Yelizovo on the Kamchatka Peninsula. That piece of land, which jutted out into the Barents Sea on Russia's west coast, was also the site of one of that country's largest and most secure submarine bases.

"How sure are you about this Intel, Barnes? I can't imagine the Russians think they would get anything out of a Canadian submariner that they couldn't get if they asked really nice," he noted. "We are their buddies now, more or less. Kind of."

"We don't think it's the Russians who have him," the Canadian replied before taking another drink. "We think it's the Chinese."

Stu looked at Cookie, wondering for a moment if he had been a little too quick in agreeing to help. Maybe the submariner had suffered some kind of breakdown and this story was all in his imagination. "The Chinese?"

"I know. You're wondering if I've lost it. Okay, here's the story but once you hear this, you're committed."

"Start talking, Canuck."

"The Canadian Security Intelligence Service picked up rumblings about a Chinese plan early last year. There was talk about a new Russian nuclear boat being hijacked and taken to China …"

"Wait!" Stu held up a hand. "You're telling me the Chinese stole a brand new attack boat from them and the Russians haven't been screaming bloody murder to the UN and anyone else who will listen?"

"Well, if you find that hard to swallow, you're gonna have a whole lot of trouble with the rest of this," Cookie replied, his face set in a deep scowl.

"Okay, go on, but man, this is starting to get weird."

"You ain't heard nothin' yet," the Newfoundlander whispered. "Apparently the plan is for the Chinese to use the *Akula* to take out one of your carriers as a show of force. Word has it that they believe your country is so tied to the Chinese economy now, you wouldn't dare do anything about it, even if you did figure out it was them. With the US Navy unable to protect its own flattops, Beijing would be well on its way to taking over as Grand Pooh-Bah of the Pacific Rim."

"And how the hell does Cole fit into this total nightmare?"

"Remember when *Corner Brook* broke through the Brit super screen around *Ark Royal* a ways back?"

"Shit, Cookie! That was OUR screen plan!" His fist hit the table so hard a fork flew into the air, did a few flips and landed on the floor causing the three people still in the restaurant to look over at them. Lowering his voice, the SEAL continued, "So they want to know how YOUR guys did it so they can slip past and clobber OUR carrier. Damn!"

Stu sat back and took a long gulp of beer before placing the empty mug on the table. "Might as well order another round my Canadian friend," he suggested. "I think this is going to be the last brew we enjoy for some time."

"AND another pizza," Cookie added.

* * *

Yelizovo Tank Factory, Kamchatka Peninsula, Russia

Chief Petty Officer Cole caught a glint of light from the corner of his good eye and instinctively turned his head towards it. The sudden move sent a bolt of searing pain shooting down his injured neck as his antagonist came back around and stood in front of him. Ugly Russian was caressing a piece of shiny metal in his hands and one look at the device told Cole that this sadist intended to do whatever it took to break him.

"So, no needles for you I think. We will …"

"Wait."

The voice came from the doorway and as Darren instinctively turned his head towards the sound, the stabbing pain again tore through his neck.

"He is almost ready to …"

"No. We have received orders that the interrogation is stopped," replied the voice. It reminded Darren of a comedian doing a bad impression of a Russian accent. He tried to move a little to see who the voice belonged to, but the bulk of Ugly Russian blocked his view.

"As you wish. I will return him to his cell."

"Wait. Blindfold him first."

"As you wish."

There was no further comment from the other man as Ugly Russian reached in a pocket for the old rag he had repeatedly used to wipe Darren's blood from his hands, and wrapped it around the submariner's eyes.

Darren pondered the blindfold, which was the first break from the usual routine since he had arrived at whatever this place was. Then he felt the ropes binding his body to the chair being loosened and strong hands helped him to his feet. Barely able to walk on legs bruised from repeated kicks, the petty officer was led out of the room and down the dimly lit hallway he had been through so many times before. He half sensed someone else in the space besides Ugly Russian and himself, but the blindfold successfully prevented him from seeing anything. Halfway to the end, the hands stood him against the wall as they always did, holding him up by the filthy, bloodstained t-shirt he had worn since his capture. He heard a key rattle in the lock on his cell door, making an odd clunky sound, much like the locks on doors leading to the dungeons in old horror movies. That's appropriate, Darren thought through the numbing pain. This experience is certainly turning out to be a horror.

The blindfold was removed at the same instant that he was brutally shoved inside the cell, falling to the concrete floor as the door slammed shut behind him. Again, he heard the metallic clicks of the old lock tumblers falling into place as he was sealed into the room. Bringing himself slowly to a sitting position, Darren tried to ignore the pain threatening to overwhelm him. Above, a single dim light bulb enclosed in a wire basket hanging from the ceiling cast haphazard shadows around the walls of the small cell. An old wooden chair in one corner and a thin mattress lying on the floor were the only things occupying the room other than himself. Once again pondering the blindfold, he surmised that whoever had saved him from Ugly Russian, and that tool, did not want to be seen.

When he had arrived the first night and had been literally tossed into the cell, the reeking stench of the old mattress had almost made him sick, but as the days wore on, he'd come to look forward to laying down and falling into a fitful sleep upon it.

Darren sat against the wall now, trying to piece together the events of the past week. This 'self-review' had become a regular routine. A regime which had been exactly the same every day since he had been brought here. He wished there was something to etch the passing days on one of the walls, but there was nothing. As he pondered his predicament, he absentmindedly started to scratch his name into the soft wood of the chair frame with a cracked fingernail.

The petty officer's days always began in the same way. A sharp yell through a small opening in the door for him to wake up, followed by a dirty metal cup full of a liquid which closely resembled dishwater, being slid through the same opening in the door a few minutes later. God only knew what the foul tasting substance was, Darren thought, but he was finding that like sleeping on the old mattress, it seemed to taste a little better with each passing day.

After what his captors had considered sufficient time for him to eat, the man who he had dubbed 'Morning Man', and who Darren was sure smelled as bad as he did, would unlock the door and once again the submariner would be led down the hall to what he imagined had once been a locker room. There, he was stripped naked, shoved against the wall, and 'showered' with cold water from a high pressure fire hose. The man holding the hose seemed to enjoy aiming the stream of water at any new cuts and bruises which had appeared on Darren's body from the previous day's 'questioning', giving him a head start to the pain that would soon come again. For good measure, his t-shirt and skivvies received the same treatment, enlarging the holes which had begun to appear in the cloth from their mistreatment and continuous use.

Morning Man never spoke, smiled, or frowned. Cole was certain he had been a Mime in a previous life. Whatever he had been, he could sure use a shower, he'd had thought.

After being allowed to dry off with a rough, dirty towel, he would be brought to the torture chamber. Morning Man would then leave him in the hands of Ugly Russian who never failed to great the submariner with a grunt that left no doubt to his disdain for him. Stumbling to the familiar chair in the middle of the room, Darren would sit down without being asked, having learned that such a simple gesture would save him from extra beatings.

The sessions in the torture chamber seemed endless. The first day, he had expected to be questioned every time the beatings stopped, but the questions never came. By the end of the second day, with nothing being asked of him, the Canadian had begun to worry that he was simply being used as a guinea pig to see how much pain a man could endure before passing out.

They must be trying to loosen me up, he'd thought the second night when they had returned him to his cell, but each successive day had continued to be one long, gruelling session of pain. Ugly Russian would methodically go through the motions of torturing him, sometimes without uttering a word. At one point, Darren had asked him what he wanted, but the man had ignored the question and rewarded him with a quick right cross to the jaw.

As he had sat down on the blood stained chair the previous day however, Darren had been surprised when Ugly Russian had left and then come back into the room carrying another chair which he had positioned so he could sit down facing him. The time for questions had finally come, the Canadian surmised. They were routine at first. What was his full name? Where was he from? The submariner had answered those, as the information had all been either on his uniform or with his belongings when they had taken him, or, and it had never occurred to him that it might make a difference, on his Facebook page. To his surprise, after answering only a half dozen, harmless questions, he had been returned to the cell, where he'd spent the rest of the day pondering what was going to happen to him. As he absentmindedly continued to scratch his name into the chair, his mind drifted to home and what Heather must be doing. If he was in Russia, she might be asleep now, depending of course what part of Russia he was in. It was a big country and ... A sudden wave of hopelessness struck him, and the petty officer realized that he would probably never see his wife again. Crawling onto the mattress, Darren fell asleep only to face seemingly endless nightmares of Heather crying alone in their apartment.

Today's session began as it had the day before with Ugly Russian sitting down in front of submariner. First had come questions about *Corner Brook*. Darren had been caught short at first by the use of his boat's name, but that was followed by simple queries they could have found the answers to in the current edition of Jane's Fighting Ships. Ugly Russian had grunted at the submariner's responses, which in Darren's mind, showed his torturer had heard the answer he expected. Then he had leaned forward, bringing his face closer, and had asked about the boat's passive sonar. Cole sat quietly with his lips pressed together. He'd cursed them for trembling slightly although it was more from the damp cold of the room than fear.

Next had come questions about how the crew of *Corner Brook* had 'sunk' a British carrier during a recent exercise and how the Canadians had managed to get so close to the Royal Navy warship. Ugly Russian was clearly more interested in that answer and Cole caught him glancing up at the ceiling at one point, probably towards a hidden camera or microphone that was recording his progress.

When Darren sat there without making a sound, the beatings had begun again, culminating in Ugly Russian shoving the newest 'tool' he planned to use in the Canadian's face. A primeval fear had gripped the submariner's body when he had seen it. He instinctively knew its intended purpose.

That was when the current reprieve had come. Ugly Russian was obviously unhappy that his day of 'fun' had been ended early. Now, as the pain slowly ebbed from his body and he tried to rest, Cole wondered if tomorrow would be twice as bad to make up for it. Reaching up, he massaged a lump on the side of his head; a reminder from his torturer a few days ago that smart-ass comments were not appreciated.

Trying to relax while thinking back to the events before his capture or kidnapping, he wasn't sure which this was, the petty office recalled the survival course with soldiers from 5th Canadian Division Support Base Gagetown. The training had gone well and he'd found himself enjoying the rigours of practicing escape and evasion tactics in the cold northern climate. His mind paused. Those guys were probably all dead.

Darren remembered the sight of their bodies strewn over the ground and the low moans escaping from a couple of them as he had been led away at gun point. For a brief moment, the possibility that this was all part of his training had entered his mind. When they had marched him over the top of a small hill, Darren had realized how much trouble he really was in. Below in the distance, the sail and upper pressure hull of an *Akula* class submarine rode low in the water.

"Shit! You guys are Russians!"

The answer had come in the form of a sharp blow to his skull, and the last sound Cole heard as he had blacked out and collapsed to the ground was laughter. He vaguely remembered waking up to find Ugly Russian standing over him, muttering something unintelligible before hitting him so hard that he had passed out again.

Again dragging his thoughts back to the present, Darren slowly lay down on the mattress. Stretching out his broken body, he begin the last part of his daily routine; moving each finger, toe and muscle to see if everything was still working. As usual, before he could finish, his body released him from his agony and he fell asleep, utterly exhausted, only to be tortured over and over again in his nightmares.

An hour later he was abruptly awoken by the door slamming open with a force so hard, one of its old rusty hinges broke apart and a piece of it landed with a metallic clunk on the concrete floor next to him. Ugly Russian kicked the useless door aside and stormed into the room followed by another man Cole had not seen before. Reaching down and roughly hauling him to a sitting position on the wooden chair, the Russian moved aside to let the other man come closer. His hand carried a syringe and before Darren could utter a protest it had pierced the submariner's neck and he could feel the fluid being injected into his body. Having finished his task, the second man left the cell, leaving ugly Russian standing over his prisoner. The torturer's face was contorted in anger and he quickly turned to leave, trying to slam the door shut behind him, but it just flopped over because of the missing hinge. Even angrier now, he made a show of tearing the door off the remaining hinge and tossing it aside as thought it weighed nothing. Before leaving, he turned and spat back into the room, "Canadian! You are lucky! I would have broken you!"

A minute later, for the first time since Darren's arrival, the light hanging from the ceiling went out. Before his eyes could adjust to the unaccustomed darkness, however, Darren suddenly felt his body go numb and he fell over unconscious.

* * *

LAX, Los Angeles, California

After their meeting at Alexanders the night before and a few hours of fitful sleep, Cookie and Stu had spent the next morning tying up loose ends before embarking on their flight across the Pacific. Emergency orders releasing Stu from the rest of the current course had come through overnight and as far as his buddies on the base knew, he and an old friend were headed to England for a close friend's funeral. Arriving at the airport shortly after nine that morning, both men, being used to the simplicity of military travel, were surprised at the confusion and intense security LAX confronted them with.

"We're looking for the United …"

"What flight?"

The young woman seated behind the information desk interrupted Stu without even looking up. She was thumbing through a fashion magazine and did not hide her disdain at the interruption.

Stu unfolded the printout he had acquired the previous evening from the United Online website. "United 891. It leaves at ele …"

"Straight down to your left," she blurted out, again cutting him off without glancing up from the magazine, while extending a finger off to her right. "The counter will be on your right."

"Thank you," Cookie quickly interjected, seeing that Stu was about to say something nasty to her.

"Man," Stu complained, as they walked in the direction she had indicated. "What a bitch!"

"Probably answers the same questions day in and day out, Cunningham. Cut the poor lady some slack."

"Yeah. She was right anyway. Here's the counter."

Walking up to the check-in together, they smiled at the agent who expressed surprise at their lack of luggage beyond the small carry-on bags they had with them. Having previously ensured they were not carrying anything other than their passports and IDs required at the airport, both men slipped through the metal detectors without mishap, although Stu had given the security guard a disgusted look when asked to remove his shoes.

"It's your funeral," he smirked. "Better plug your nose, man."

"No problem. I'm sure I've smelt worse," the guard replied, his face devoid of humour.

"You know," the SEAL commented when they were out of earshot. "I'm gonna hug the next air force puke I run into after this. This civvy flying sucks."

Once settled into his seat in Row 40 of the Boeing 747 Jumbo Jet's Economy Plus section, Stu had admitted that these surroundings were much nicer than the last time he'd taken an overseas flight on a military transport. That had been a bumpy hop on a Marine C-130 from the Royal Navy base at Gibraltar, back to Norfolk, Virginia. Of course, he reflected, there had been the advantage on that flight of endless leg room afforded him by the stretcher he was strapped to due to the wounds he had received during the op in France.

Twelve hours after their departure from LAX, the United Airlines Boeing 747 made a smooth landing onto runway 34L at Narita International Airport in Tokyo. The huge aircraft taxied up to the gate 33 jet bridge at Terminal 2, where Stu and Cookie deplaned and were quickly checked through customs; their military IDs given only a cursory glance by the security agent long used to servicemen rotating through the country.

"That was pretty painless," Stu commented, tossing the carry-on over his shoulder, "and I got to keep my shoes on this time."

"Yeah, they must have higher pollution control standards here than in the US." Cookie ducked the playful punch thrown at him before adding, "Hey, you really have healed. You move much faster than an old man now."

"You should know old man! So where do we find this buddy of yours who's going to pick us up?"

During the flight, Cookie had explained that someone would meet them at the airport who would then take them on the next leg of their journey. The admiral had not gone into further details explaining that parts of the plan were still being 'worked out'.

"We don't. He's going to find us."

"Oh."

"Don't worry. He'll be here," Cookie answered the doubtful expression on the SEALs face. As they scanned the row of cars outside the terminal for anyone trying to get their attention, neither man noticed a figure quietly approach them from behind.

"O'Hanlon was right," a female voice startled them. "You two do look like a couple of vacationing men in the throes of a mid-life crisis."

In unison they turned and stared. The woman standing before them in a lose-fitting top and tight, but not too tight, blue jeans was beautiful. At five eight, she was slightly taller than Cookie. Locks of reddish-brown hair framed a beautifully sculpted face before flowing in waves to the middle of her back. Her eyes, accenting the colour of her hair, were a deep, sensual brown. She wore no makeup. She didn't have to.

Stu found his voice first. "And besides beautiful, you would be?"

"Ah, you must be Ensign Stu Cunningham," she laughed, holding out a hand in greeting. Stu took her hand in his, holding it longer than he should have, but not wanting to let go. Turning to Cookie, she continued, "And that would make you the gentlemen of the two, Chief Petty Officer Cookie Barnes. I am Yelizaveta Nikolev."

The Canadian took her outstretched hand and was surprised by the woman's firm grip. All he could say was, "From?"

"Russia. That is all you need to know for now."

"So where are we off to from here?"

29

"My car. This way." Her English was concise; carrying only the slightest trace of a Slavic accent. They walked a short distance to an older model light blue Toyota Corolla which beeped and flashed its lights as they approached.

"Nice car, Yeliza-veta?" Stu stumbled over her name, dropping into the front passenger seat.

"Thank you, and please, call me Liza," she replied, sliding behind the wheel while Cookie seated himself in the back and buckled his seatbelt. "How was your flight?"

"Great, but long," Cookie answered. "Security was a pain. It's like they don't want to let you on the plane. That must be really popular with the public," he noted. "Makes you want to just drive instead except for the damn ocean …"

They all laughed at his comment. Yelizaveta manoeuvred through the airport property and after what seemed like an eternity they finally reached an exit. Taking a nearby ramp at a good clip, they were soon northbound on the Tohoku Highway.

"We are going to a small airfield at Utsunmiya. I have a plane waiting there to take us to Yelizovo. It is important that you do not talk when we get there," she cautioned. "My contact believes you to be Russians."

"No problem, Yeliz … Liza," Cookie replied while watching the scenery along the highway pass by. He had never been to Japan and was surprised at how much it looked like home. "Mom's the word."

"Mom?"

"A figure of speech," Stu explained. "It means we'll keep our traps shut."

"Traps? Never mind. I do not want to know."

A few hours later Yelizaveta exited off the highway and drove through the outskirts of Utsunomiya into an industrial area. Turning into an empty parking lot adjacent to what appeared to be an abandoned airport, she pulled up next to a dilapidated old hangar and turned the car off.

"We are here," she announced while getting out. "Remember, as you say, mom is the word."

Following her towards a door in the side of the building, which appeared to be barely standing, Stu rushed ahead to open it for the Russian. Cookie smirked at him as he also stepped through the open door and slowed to allow his eyes time to adjust to the gloomy interior. An aroma of gasoline, oil and an odour he didn't recognize permeated the dank, rundown structure. As his eyes adjusted to the dark space, the Canadian noticed an old white De Havilland Twin Otter parked in the opposite corner. Even in the dim light of the hangar it was obvious that the aircraft had seen much better days.

"Holy shit," Stu breathed next to him. Cookie elbowed him, shooting the SEAL a stern look. Yelizaveta was speaking with a man leaning against the aircraft who they assumed was the pilot. Trying to appear nonchalant, the two men looked over the aircraft which appeared more dilapidated with every glance. One end of an HF wire antenna hung from the top of the fuselage, reaching the cracked concrete floor of the hangar. The tire nearest them had exposed steel belts, and so much oil dripped from the bottom of the left engine nacelle before forming into a pool on the floor, the two men wondered if there was any left in the engine.

The pilot, they noted, didn't appear to be in much better shape than the aircraft. The leather jacket he wore looked to be military surplus from the forties and was covered in patches and repairs, along with a couple of holes and tears still waiting their turn to be mended. He had not shaved in a few days and his hair looked as though it had been styled with some of the oil dripping from the engines.

"Come! Get aboard," Yelizaveta commanded them in Russian, gesturing with her hands towards the Twin Otter's door so they would understand. The pilot crossed the hanger to open the main doors, one of them resisting his attempt until finally it swung out with a rusty squeal.

As daylight filled the hanger, Cookie and Stu stepped aside to let Yelizaveta hesitantly climb the rusted steps into the aircraft, being prepared to catch her if the steps broke off. Surprisingly, she noticed that the Twin Otter appeared even more decrepit on the inside. Only one set of seats remained behind the pilot and co-pilot's position while the rest of the fuselage had been stripped bare except for a few cargo nets. Strapping herself into the co-pilot seat, she could feel a few springs pushing through the thin fabric into her back. As the submariner and SEAL strapped themselves in, the pilot entered and pulled the steps up to close off the aircraft before coming forward and sitting in the left seat. Without bothering to strap himself in, he flicked a few switches and then proceeded to pound on the instrument panel with his fists. Satisfied that the desired result was indicated on one of the instruments, he finally strapped himself in. Behind him, both men were sure this would be the last flight they'd ever make as a thin cloud of blue smoke filled the cockpit shortly after the pilot started the starboard engine. Stu glanced over at Cookie; a questioning look on his face. The Canadian shrugged and looked up as the port engine caught on the third try, sounding like it was about to fall off the wing.

The pilot seemed unconcerned with the smoke and various rattling sounds emanating from all corners of the aircraft as he taxied out of the hangar and onto the ramp. The Twin Otter's fuselage shook violently as the plane rolled over patches of broken concrete. It appeared as though the airport had long been abandoned by the previous tenants and this was confirmed as they swerved to avoid a deserted, rusty fuel truck stuck in the dirt alongside the taxiway they turned onto. With a bone jarring crash and squeals of protest from its old tires, the twin engine aircraft bumped along another few hundred feet before finally reaching the runway.

With no hesitation, the pilot lined up with what remained of the centre line and shoved the throttles forward. Without either running up the engines or speaking into the radio, he released the brakes, allowing the old plane to leap forward, bouncing on the occasional heaves in the runway's cracked asphalt. Just as the two men strapped into the back seats thought a wing would surely break off, the Twin Otter staggered into the air, seeming to hesitate a few moments as though trying to decide if it really wanted to fly. The pilot finally muttered something into the radio; the response an unintelligible noise from the speaker over his head. Hopefully he was receiving flight clearance and not radioing a Mayday, thought Stu, as his hands clenched the ratted armrests of the seat.

Surprisingly, the old aircraft began to climb its way into the cloudless sky. The engines settled into a steady drone, and although the cabin temperature dropped steadily with no sign of any heat source to control it, the flight was relatively comfortable.

No one aboard the aircraft spoke again until a few hours later after they had crossed into Russian airspace. The pilot uttered something indecipherable into the microphone and apparently did not approve of the response, beginning an argument with whoever was on the other end of the radio conversation. A few moments of bantering back and forth ended with a grunted acknowledgement into the mike which was then tossed to the floor. Cookie and Stu exchanged glances; both wondering if a Russian Mig-31 was on the way to send them to a watery grave. The SEAL had found it odd they had so easily crossed into Russia's air defence zone.

His thoughts were abruptly interrupted by the sound of the hum of the engines dropping as they were throttled back and the Twin Otter began a steep descent. Deciding that he had more to say to whoever was on the ground, the pilot flailed around the cockpit floor beneath his seat for the microphone, and bringing it to his lips, spoke the first intelligible sentence they had heard from him.

"RA-362773–Understood. Cleared to land runway one six. Wind one five zero at five."

Looking out the port window, Stu noted the ground rushing by faster and faster as the Twin Otter settled to the runway with a thunk, a small bounce, and finally another thunk as though it had finally decided to stay on the ground. He noted a smattering of jet interceptors parked off to right. Some of them were in about the same condition as the Twin Otter, with rust streaks curving below their sleek fuselages, but as the aircraft slowed, he saw newer Mig-31s, sitting ready, with APUs plugged in and what the SEAL presumed were live missiles hanging from hard points below their wings. All of them bore the Red Star Insignia of the Russian Air Force.

Slowing the Twin Otter to a crawl, the pilot continued down the runway before turning right onto a short taxiway to the terminal building. Interceptors seemed to be parked all over the field and both Cookie and Stu were surprised they had been granted permission to land here at all considering the heavy military presence on the field.

"Welcome to Petropavlovsk-Kamchatsky Airport, my gentleman," the pilot called over his shoulder in broken English. A broad grin covered his face at the shocked expression on both men. "I hope you found flight to be pleasant one."

"Yeah," Cookie grunted. "Great flight."

"You knew?" Yelizaveta accused, slapping the pilot's arm.

"Of course, Liza!" he laughed heartily, showing gaps where teeth had gone missing. "Do they look Russian to you?"

"No, not really," she admitted with a smile. "Come, my friends. We must go before he increases the price."

Climbing stiffly from the aircraft, they walked slowly towards a building where automated doors opened at their approach. Stepping inside, both Cookie and Stu were surprised to find a brightly lit, attractive lounge filled with people, mostly in uniform, milling about. It could have been any airport in the United States or Canada.

"No customs clearance?" Stu asked.

"No, that was taken care of."

The people milling about paid no attention to the strangers in their midst, as Yelizaveta escorted them through the lounge and baggage area to the main terminal entrance and back outside. Looking around at the people standing along the sidewalk, she spotted the person she was looking for and called out.

"Asimov!"

"Liza!"

The man rushed over and embraced her, bringing a glare from Stu. Noticing the look on his friend's face, Cookie smiled at the SEAL. At first glance, Asimov did not stand out from anyone else around, unless you noticed how the polo shirt and jeans he wore accented his muscular physique. Letting Yelizaveta go and kissing her cheeks, he turned towards the two men, his light brown eyes sizing them up.

"So these are Americans?" He asked, while running a hand through his thick brown hair and smiling.

"This one is Canadian," she replied, glancing towards Cookie. "Stu, Cookie; this is my friend Asimov. He is going to help us."

"Good to meet you," Cookie took the man's outstretched hand.

"Yes," Stu forced a smile while sizing up the Russian and reluctantly offering his hand. "Good to meet you."

"Come this way," Asimov directed. "I have a car for us."

They walked towards a group of parked vehicles. Reaching a Lada that appeared to have been painted with a brush and roller, Asimov waved them inside. "The others are waiting," he announced.

"How many?" Stu inquired.

"Two."

"Two ...," the SEAL echoed.

"It will be enough," Asimov assured him, reading the disappointment in his voice.

"Who are they?" Yelizaveta asked.

"Alexski and John."

"Good," she commented, looking at the two men in the back seat. Seeing the concern etched on their faces, she added, "They will be sufficient; do not worry."

"Sufficient," Stu mouthed to Cookie, although he was thinking, not likely.

The Russian drove out through the airport's security gate with a wave at the guards while Cookie and Stu scrunched down in their seats, half expecting a barrage of bullets to tear into the car.

"IL-38s," noted Cookie, pointing to a few of the Russian anti-submarine aircraft parked in the distance on their right. "I'm usually trying to hide from those things."

Less than half an hour later, Asimov drove across a bridge leading into the city of Yelizovo, and made his way through narrow streets to an industrial area. Finally pulling up to what appeared to be a warehouse, he slowed the car down as a loading door in the side of the building opened. Driving into pitch blackness, he stopped inside and shut off the ignition, although the motor continued chugging for a few more revolutions.

"We are safe here," he announced opening the car's door. "You are among friends."

"Sure," Cookie replied, trying to sound as though he trusted him— and failing. After getting out of the car, he stopped for a moment while his eyes adjusted to the darkness. There seems to be an awful lot of dark buildings in this mission, he thought. Just as the submariner was able to make out a few features of the building's darkened interior, three bare light fixtures mounted on the opposite wall came on, temporarily blinding him.

A few moments later, with his eyes adjusted once again, he saw a man walking towards them. His head was shaved and he wore a baggy shirt hanging over a pair of cargo pants that hid any indication of his physique. He was just barely taller than the Canadian.

"John!" Yelizaveta exclaimed. "It is so good to see you again!"

"And you my dear … it was what?" He paused for a moment, trying to remember where they had last met and as it struck him, he blurted out, "Syria!"

Yelizaveta shot him a stern look.

"Of course, I could be wrong," he said, winking at her with his soft brown eyes.

"No wonder we lost the cold war with the likes of you on our side."

They embraced and kissed each other's cheeks. Once again a look of disappointment crossed Stu's face.

"I guarantee she's ex-KGB or whatever the hell they are now, Stu," Cookie whispered. "The SEALs won't buy into that so forget it. Now stop thinking with Mr. Happy and let's get to work, and besides," he added, "she's too old for you anyway."

"You said 'ex' my friend," the SEAL whispered back, "and she is not too …"

"Okay, come," Asimov interrupted. "We have weapons here. John, this is Stu and ... Cookie."

"It is good to meet you," said John, reaching out to shake hands. The firmness of his grip left no doubt that he was in shape. Leading them into an office, he flipped a light switch alongside the door and a bare light bulb hanging from the ceiling illuminated the room, casting strange shadows over a cache of guns and explosives laid out on an old desk.

* * *

Yelizovo Hospital, Kamchatka Peninsula, Russia

"NO!!!"

Darren had screamed out in the darkness, still living the nightmare which had once again invaded his fitful sleep. Ugly Russian had been coming towards him with the torture tool in his hand and a horribly evil smile on his face. Now the dream had vanished and he was awake. Unlike the other times when he had awoken to the sound of his own screaming and bolted up on the old mattress, it seemed as though his body now weighed a ton, and refused to move. Darren fought back the panic that welled up within and tried to relax, focusing on getting his arms, legs, and fingers to move, but they all seemed to mock his attempts to make them respond.

Panic started to take hold. Had he been tortured again and paralyzed? His mind started to clear, and relaxing again, he noticed the smell. What is that? A flower? It felt as though he was drunk and his senses and muscles protested every attempt at thought or movement. There, he could feel his left arm again. Sensations were slowly returning to his body and by concentrating harder, he moved a finger on his left hand, then the hand itself, and finally, he was able to lift his arm a little. Something was wrong though. His fingers were not working properly. Their sense of touch was off. This wasn't ... isn't ... couldn't be the old, tattered mattress he'd fallen asleep on. He was laying on something soft … warm … Wait, he thought, memories hesitantly filtered into his mind. He hadn't fallen asleep. He remembered now. The syringe. He remembered the feeling as a warm liquid had been shot into his neck. They had drugged him. Had he talked? Did he tell them what they wanted to know? A sudden pounding in his head disrupted the attempt to remember. It felt as though a little person inside his skull was trying to pound his way out with a hammer, and through the waves of pain he now remembered how Ugly Russian had come into the cell with someone else. The little man in his head began to pound harder now. Searing pain shot through his body and then … blackness.

Hours later, the submariner awoke again, but not from the nightmare this time. He could hear voices in the room. Darren tried to speak but his mouth would not cooperate. The panic returned. Where they going to torture him again? Drug him? Was he dead? Feel, his mind screamed! Feel the bed. It has to be a bed. It is warm and soft! He tried to open his eyes but they would not move. At the realization that he might be blind, another wave of panic washed over him before he passed out again.

"Has he come to?"

"No," the nurse standing next to Cole's bed replied in heavily accented English. "He begin but fall asleep again."

"Increase his medication by five ccs and monitor him closely," the doctor ordered. He was concerned for this young man. The barbarian, he thought, but dared not say. As a doctor, he could never concede the necessity of torture. I've been at this for too long, he thought, reaching for the door. Then, turning back to the nurse, he added, "Contact me immediately if there is any change, and if he does come to, do not speak to him."

"Yes doctor."

The nurse punched a few keys on the control panel built into the IV station alongside Darren's bed. The machine's display registered the programmed change and satisfied that it was correct, the woman returned to her chair next to the bed and continued reading a book she had found at the nurses station. She had watched over the young man since they had first brought him in two days earlier. As she had assisted the orderlies moving his broken and limp body onto the bed, she had noted that he was handsome, or at least he would be again someday, once the damage caused by those who had tortured him fully healed.

Looking up, she noted that his breathing had fallen into a regular rhythm. The facial muscles around his undamaged eye twitched however, showing he was dreaming. Nurse Su stood and touched his hand. She hoped it was a good dream this time as he had been suffering from nightmares since his arrival.

"Torpedo! Bearing 280 degrees! Zero aspect change!"

"Deploy countermeasures! Emergency blow!"

HMCS Corner Brook heeled over and Darren could feel the submarine's bow rise sharply.

"Damn! It's too close!"

"NO!!!"

In slow motion, the side of the hull collapsed inward and water cascaded into the control room. As the level rose he could see the bow start to drop as though he was both inside and outside the submarine at the same time. It continued to drop lower until he knew his boat would soon be diving to her death. The water rose to his waist and the control room crew looked at him, waiting for him to say something … anything.

"I'm sorry … It's my fault. I …"

Someone was holding his hand as the water rose past his chest. He looked down but in the dream there was no one next to him and yet he still felt it. A warm hand was caressing his. Suddenly *Corner Brook* had disappeared and he felt himself once again in the warm bed. Shaking off the remnants of the nightmare, Darren lay still. The hand was still there. So was the little man pounding away inside his head. He tried moving his legs again and this time they reacted, albeit barely. Slowly opening his good eye, he was blinded by the brightness of the room. The light sent a bolt of pain through his already throbbing head and he instinctively reached up with both arms to cover his eyes.

"Oh!"

The nurse was startled by his hand jerking away from hers. She reached over and pressed the buzzer fastened to the footboard as she composed herself. She was embarrassed by the realization that he had probably felt her hand on his.

"We worry about you and … Oh, I sorry," she apologized, seeing the grimace on Darren's face and quickly moving to turn down the lights until the room was bathed in a soft glow.

Within seconds the doctor strolled casually into the room.

"Well, Mr. Cole. I see you have returned to the living," he announced, a huge smile covering his face.

Darren lowered his hands and tried to open his good eye again. The light was dimmer this time and his eye slowly focused on the room. The voice had come from a middle aged Asian man wearing a lab coat. Small in stature, he had a kind face and his black hair was flecked with grey. Something was written above the right breast pocket of his coat in Chinese characters and what he assumed was the logo of a hospital appeared below them. His English was good with only the slightest hint of an accent.

"I am Doctor Hue Chou and this," he gestured towards the woman who had been holding the submariner's hand, "is Nurse Su."

"You arrive here early two days now." She bowed slightly and spoke softly, shyly brushing the hair away from her face. "You been unconscious until now."

Cole tried to speak but his mouth was dry and all he managed was an awkward cough.

"Please do not try to speak," she held her hand up. "You have been through much but you safe in China now." Her English was not bad in spite of the strong accent, Cole noted.

"Someone from the Canadian Embassy will be here to speak with you shortly," the doctor noted. "Your other eye will be fine when the swelling goes down and other than some fairly bad cuts and severe bruising, you are okay." The doctor smiled at the look of relief in Darren's expression. "Sleep now," he commanded. "You need rest more than anything I can do for you now."

Sleep. The bed was so soft and through the corner of his eye he could see Nurse Su looking at him; a concerned expression on her face.

She was pretty and the jet black hair flowing from under her nurses' cap reached just past her shoulders. He tried to mouth a 'thank-you' to her, but all that escaped his lips was a murmur and in seconds he was out again. This time his mind relaxed and slipped past the recurring nightmares into a deep, restful sleep.

* * *

K-335, Pacific Ocean, West of San Francisco

As Darren fell into a state of near unconsciousness, *K-335* slithered silently through the black depths of the Pacific Ocean. Technologically the most advanced submarine built by Russia to date; the upgraded *Akula II* attack boat was much quieter and far more deadly than all of the previous classes built in the former Soviet Union.

In the boat's control room, the Chinese captain, an unpleasant, little man who ruled over his men with an iron fist, stared intently at the sonar displays which were both his eyes and ears to what was happening outside the thick steel hull of the nuclear powered submarine. He was driven by a patriotic desire to please his admiral who had given him command of this weapon after it had been acquired from the Russians. Perhaps acquired was not the right word, he thought, thinking of the boat's previous crew who were all dead except for a few who'd been bought off and were now commanded by him.

Fortunately for him and his men, the Russian Naval Infantry unit protecting the submarine had been found lacking by the Sea Dragon commando force, and had paid dearly for that shortcoming. He harboured no sympathy towards them however. The Chinese naval officer could taste the bitterness he felt for the people of Russia. Like sheep, they had bowed before the West and capitulated, almost starving to death in the leadership vacuum which had followed the celebrated tearing down of their 'wall'. His own country however, continued to stand strong against the Americans and her Western puppets, and China was now a world economic power to be both respected and feared; something Russia would never accomplish now. With the country's improved economy had come the ability, and finances, to take on missions like this one. Hopefully, the captain thought, this was only the beginning of China flexing her new-found muscles.

The hateful Americans possessed only one weapon with which to flaunt their power worldwide that China did not yet possess; the aircraft carrier battle group, and now he would eliminate one of those thorns in the side of the rest of the world.

Their earlier mission to the Canadian north had been fraught with danger and had his submarine been discovered, would have ended in disaster. Although the Americans and British no longer kept half a dozen nuclear submarines constantly patrolling the Arctic Ocean as they had during the Cold War, the two boats regularly stationed in the area were far more capable than those older submarines had been. His mission had succeeded however, and now it was time to show the United States Navy how impotent it truly was.

When first told of the plan by Admiral Quong Dai at the Yulin Naval Base in Southern China, he'd been taken aback by the daring plot to kidnap a Canadian submariner, and had verbalized his concerns regarding the plan. The admiral had assured him that no one would ever discover their presence and if someone did see them, the Russians would take the blame. In spite of the boat and crew's probable demise, his homeland would still benefit from the adverse press that a Russian submarine discovered within Canadian northern waters would cause.

So far now, everything had gone according to plan. They had eliminated the witnesses who had been with the Canadian submariner. More importantly, no one had spotted the submarine during its rendezvous with a Chinese destroyer to which the prisoner was transferred, and now a team in Russia was extracting the information he and his crew needed to successfully complete their quest. Having the interrogation take place in that country would place the blame squarely on Moscow if anything went wrong, even at this stage.

Zhong Xiao Liu Chong's orders were relatively simple. *K-335* was to remain in its designated patrol area and above all else, not be detected. When the attack information he would use against the Americans was acquired by his comrades, it would be transmitted to him along with the co-ordinates of an American carrier battle group.

Unlike the earlier success the Peoples Liberation Army Navy had enjoyed against the *USS Kitty Hawk* battle group a few years ago, this would not be a 'show' of trailing the carrier and simply coming within firing range. No, he thought, smiling. This time the aircraft carrier would be obliterated.

* * *

Yelizovo, Kamchatka Peninsula, Russia

"Nice," Cookie remarked to Stu, holding an Uzi at eye level. He was surprised at how little the deadly weapon weighed. The stubby little submachine gun had been chopped down even further from its original compact size, allowing it to easily fit inside a large coat pocket or smock. Working the bolt, he noted that although the action showed signs of wear, it still functioned smoothly, and equally as important, it was clean and properly lubricated.

Stu slid a magazine into the MAC-10 he held. Although not his weapon of choice, it did offer a massive rate of fire, and for this mission, that might be crucial. He had smirked upon noticing that every second 9mm round in the magazine was a jacketed hollow point with the rest being standard military issue ball rounds. "Nothing like making sure," he'd muttered, making a mental note to share this concept back home.

"Please take many magazines as you feel you can carry," Asimov requested. "The weapons all use 9mm ammo," he continued, waving his hand over the stockpile. "This way we can share if someone runs low." After they had all selected their guns and pocketed a half dozen extra magazines, he waved them to the door before reaching up and turning off the light.

"Come," Yelizaveta gestured to the group. They followed her outside to an old truck, which like the Twin Otter they had arrived in, had seen better days. Green paint had flaked off in swathes from the sides and faded markings around the doors and fenders indicated that the vehicle had once belonged to the Russian Army.

"Shit," Cookie yelped as the metal step he climbed up on to reach the cargo area broke under his weight, causing his knee to strike the bumper hard. "Is there nothing in this country that isn't falling apart?"

Yelizaveta looked over to him and the hurt expression on her face caused the Canadian to regret his comment. He knew Russia had gone through tough economic times since the breakup of the old Soviet government, but fortunately they were recovering, albeit slowly, with the funds from their massive oil reserves.

"I'll have to diet when I get home, Liza," he joked, smiling at her. Her eyes softened and she returned the smile.

"You look fine."

Cookie blushed at the compliment while Stu gave him a disgruntled look. With everyone aboard the truck, Asimov started the engine and after waiting a minute for it to warm up, threw the transmission in gear and drove slowly away from the warehouse. Turning onto a side road, he continued for a few miles being careful not to push the old vehicle too hard.

As they drove along, Stu pointed out what appeared to be a communications base to Cookie; its many radio towers reached into the sky while a group of satellite dishes, forming a half circle, sat next to a huge brick structure. The old Soviet Navy ensign had been painted on one of the building's walls, but weather and neglect left it almost unrecognizable now, as much of the paint had faded and peeled away.

"Nothing is secret anymore," remarked Stu. "At least nothing in the way of permanent installations. With Google Earth, anyone sitting in front of a home computer can examine bases once seen only by the people working there, analysts privy to satellite photos, and of course, spies."

The rest of the trip was made in relative silence as Cookie and Stu constantly gazed in wonder at sights they never dreamed they'd actually see in person. While they watched the landscape go by, the old truck rattled over roads that nature seemed intent on reclaiming.

Plant life grew through the cracks that spread all over what remained of the asphalt. As the sun was setting, Asimov turned into a parking lot alongside an older, ornate building. Although age and neglect had allowed the building to deteriorate, enough remained of the structure to show that it had once been a fine hotel. Parking close to the entrance, he yanked hard on the parking brake lever and turned off the engine.

"We stay here."

"Nice," Stu smirked. "Wonder how many stars this place has?"

"Not many," John responded without smiling, "but two out of three cockroaches surveyed responded favourably."

They all laughed at the joke and walked slowly up to the dimly lit entrance where stepping inside, they made their way to the front desk. Stu noted that in spite of the building's rundown condition, it really was still a hotel. A large sign behind the check-in desk pronounced that they had arrived at the Hotel Yelizovo. Asimov checked them all in and handed the man behind the desk an envelope. There was no signing of the registrar and the man did not request a credit card deposit from the Russian.

"Looks like we were expected," Cookie noted.

"Yes, you were," snorted a voice from behind a nearby column.

"Alexski! You made it!" John walked over and embraced the man in a bear hug. Although Alexski was shorter than the rest of them, he was built like a small tank. He wore his blonde hair long, almost to his shoulders and his bright blue eyes twinkled as he smiled broadly, belying a serious side that was all business when the situation called for it.

Cookie and Stu exchanged glances, unused to the Russian tradition of hugging amongst men.

"Alexski, this is Cookie and Stu."

"Good to meet you," Stu reached out a hand which the Russian ignored before embracing Cookie.

"You are Canadian submariner?"

"Er ... yeah."

"Good!"

He hugged the portly cook without saying anything further. Stu shrugged his shoulders and ignored the snub. Probably has a thing about Americans, he surmised.

"Now come," John commanded. "We must rest as we will need to be up at dawn to rescue the Canadian."

* * *

HMCS Victoria, Pacific Ocean, West of San Francisco

"Still have the contact?"

"No, I just lost him, but if we maintain this course, I'm sure he'll pop up again."

Petty Officer Alexander Yokov listened intently, his pale blue eyes constantly switching from gazing out into space and staring at the passive sonar waterfall display on one of the monitors in front of him. *HMCS Victoria* was entering the third week of her second post-refit patrol, and her sonar crew had been chasing an elusive contact on and off for the past eighteen hours. Yokov was nearing the end of his watch, and although the chair he sat in was designed to be comfortable over long periods of sitting, it now felt like he was perched on a rock and his butt was killing him. His watch had ended a couple of hours ago, but he was intent on not losing this contact.

The fact that the contact's ID was not coming up on the acoustic database, along with how quietly it moved through the water, made it pretty certain to Commander Rene Bourgeois, *Victoria's* forty-six year old captain that it was probably one of the new American *Virginia* class boats.

"Keep listening, Yokov. Sing out if you find him again."

Rene ducked to avoid a fixture protruding from the overhead. At 6'2", his height was not conducive to submarine duty, and his shaved scalp was adorned with numerous scars from injuries he'd acquired while working within the boat's tight confines.

HMCS Victoria was the name ship of the four boats Canada had acquired just under two decades earlier from Britain. Along with *HMCS Chicoutimi*, which had recently joined the fleet after completion of repairs to damage caused by a horrific, deadly accident that had occurred aboard her years earlier, and *HMCS Corner Book*, *Victoria* formed an important part of Canada's naval force in the Pacific.

Rumours, which had recently been proven true, had abounded that *Corner Brook's* refit had been a preamble to the boat being permanently assigned to British Columbia, as Canada, like its neighbour to the south was slowly moving the bulk of its naval forces to the west coast. The cold war with the Soviet Union was long over and the newer naval threats to world stability were almost all Pacific Rim based, at least for now. Recent activities in Russia were garnering close attention by all NATO countries who feared increased tensions would bring about another undeclared conflict with the huge country.

After the expected teething issues with their reactivation, along with delays brought on by Canada's involvement in Afghanistan, the *Victorias'* were now earning their keep. The 'star' of the class of SSKs, *HMCS Corner Brook*, owned the bragging rights for most of their successes to date, but Rene and his 'Raiders' as the crew liked to call themselves, were determined to change that, especially now that their competition was tied up with her own updates and repairs.

* * *

MARLANT, CFB Halifax, Nova Scotia

Petty Officer Jody Fletcher sprang from his chair as a figure stormed into the reception area of the MARLANT offices in Halifax, Nova Scotia and headed straight for Admiral Brent O'Hanlon's door.

"Sir! Just a minute! You …,"

The tall, unshaven man in wrinkled clothes stopped and turned towards the young man, stopping Jody in his tracks.

"Oh, I'm sorry Admiral Carroll. I didn't …"

"Still doing weird things with you hair, eh Fletcher?" He feigned disgust at the current version of multi-coloured hair being sported by the petty officer. "I can't believe O'Hanlon lets you get away with that."

"Er … no, I mean yes, sir. Please, go right in. The admiral's expecting you."

Shaking his head again at Jody's latest hair colour creation, Carroll threw the door open, his voice booming around both rooms as he entered Brent's office.

"Brent! I got here as fast …"

The rest was drowned out as the door slammed shut behind him. Jody returned to his desk, still slightly shaken by the sudden appearance of Admiral George Carroll. The retired Chief of Naval Operations for the United States Navy had arrived at Halifax's Stanfield International Airport after a nightmare of connecting flights, and had exhorted a taxi driver at the terminal to get him to Atlantic Fleet Headquarters as fast as he could. Recognizing the authority in his passenger's voice, the cabbie had ripped down Veterans Memorial Highway like a madman, weaving amongst the traffic making its way into Halifax, before pulling up to the main gate at the east coast navy base.

"George!" Admiral Brent O'Hanlon came around the desk to warmly shake his friend's hand. "Damn it George, I'm glad to see you again. I only wish it was under difference circumstances."

"Anything new since we last spoke?" Carroll asked before sitting in the chair Brent motioned him to.

"They're on the ground in Russia. That's all I know right now," O'Hanlon responded. "Have you spoken to Heather?"

"Yeah, I called her from the airport," he replied, sinking into the chair as he recalled the short conversation with his daughter. "She's pretty shaken up, Brent. I told her I'd be right over after speaking with you. She begged me to find out anything I can."

"I called her myself this morning and let her know they had landed in Russia but I didn't want to go into any more details. I thought she would just worry that much more."

"Right thing to do," George agreed. "She's been a sailor's kid long enough to know that sometimes you just have to sit and wait. Her mom has been doing that for a lot of years."

"How is Debby?"

"Good. Worried about her son-in-law, as you can imagine." George paused, making a mental note to call his wife and let her know that he had arrived safely. "Any idea how they knew he was up there?"

"None. There is a special team from CSIS working on that. Hopefully they'll find out." Brent could not say any more and was relieved that his friend did not pursue the subject. The Canadian Security Intelligence Service, in spite of recent contemptuous stories in the press, was in fact one of the world's most effective spy agencies.

Months earlier, a communications intercept had led to the discovery of an operation involving China and a Russian submarine. Further investigation by CSIS operatives uncovered more details of the plot and a few non-descript references to Canada. The situation had continued to be closely monitored by the service with regular reports being made to the Prime Minister's Office. Now the men and women working on the case hadn't left their own offices since the first reports of Cole's abduction had come in. Information from an overseas asset was trickling in, but in painfully small amounts.

"I'd better get over to Heather's," said George, his voice tinged with exhaustion. "You'll call if you hear anything?"

"I will," Brent replied, "and George? Tell Heather we'll find him. One way or another, we'll get him back home."

"Thanks, Brent. She knows you'll move heaven and earth to …" His words trailed off.

"We will get him out, George."

"I know you will," he added, leaving the office. Carroll didn't believe that for a minute, although he desperately wanted to—had to—for Heather's sake.

Twenty minutes later, he turned onto Chadwick Place, a short street lined with townhouses on one side and apartment buildings on the other, and found a parking spot in the visitor area of the apartment complex his daughter and Darren called home. Typing her apartment number into the intercom system, he was immediately rewarded with a buzzing sound as the electronic lock on the front door released.

Walking slowly up the stairs, George took a few moments to compose himself. As Brent had just done with him, he would have to try and give Heather hope that her husband was okay and would be home soon. He wanted to believe that would be the case but the same thoughts which had permeated his mind in O'Hanlon's office still dug at him. Darren was in deep trouble and this time it wasn't with him.

The retired admiral thought back to the first time he had met the young petty officer who was going out on a date with his daughter. Darren had impressed him with his manors and more importantly, his genuine respect for Heather. The fact he had lied about his occupation while on a 'spy' mission in Virginia for the Royal Canadian Navy had been quickly forgiven. George smiled as he recalled the afternoon he had attended a briefing with one of the SEAL teams about to embark on a mission to French waters. The Canadian, having joined them prior to their trip to Nova Scotia and being unaware of the position Heather's father held in the US Navy at the time, had been shocked when he had entered the room. The expression on the Cole's face had been priceless.

Darren's relationship with Heather had blossomed and the young couple had been married eight months later at a beautiful wedding on the grounds of the Carroll estate in Virginia. Now as he approached her door, he stopped for moment, pondering what he would say. Before he could form the words however, the door swung open.

"Daddy!" She embraced him and deep sobs shook her body as she clutched her father tightly. George held her in his arms, feeling totally helpless. Looking down at her and brushing the tears from her cheeks, he was reminded how much she looked like his wife had when she was that age. She wore her long brown hair the same way Debby had and they shared the same doe-like brown eyes.

"It will be okay, honey. He'll be fine. You know Darren; if the SEALs couldn't kill him, no one can."

* * *

HMCS Victoria, Pacific Ocean, West of San Francisco

"He's back. I've got him."

"How far?" Rene asked in response to the hoarse whisper from *HMCS Victoria's* sonar operator.

"Three thousand yards. Right on our bow. Damn, he's quiet!"

"Is the range increasing?"

"No, decreasing. Looks like we may have a couple of knots on him," Yokov replied. "I don't know what the Yanks did, but that is one quiet boat. I'd almost swear it was a hybrid." He used the automotive term which had become a joke amongst the Canadian submariners who referred to their boats as 'Green' due to their hybrid diesel/electric power plants.

"Helm, steady on this course." Rene looked over his shoulder to the helmsman calmly manoeuvring *HMCS Victoria* through the depths. He could taste the tension in the air. The entire crew was intent on being the first to bag one of the new *Virginia* class SSNs. For Rene, the ultimate joy would be calling his buddy, Commander Mike Simpson, and asking what he and *Corner Brook* had done lately. Then he would fill him in on how *Vic's* crew 'took out' the American SSN.

A short distance ahead, *K-335's* captain, unaware of his stalker, carefully checked the sonar screens, and noting they had no contacts anywhere close by, ordered the boat brought around to clear their baffles.

"Aspect change!" Yokov announced.

"Helm! All stop!" Rene called over his shoulder.

"He's coming hard right! Really hard!" the sonar operator warned. "Geeze guy, that's mighty Russian of you!"

Commander Bourgeois patted the man's shoulder. "Looks like they learned something from the other side over the decades. The Americans are trying out some of the old Soviet tactics it seems."

HMCS Victoria slowed to a crawl as the Russian submarine changed course and literally circled the Canadians before returning to its previous course.

The other boat's manoeuvre did not sit well with Petty Officer 2nd Class Alexander Yokov. The only son of immigrant parents, he often chatted with his US Navy counterparts during online war games and the subject of the dangerous 'Crazy Ivan' tactics the Russian Navy still employed often came up. 'Ivan' would suddenly bring his boat around in a sharp 360 degrees turn to clear their stern of a possible stalking submarine hiding in the sonar 'blind spot' behind them. There was a high risk of collision using the tactic and this forced shadowing boats to give their Russian prey plenty of breathing space, which is exactly what the old Soviet captains had counted on.

The Americans had also told him repeatedly that there was no way they would ever employ that tactic. A rumour was floating around the American fleet that a submarine collision with an underwater mountain that had occurred quite a few years ago was caused by her captain trying to replicate the dangerous move.

"I don't know," Yokov replied, hesitantly. "I've heard they're not allowed to perform that manoeuver because of what happened to one of the *688s* a few years back."

"Oh?" Rene looked down at him.

"The guys I talk with at Groton say the rule is written in stone."

Rene pondered the possibility that perhaps this wasn't one of the new American boats after all. But if not them, who? A Russian sub perhaps? That prospect didn't seem likely. Almost all of their boats were tracked regularly since the Russian President had begun his sabre rattling as of late. If it was Russian, he thought, it was the quietest Federation boat ever tracked, and worse, they might not be the first to nail one of the new American SSNs after all.

"Okay, Yokov. Keep on him. Try washing him through your cards again. Maybe we missed something there," he said before adding, "Expand the POE by five percent and see what that kicks out."

The 'Probability of Error' was a fudge factor that could be calibrated when comparing the sound signature of a submarine with the acoustic signature recordings on file. This way, a modified boat of a given type which might have a different but similar sound signature from the rest of the class could be more easily identified.

"Aye, sir. Give me a few minutes."

* * *

Yelizovo Tank Factory, Kamchatka Peninsula, Russia

Standing to one side of the building's entrance with his weapon hidden between his arm and body, Stu looked over to Cookie and signalled that everyone was in place. Taking a quick look around the area for anything out of place and satisfied that no one was around, the submariner took a few steps back, and with a well-aimed boot, kicked the door open.

Stu rushed past him through the opening and dropped to the floor; his MAC-10 ready to cover Alexski who literally jumped over the SEAL before throwing himself against the wall to his right. Sweeping the area with his gun, the former Spetsnaz commando saw that the room, which appeared to have been a reception area at one time, was now empty except for a pair of garbage cans. Following close behind Alexski, Yelizaveta stormed into the room with John right behind her; both of them covering the exit in case they would have to fight their way out. Last of all, Asimov entered slowly, cowering behind the garbage cans in case cover was needed for them to escape. His nose wrinkled as he crouched; the cans had obviously not been cleaned in some time.

The space was empty, and the only thing visible in the light streaming through a pair of windows on either side of the room was a closed door opposite to where they stood. Stu rose and slowly moved towards it, hugging the wall on his left. Reaching over, he carefully turned the knob and was rewarded with a click followed by the door slowly swinging out. Peering into the opening, he could see a dark hallway stretching into the distance. Feeling for a light switch and not finding any, he looked back.

"Damn," he whispered, his mind racing back to a similar situation aboard a North Korean cargo ship.

"Asimov, John, Alexski, stay to the right," Stu ordered. Reaching down and propping the door open with a piece of two by four laying on the floor, he noted the light from behind barely lit the space ahead. "Cookie, Liza and I will stay left and ten paces behind you. Feel along the wall for any openings as you move forward."

Moving into position and slowly making their way down the corridor, Stu wished now that they had been able to acquire communications gear along with the weapons. At least then they could have formed two independent teams to search the premises, but if they separated now, he knew that trying to find each other again in the huge expanse of the building would be a nightmare.

They had arrived at the old factory that morning just as the sun began to rise over the horizon. Parking the truck a block away, they'd quickly headed straight for the entrance, forgoing the usual procedure of staking out the area first to spot anyone coming or going. They were aware that, with Cole's life hanging in the balance, time was not on their side.

Now, making their way down the corridor, they were surprised to find no doors breaking the expanse of wall on either side. Reaching the hallway's end, they came upon another door; this one locked.

"It opens in," Stu noted. "We'll have to kick it."

"Wait!" Yelizaveta whispered harshly. "That will make too much noise and we do not know what is on the other side." Retrieving a small pencil flashlight from one of her pockets, she produced an odd looking tool and slipped it into the lock.

"Do you really think …?" Stu began but was interrupted by a click of the lock opening.

"I am sorry," she whispered. "What were you saying?"

"Nothing," Stu replied quietly. "I was just going to offer to hold the light for you."

She smiled and turned the knob while stepping back and slowly pushing the door open. A brightly lit corridor with rusty metal doors lining the walls on either side stretched out ahead. Small openings with bars on each door made it clear that this section had been built to confine people. The last door on the left hung from one hinge, looking as though someone had tried to rip it from its frame. The opposite end of the corridor was open, leading into a much larger room. Odd thing to have in a factory Stu pondered, but then again, this building did date back to the old Soviet Union.

Realizing Darren could be in one of the cells, Cookie's heart was racing. Checking first for any kind of security camera or detection system and not seeing any, he entered the hallway followed by the rest, slowly opening the doors which all turned out to be unlocked. Peering into each of the darkened cells, they found the small rooms were all empty, except for the last one with the damaged door. A well-worn mattress lay on the floor and an old wooden chair leaned against one wall. A strong, pungent odour of human waste and sweat permeated the room, indicating that someone had recently been detained there.

"Damn!" Stu exclaimed, pointing down at the chair. "Look!"

Five pairs of eyes followed to where his finger pointed at the letters DARRE, crookedly scratched into the chair's frame.

"Has to be him." Cookie stated firmly.

"Perhaps," Alexski noted, "but let us continue search."

Leaving the cell and moving towards the opening at the end of the hallway, they entered what had once been a locker room. Rows of battered lockers lined the walls on both sides with their doors hanging open or laying on the painted concrete floor below. A few crude wooden benches sat haphazardly around the room; most of them knocked over, and one reduced to splinters. Again, because of the lingering odour, it appeared someone had been here recently, but also because a dirty, still damp towel hung over one of the benches in the middle of the floor. A fire hose lay coiled in a corner nearby with water dripping from its nozzle, and although none of them spoke it, they all surmised what it had been used for.

The locker room stretched out over a hundred feet from the hallway before ending in a large brick wall on which the old Soviet flag had once been painted. Its hammer and sickle were barely visible now; the paint mostly fallen away, forming a small pile of red flakes on the floor. Below the faded image of the banner, a single door, slightly ajar, beckoned to them. Moving cautiously with their guns ready, Stu, John, and Asimov approached the opening, crouching along the rows of lockers on either side of the room. Alexski and Yelizaveta remained by the entrance to cover the opening behind them, least someone come from that direction. Cookie took up station behind one of the benches where he would have a clear field of fire in either direction.

Watching for any movement through the narrow opening, Stu moved further along the wall of lockers, stopping a few feet away from the doorway. The space inside was brightly lit but all he could make out through the small opening in the door was a wooden work table against the back wall. Moving closer, he listened for a few moments, and hearing nothing, signalled John and Asimov that he was going in.

Diving at the door, and shoving it open hard, he dove to the floor and was surprised to find himself sliding in a slippery liquid which seemed to coat the bare concrete surface in the middle of the room.

"Shit!"

Quickly scanning the room, he yelled, "Clear!"

Entering slowly, his eyes scanning the scene; John looked at the SEAL and started to say something when Stu cut him off.

"Yeah, blood. Lots of it," he noted, gesturing at two bodies lying slumped against the wall to the right. Both men had been shot once in the back of the head by a large calibre round and their faces were literally blown away. Asimov walked over to a chair lying on its side in the middle of the room as Stu reached down to set it back on its legs. The chair had been modified with leather fastenings and ropes to constrain a person. Patches of dried blood covered the chair, and the floor around where it had lain was covered with blood spatters. Thick pools of blood which had flowed from the corpses, and had sent the SEAL sliding across the room, covered the rest of the floor.

Kneeling to examine the dead men, Asimov checked their pockets and as he expected, found them empty.

"The men have each been shot once and there is no other apparent harm to the bodies. The blood there," he waved at the chair, "is not theirs."

"I have a feeling we won't find anyone else in here," said John.

"Yeah," Stu remarked, disturbed by the gory scene. "I think you're right."

After returning to the truck, they watched the building's main entrance for almost an hour in case someone showed up until finally Cookie hit the dash with his fist so hard, he left a small dent in the green metal.

"I KNOW he's not dead!"

"I know, Cookie. I know," Yelizaveta responded, reaching over and touching his shoulder. "We will go back to the hotel. Hopefully there will be word."

"Word?" Cunningham asked.

"Yes, Stu," she smiled. "Word."

They drove back in silence, each of them picturing in their mind's eye what might have taken place in the blood covered room.

* * *

Yelizovo Hospital, Kamchatka Peninsula, Russia

Darren awoke, and remembering where he was, lay still, enjoying the warm comfort of the hospital bed. His head was finally beginning to feel clear for the first time since one of the Russians had clubbed him back in northern Canada. Slowly opening his good eye, the submariner was pleasantly surprised to find both of them working. A wave of relief washed over him as he lifted his head slightly to examine his surroundings. There was an older man reading a newspaper sitting in the chair Nurse Su usually occupied. Dressed in a dark blue suit, he was the first Caucasian Darren had seen since arriving at the hospital.

"Who are you?" Cole asked, surprising himself with the strength and clarity of his voice. The long sleep had obviously done him some good. Startled by the unexpected sound, the man dropped his paper and jumped up from the chair.

"Good morning, petty officer!" He reached out a hand; his thin, pimple scarred face reminding the submariner of a politician out on the hustings. "It is so good to see you awake!" The man's smile seemed genuine. Almost.

"Frankly, forget awake," Darren responded, shaking the stranger's hand. "It's just good to be alive."

"I am sure it is, Mr. Cole. I am the Charges d'affaires assigned to the Canadian Embassy here in Beijing. Anthony Westmorland; at your service, sir." His voice conveyed a great deal of pride in his position. "Ottawa has been negotiating for your release between the Chinese and Russians for a few days now," he noted with even more haughtiness, "and after much effort, we successfully managed to secure your freedom."

"Thank you," Darren replied, his voice dropping as the realization that he was finally safe and would soon be going home flooded his thoughts.

"You are quite welcome. The Prime Minister's Office made it quite clear that we were not to cease pushing for your release until we had you safely on Chinese soil."

"Please thank him for me," Darren replied sincerely. That meant he had been in Russia, as he had surmised from Ugly Russian's accent. "Would it be possible to speak with my wife?"

"Not yet Mr. Cole, but soon. The Chinese would like to debrief you first. They are concerned about what kind of information the Russians were after and we have assured them that they would have your complete cooperation. This was of course cleared through both the Minister of Defence and Chief of the Defence Staff," he added.

"I understand. Does Heather know I'm safe?"

"Oh yes, of course! She was notified the moment your plane landed and she is quite thrilled at your release!"

Darren relaxed, knowing that she must have been worried sick over his disappearance. Then he remembered. "The others who were with me ..." His voice trailed off.

"I am sorry Mr. Cole." He paused, a look of angst in his eyes. "I'm afraid they are all dead. It appears the Russians were only interested in keeping you."

A feeling of helplessness washed over Darren as he recalled the time spent training with the small group of soldiers from Gagetown. After much good natured ribbing about the chance a submariner would have surviving in the real world, the troops had quickly grown to like him. More so, they had been impressed by his willingness and capacity to learn their trade. A strong friendship had developed amongst them during their short time together, and plans had been made for a party in Halifax when the exercises were completed.

Cole's indoctrination had begun at the sprawling 5th Canadian Division Support Base in Gagetown, New Brunswick, where he had received three weeks of basic survival skills training. Next had come, as the instructor jokingly put it; 'Learnin' to leave a perfectly good airplane for no good reason!' After successfully completing three jumps, he and the rest of the class, who were going through the course as a refresher, were flown north in a CC-130 Hercules transport aircraft where they would test their skills in the frozen lands of Nunavut. Cole remembered how not long after they had set up camp on the fourth day, while joking about the quality of their survival rations around a roaring fire, the Russians had materialized out of nowhere; their AK-74s pointed at the Canadians.

Darren had been immediately singled out and separated from the soldiers before being led away. A few minutes later he'd heard short bursts of automatic rifle fire behind him, followed by silence. With only small LED lights showing the way in front of them and guided by a handheld GPS, his captors moved quickly, prodding the submariner along over the uneven ground. Finally, stopping at a location where they had left supplies earlier, Darren had been given a small amount of food. Noting the Cyrillic writing on the packages which were similar to the MRE's his group had carried with them, he knew enough to accept the meal. Only movie heroes refused food and water in this kind of situation.

After eating, the men had sat around talking, ignoring their captive. Cole understood a stray Russian word here and there, but nothing which explained the reason for his capture. One of the men, apparently their leader, had stood a few moments later and uttered a command. The others got up and one of them motioned to Darren with the barrel of his weapon to stand and start moving.

Just under an hour later they had walked over a hill, and off in the distance, Darren could see the coast, and beyond that, a submarine laying low in the water. After that had come the blow to his head and what he assumed must have been days later, his arrival somewhere in Russia. The missing piece to all of this was why? In spite of all the rhetoric from Moscow as of late, Russia was, more or less, on good terms with the West. The Embassy official speaking broke through the submariner's thoughts.

"Again, I am sorry. There was a burial with full military honours for them and they were all laid to rest at the National Cemetery in Ottawa," he continued in a solemn tone. "Their families were flown in and they all attended the service. I was able to view it on satellite television. The Prime Minister was there as well as the Governor General."

"That's good. They would have liked that." Darren looked down, trying to fight back the tears welling up in his eyes. Through the emotional pain, something was eating at him. Something in what the man had said, but he couldn't put his finger on it. He looked up at Westmorland. "How long was it before they realized I was still alive?"

"Oh, they expected you were alive the minute they discovered you missing, Mr. Cole." He responded with the same note of self-confident back in his voice. "When you were not found with the rest of the soldiers, Ottawa was pretty certain you were alive and had been taken prisoner."

Darren knew all hell would have broken lose when the men he had been with were found dead, and more again when they realized he was not amongst them. Heather would have been devastated when they told her the news.

He remembered the moment when, during one of the beatings, she had 'appeared' in his thoughts. He knew she had somehow connected with him at that moment and that it had saved his life. Ugly Russian's eyes had shown disappointment in the expression he saw on the submariner's face. Although his tormentor had tried to hide it, Cole knew that for the moment at least, he had won.

"How much longer before the Chinese ..."

His sentence was interrupted by Doctor Chou entering the room followed by two older men, both looking uncomfortable in badly fitting suits. "Good day, Mr. Cole," the doctor greeted him. "These men are from the Chinese Government and will be conducting your interview. I present Mr. Wei Kuai and Mr. Dong Seto. They are with our Foreign Service and wish you to be comfortable during your talk with them."

They both shook Darren's hand warmly as their names were announced. Darren smiled up at them and resisted the urge to ask how the spy business was these days. He couldn't help but think of Laurel and Hardy as one of the 'spies' was tall and slim while the other was short and fat, complete with a little moustache.

"We have prepared a room down the hall where you may be comfortable while they speak with you," Doctor Chou continued. "Do you feel able to stand?"

Getting up carefully, Darren gingerly stood beside the bed; steadying himself against it. The pain from his many wounds, along with the long time spent recuperating in bed, made him a little queasy.

"I think I'll be okay. I really want to try and walk."

"Fine, but please be careful," the doctor replied, watching carefully for any sign of duress from the submariner. "Please accompany me this way."

Thankfully, Darren noted, everything seemed to be working and he slowly followed the doctor out of the room into a spacious corridor, with the two men trailing closely behind.

Kuai stopped abruptly and turned towards the Canadian Embassy official. "Would you come with us as well, please, Mr. Westmorland? Our government would like you present to observe that the interview is conducted properly."

"Yes. Of course," Westmorland replied, apparently surprised by the request and quickly joining the men in the corridor.

The doctor led them down the hallway a short distance, stopping at a door he unlocked with a key from his pocket. Standing aside, he waved them all into the room which Darren saw was furnished with comfortable chairs and a large table. An ornate silver tray with matching tea and coffee pots surrounded by cups and saucers sat upon a stand in one corner. As they all found a place to sit, Nurse Su entered the room and asked around as to what the men would like to drink.

Darren looked up at her and asked for a cup of coffee, bringing a smile to her face. Later, as the men relaxed with their beverages, she left the room, closing the door behind her. Doctor Chou was the first to speak. "Mr. Cole, if you feel uncomfortable or ill at any time, please let me know and we will bring the interview to an end."

"Thank you, doctor," Darren replied. "I appreciate your concern but I feel fine. Please go ahead gentlemen, but first, I wish to thank you for your help getting me out of Russia."

"Petty Officer Cole, you are most welcome and we congratulate you on your freedom," Mr. Kuai responded. "The Russians were not impressed with our stepping in and demanding your release. Our negotiating team indicated that they were unhappy, leading us to believe that you did not disclose the information they were looking for."

"Not that they didn't try," the Canadian commented before sharing his experiences with them. They appeared genuinely disgusted while he recounted the numerous beatings, and Westmorland visibly paled when Darren described the device Ugly Russian was about to use on him.

* * *

USS Enterprise, San Diego Harbour, California

Halfway around the world, off the coast of Southern California, the sun glinted off the small waves rolling across the water just outside San Diego Bay.

"Sir, we have cleared the outer harbour buoy."

"Thank you, Mr. Douglas. Helm, bring us left to heading three one zero."

The *USS Enterprise's* captain could not help but smile. Exiting the harbour had gone perfectly, and with all of the pre-departure ceremonies behind them now, he and the crew could get down to business. Looking out the row of windows lining the front and sides of the ship's bridge, he could see large groups of people lining the shore trying to get a glimpse of the carrier as it sailed out of San Diego harbour for the last time. Besides the usual family and friends of the ship's crew, a large number of other spectators waved towards the ship along with a smattering of reporters and camera crews. They stood upon every available perch and snapped pictures and video as the carrier began to pick up speed; the eight Westinghouse nuclear reactors buried deep in her hull creating the steam necessary to drive the huge ship. One older man in the crowd of people, his worn and weather beaten leather aviator's jacked covered in patches denoting half a dozen different navy squadrons, looked up at his son standing beside him and smiled.

"She looks good. I'm glad they stopped here on the way over to Norfolk," he noted before adding. "I'd rather not see her after they're done."

USS Enterprise, CV-65 or as he and his buddies had called her back during their deployment to Vietnam, *The Big E*, was sailing from San Diego under her own power for the last time. The largest aircraft carrier in the US Navy was heading for the east coast, where, after a decommissioning ceremony in Norfolk, Virginia, the ship would be brought alongside at the sprawling Newport News shipbuilding facility where everything that could be removed, along with her nuclear fuel, would be taken from the ship until all that remained was an empty, lifeless hulk. Afterwards, the remains of the once proud warship would be towed back to the west coast to be cut up for scrap—recycled they called it these days, the old man knew—and what had once been the second oldest commissioned ship in the US Navy, would soon become a distant memory, as those other '*Enterprises*' had before her. The aircraft carrier, as usual, was the last of the battle group to leave port and everyone, even if they had no friends or family aboard the majestic ship, had waited to see the huge, gray beast slowly make her way past the breakwaters. Unknown to all but a half dozen officers on the bridge however, the carrier and her escorts would not be heading straight to Norfolk—not yet.

Unnoticed amongst the throng of people, a man of Asian descent sitting on a park bench just below the Old Point Loma Lighthouse, casually put down the paper cup of fries he had been holding and turned on his cell phone. Bringing up a number from the phone's memory and dialing, he then typed a five letter code on the keypad, pressed the send button, and casually returned the phone to his shirt pocket. Tossing the remaining fries at a pair of seagulls who had been hungrily staring at them since he had sat down, the man smiled as they began to fight over the greasy morsels. Dropping the now empty cup into a nearby trashcan, he slowly walked back along the pathway to his car, stopping now and then to turn and watch the warship slowly fade from sight over the horizon.

Aboard the subject of the man's attention, surveying the area around him from his perch in the commanding officer's chair, Captain Nelson Craig felt the familiar tensioning in his muscles as the ship began to plough into the Pacific Ocean swells. They would stay that way until the ship was tied up again at her destination, assuming she made it there. Whoever had come up with this plan should have their head examined he thought, turning to the young sailor manning the ship's wheel.

"Helm, increase speed to ten knots."

"Increasing speed to ten knots, aye," responded the seaman holding the ships wheel.

An hour later, the ships of *Enterprise's* ceremonial battle group, supposedly running a combination NAVEX and special escort for the old carrier's final cruise, had reached their positions spread out over a dozen square miles of ocean, their weapons systems fully armed and manned. Unlike World War II, when carrier task forces kept their escorts snuggled in close to the flat-top to afford extra anti-aircraft fire for her protection, the modern carrier battle group's ships sailed almost out of sight of one another. The speed and technology of today's weapons necessitated that the formation be able to deal with threats long before the carrier was in sight. If the enemy was able to get close enough to see the ship, it was too late to save her.

On *Enterprise's* flight deck where her knockout punch would normally be parked from bow to stern, two older model E-2C Hawkeyes were tied down alongside a row of MH-60F Oceanhawks, pulling double duty as hacks and submarine killers.

Also part of the battle group, but not seen by the crowds ashore as she had already been out on patrol when the her assignment had arrived, the *USS Hawaii*, a *Los Angeles* class fast attack submarine, cruised below the surface of the ocean a few miles ahead of *Enterprise*, her sonar crew on a constant lookout for anything that might pose a threat to the carrier.

As *Enterprise's* captain settled into his chair with a steaming cup of coffee, he glanced down at the surface radar repeater in front of him and noted only his own ships showing on the screen. So far, everything was going fine, he thought. He was not happy with this mission, but like his father had before him, and his father's father before him, he would follow orders. Although he appreciated why *Enterprise* had been selected for this mission, Craig felt the nuclear powered aircraft carrier was far too valuable historically to be used as bait. Like many others, he had his fingers crossed that something could be done to turn his ship into a museum; a shrine perhaps to the thousands who had catapulted from her decks into harm's way.

"Well, it's time to upset the VIPs," he noted to the XO, who had been watching the radar repeater as the last of the escorts took their positions. "Send to *Spruance*; enact engineering casualty and return to Diego."

The special guests and VIPs aboard the Arleigh Burke class destroyer would not be happy that their cruise escorting *Big E* for a few hours was about to be cancelled due to a mechanical failure, Craig knew. But if they had any idea what was waiting out there, they'd probably jump off the ship and swim back to California.

* * *

Hotel Yelizovo, Kamchatka Peninsula, Russia

In Russia, emotions were running high among the insertion team after not finding Petty Officer Cole at the tank factory. Parking the truck behind the hotel, John shut off the motor, exhaled a deep sigh and looking over at Stu, sank back into the tattered seat while Alexski climbed out and headed for the hotel's rear entrance.

"Yeah, I know what you mean," Stu muttered, reading the disappointment in the Russian's face. "That wasn't what I was expecting to find either. Maybe they knew we were coming."

"Maybe," Cookie replied from the truck's back seat, removing the magazine from his Uzi and clearing the gun's action. "They didn't even dump their stuff though. It's as if they didn't care whether anyone came across it."

Discovering the torture tools in the blood splattered room had come as a shock. When Cookie had opened the box he'd found sitting on the bench and seen the pliers-like device inside, he had dropped it to the floor. A flood of relief had struck him as he noted that unlike the other items laid out on the work table, this one was clean and not covered with bits of flesh and dried blood.

"Come," Yelizaveta touched Cookie's shoulder, interrupting the gruesome picture in the submariner's mind. Gently nudging him out of the truck, she added, "We will sit inside and discuss our next action."

"I don't know, Liza. He could be anywhere by now."

"No, he is somewhere close. This is still a secure military area and they could not move him around easily. We will be told," she added; a slight smile crossing her lips.

"I wish I had your confidence," Stu responded while handing his MAC-10 over to Cookie, who safely stored it along with his own weapon in the truck's toolbox. As they headed up the steps to the hotel and reached the door, it opened, and Alexski stepped outside.

"Liza, there is message for you," he said, handing her a folded piece of paper.

She took the note and read it; a concerned expression momentarily crossing her face. "Okay, I will go now. All of you get some rest," she commanded. "We will be moving again soon."

"What is it?" Cookie asked, having caught the guarded look on her face.

"I will return soon."

Yelizaveta climbed back into the truck and drove quickly from the parking lot. Cookie and Stu exchanged troubled glances and headed into the hotel.

"She will be fine," John assured them. "Come. Have some coffee with me. It is time I properly introduce you to our little group."

Entering the dining area, they sat together at a table in a corner of the room, opposite the entrance. The ornate carvings and fine details adorning the walls and ceilings indicated that this had once been a rather swank spot, Stu noticed. None of the other tables were occupied and once they sat down, an older woman came and took their order. She returned within minutes with two pots of coffee and a tray of old mugs. She did not offer to bring cream or sugar and there was none of either on any of the tables.

"I guess we drink it black," Stu noted with a smirk.

"Black?" Asimov asked.

"The coffee."

"You have coloured coffee in America?"

"Err, no," Cookie explained. "We sometimes add cream or sugar to it."

"Why?"

"Never mind. We're just weird that way. So, John," he began, changing the subject, "you were saying something about introductions?"

"Ah yes; proper introductions." John took a long sip of coffee and lowered the cup slowly as though he was pondering what words to use. "Asimov and Alexski here were both with Spetsnaz before their units were eliminated—no, that is not the word—they were what you call 'downsizing' I believe."

"But Russian army is growing strong again and I expect to be back with my comrades again soon," Alexski quickly added. He was proud of his country, and clearly did not want the foreigners to think it weak.

"Yes," John continued. "Alexski comes from a long line of soldiers. His father was ..." He stopped in mid-sentence, trying to find the right words.

"Killed!" Alexski finished the sentence while glaring directly at Stu. "He was killed by American SEALs in Vietnam while helping unification."

Stu looked at him, not knowing what to say. Now he understood the reason for the cool reception he had received from the Russian earlier. "I'm sorry ..."

The room was silent for a few moments but the tension in the air made it seem like an hour.

"No." Alexski sighed, "It is not your fault, Stu. It was long time ago. A different time." The Russian stood and slowly reached his hand out to the SEAL, who instead of taking it, came around the table towards him, causing the Russian to take a step back.

"I've learned one thing since arriving here," Stu said, before grabbing Alexski in a huge bear hug. The tension between the two which had hung heavy in the air since they'd met, melted away. As the two men returned to their coffee, John continued.

"Asimov, on the other hand, is happy with his departure from the army and has become an independent. He is for hire but not by just anybody." John laughed, clapping his friend on the shoulder. "He is what you call a soldier of fortune, but a picky one."

"You are upset that you still work for living," Asimov accused him jokingly.

"Perhaps you are right. So, now it is my turn. I am with the FSB and ..." He laughed heartily at the reaction on both Stu and Cookie's faces. "Oh do not worry my friends! I am here under orders from high up."

"Yeah okay," said Cookie, although he didn't really think that it was okay. When the KGB was disbanded about the same time as the Soviet Union, it had been replaced by a new security organization, the Federal Security Service of the Russian Federation or FSB. Some thought it every bit as ruthless as its predecessor, the KGB, and the jumble of other organizations which had been dissolved into the new organization. O'Hanlon must be aware of what was going on and who they are working with over here, he realized, and this did answer one nagging question which had been troubling him and Stu since their arrival. Why they hadn't been stopped by security forces as they arrived at the airport and traveled around the city.

Since John was here with the FSB's blessing, thought Cookie, this operation must be really high profile on both sides of the ocean. "So, John," Cookie began, looking him straight in the eye. "How did FSB get involved in this? I was under the impression that we were flying under the radar here."

"We are," replied John. "But your Admiral O'Hanlon has some friends in high places in the Russian military."

"High places?"

"Very high places."

* * *

MARLANT, CFB Halifax, Nova Scotia

As Cookie's was wondering just how high 'very high' was, at MARLANT headquarters in Halifax, NS, Petty Officer Jody Fletcher was about to find out. He was reaching for a file on his desk when the door leading in from the foyer swung open and a man he did not recognize walked in with a Military Police officer following closely behind. Slightly overweight and wearing a rumpled, older style suit, the burley stranger looked like a character from an old 30's gangster movie. Jody stood and came around his desk, ready to assist the MP as it appeared from the expression on his face that the 'gangster' might be trouble.

"Can I help you find …?"

It was all Jody was able to get out before the door behind the 'gangster' and MP opened again and a tall, muscular man wearing the uniform of a Russian general walked in. Ignoring both the MP and the gangster, the general walked over and stared down at the petty officer who had come to rigid attention upon seeing the single large star on the man's shoulder boards. Not sure what general rank that translated to in the Canadian military, Jody realized that regardless, it was far above his pay grade.

"At ease petty officer," the man commanded in a heavily accented voice while removing his hat. Then smiling at the young man's hair, he held out his hand. "You must be Jody Fletcher."

"Yes, sir …" Jody's face was a contradiction of relief and shock at the officer knowing his name as he limply shook the offered hand. He couldn't help but stare at the officer's red hair. That was odd. He didn't think Russians had red hair.

"Admiral O'Hanlon has spoken good of you. I am General of the Army, Kristoff Nikolev. Brent is in?"

"Yes … sir." Giving up on his voice, Jody tapped on the admiral's door and stood aside. Without thinking, he ushered the general inside by pointing through the doorway. Damn, Jody thought. He wasn't sure what the protocol was for the highest ranking military officer of the Russian Federation's armed services showing up unannounced in the office, but he was pretty sure it didn't include pointing.

"Nikolev! Damn it's good to see you!" O'Hanlon hollered as he rushed around his desk to greet the Russian while reaching to close the door.

Jody returned to his desk and wondered anew as to what was going on. Russian generals did not just show up at MARLANT without advanced notice. No, that's not true, he thought; Russian generals did not show up here ever! This must have something to do with Cole's disappearance which had weighed heavily on his mind since word had arrived from Gagetown. Try as he might, he could not shake the feeling that he might never see his friend again.

The Military Police officer, seeing that all appeared to be in order, chatted with the petty officer for a moment and turned to leave. As he was going through the door, Jody suggested that it might be best if no one knew of the Russian's visit for now and the officer nodded in agreement.

Looking at the 'gangster' who he supposed was some kind of security detail for the general, Fletcher noted the man had not sat down, but seemed content to just stand inside the door. Pointing to a chair, Jody asked if he wanted to sit down, to which the man shrugged his shoulders before lowering his bulk into the seat. As he seated himself, the gun he wore inside his suit jacket was visible and he made no effort to conceal it.

"Coffee?" Fletcher asked.

"Da. Thank you." The man smiled before catching himself; his face returning to the suspicious expression he'd exhibited since entering the office.

"Black?"

The man's suspicious expression changed to one of puzzlement.

* * *

Hotel Yelizovo, Kamchatka Peninsula, Russia

Sitting across from John at a slightly battered table in the hotel restaurant, Cookie tried to hide the surprise in his voice but failed. At first he thought the Russian had been just pulling his leg about O'Hanlon having friends in 'high places' within Russia, but then again, even he didn't know everything about the admiral's mysterious past.

"Oh?"

"Yes, Cookie. Your Admiral O'Hanlon is a good friend of Liza's father. Did you know her father is General of the Russian Army," he asked, enjoying the stunned expression the information brought to the Canadian's face.

"What?" Stu was equally shocked. "Your army knows about this?"

"Yes, of course. It is how we all came together." Reaching for his cup, John took another long drink. "Liza joined the KGB just before they disbanded into the FSB. She stayed for a little while but left to join private sector as security specialist."

"Damn." The world really has changed, thought Cunningham. Not all that long ago these people were his sworn enemies.

"O'Hanlon," John continued, "has been friends with General Nikolev for a long time. They became friends after incident that took place in 1966."

"They were on different sides back then," Cookie noted.

"Oh yes. It seems to me the story goes that your admiral tried to sink the Soviet submarine which was to remove her father from Canada."

"I see," Cookie responded after a long moment of silence, although he didn't really 'see' at all. O'Hanlon had neglected to share THAT little sea story with him.

"It is all about the secrets, is it not?" John roared with laughter, ignoring the looks given him by the waitress who had returned to replace one of the coffee pots.

"I supposed we should tell you a little bit about us," Cookie began, not at all sure that he should.

"You do not have to," Alexski remarked.

"No," Asimov cut in. "We heard story about your submarine mission to France and we want to hear more. You and Stu were together there, yes?"

"You know," said Stu, his face contorted in fake pain, "There are days I miss the Cold War when everybody didn't know what you'd been doing for the past few years."

They all laughed at his remark and toasted the comment with their coffee. As they were sharing more stories from their past, Yelizaveta entered the restaurant. One look at the expression on her face told them the news was not good.

"What is it Liza?" Cookie asked, bringing a chair over for her.

"The Chinese have moved him." Sitting down heavily, she added, "Our people do not know where."

"That's not good," Stu noted.

"No, but they will find out where he is," she replied before taking a sip of coffee from John's cup.

"Okay," Alexski commanded, bringing the meeting to an end. "We rest this evening and perhaps there will be news tomorrow."

No one spoke as they separated and headed for their rooms. Stu followed Cookie into his room and sat on a worn out chair against an old bureau.

"So, what do you think?" the Seal asked.

"I don't know, but what a bunch they are. I guess they're all we've got though."

"Yeah."

"I'll have to get O'Hanlon to tell me the story behind the Russian General. I bet there's a good yarn there, eh?"

"So it seems," Stu laughed. "Well, I guess we'd better rest up. God knows what we'll be doing tomorrow."

"Yeah," Cookie replied, and his voice trailed off as he continued, "hopefully we'll be doing something ..."

* * *

CSIS Headquarters, Ottawa, Ontario

Standing in front of the headquarters building of the Canadian Security Intelligence Service, one would be impressed by its modern, almost art deco, appearance. From the air, the structure has an arrow shaped design, pointing off to the north-west, coincidentally perhaps, directly at the heart of Russia. In a windowless office on the second floor, a young woman seated at her desk was jolted from the mountain of paper work in front of her by a harsh buzzing. Accompanying the annoying sound, a strobe light on the multiline phone in front of her was visible beneath the two layers of pages covering the device. Reaching through the reports for the telephone's headset, she pushed the flashing button and spoke only one word.

"Yes?"

She listened to the voice on the other end of the call without speaking, carefully taking notes. Although the call, as all communications into and out of this room, was being digitally recorded, a shorthand transcript was always made as a backup. When the person at the other end had finished, instead of good-bye, they closed with a prearranged code word signifying that the call was complete and that neither of them were under duress. No one dismissed the possibility that even CSIS headquarters could be breached, and agents in the field needed to know if that had happened. As the line went dead, the woman transcribed her notes into the full message and disposed of the original piece of paper in the safe disposal bin next to her cubicle.

Recruited while in her final year of political science at St. Francis Xavier University, Tara had been with CSIS for six years now and yet she still found herself pondering what kind of inner strength motivated the operatives she regularly spoke with. Well, almost spoke with. The conversations, if you could call them that, were only a couple of minutes at most and her part usually consisted of no more than one or two words. Saying a silent prayer for this woman who she knew only as a voice on the phone, she pressed the intercom.

"Sir, I have traffic from Delta Sierra."

"On my way."

Through the intercom, she detected a ring of anticipation in her boss's voice. Tara hoped the coded information she was about to give him was good news.

It was.

* * *

MARLANT, CFB Halifax, Nova Scotia

Before the sun had risen the next day in Halifax, Admiral O'Hanlon and General of the Russian Army, Kristoff Nikolev were sitting in Brent's office discussing the turn of events from the previous day. Neither had spoken for a few minutes; both lost in their concerns for the group in Russia. Cookie had called earlier, reporting what had happened during the failed rescue attempt, ensuring them that the team still had high hopes they would find Cole alive. Their earlier expectations for a quick and successful mission dashed, the two men sat quietly, a feeling of helplessness permeating the room.

"If they've flown him into China, our chances are not good," O'Hanlon sighed, breaking the uneasy silence.

"I do not think they would do that. It would be a great risk trying to fly him out of the country," Kristoff explained. "Russia is much easier to fly into than out of, my friend."

"I hope so. Our contact overseas should be reporting soon. Hopefully they'll have some …"

As if on cue, the buzzing of the phone interrupted his sentence. Brent grabbed at the receiver and bellowed his name into it.

"When?" He asked after listening for a few moments. "Do they have the info yet?" Another pause. "Great! That is good news! Thank you!" He slammed the receiver down and turned to his Russian friend.

"What is it?" Nikolev asked.

"Our group over there will be going to work when they wake up. The Chinese have Cole at a deserted hospital only half a kilometre from the original site," Brent explained. "It looks like they're trying the 'good cop' approach now."

"Good cop?"

"Yeah, the report from our CSIS operative says they brought him in pretty badly beaten. That's good news," O'Hanlon noted. "It means they haven't gotten what they're after yet. There's a good chance that will keep him alive."

"And the 'good cop' part?"

"Oh, sorry. Now they're probably going to try being nice to him and see how that works. Our operative on the ground thinks they're trying to convince him that the Chinese have saved his ass."

Kristoff pondered how reliable the source of the information was, but O'Hanlon was obviously certain of its accuracy. The Russian government was being careful as they had a long history of joint animosity with the large country to their south and they didn't want this incident to explode into a shooting war. China and Russia had been practically at war, in one form or another, for so long, no one really knew why anymore.

Kristoff thought back to how his being in Canada this day had come about. Almost three decades ago, after an afternoon of searching through old classified files from the days of the Soviet Union, the ex-Spetsnaz commando had found one containing information about an operation he himself had taken part in decades earlier. Googling *HMCS Margaree*, the Canadian destroyer which the file indicated had intercepted, and saved, the Soviet submarine tasked with picking him up, from being sunk by the Americans. He had noted a link to then Commander Brent O'Hanlon and on a whim, after finding the commander's office number through Canadian directory assistance, Kristoff had called him.

"Commander O'Hanlon," Brent had answered in what Kristoff would learn was his characteristically gruff telephone voice.

"Commander Brent O'Hanlon?"

"Yes. Who is this?"

"We have never met commander, but we share a past. You were of destroyer *Margaree*?"

"A long time ago—who is this?"

"I am Colonel General Kristoff Nikolev of the Russian Army," Kristoff had replied, expecting the Canadian would immediately hang up.

"Yeah, sure you are."

"The submarine you protected from the Americans in 1966. It was there to pick me up."

Brent had stared at the receiver clutched in his hand, not believing what he'd heard. Slowly bringing it back to his ear, he was unsure if he should hang up or continue talking with this man.

"A submarine you say?"

"Yes Brent. I know this is unusual, but I wanted to thank you for my submarine's crew. Your ship is still spoken of fondly when they have reunion in Russia."

"I see …"

"Perhaps someday, I will be able to return the favour my friend."

They had spoken for a few more minutes and after saying goodbye, Commander O'Hanlon had immediately contacted the newly formed CFNIS, the Canadian Forces National Investigative Service, who researched and verified for him that there was indeed a Colonel General Kristoff Nikolev, and that he had been a member of Spetsnaz in 1966. Thinking back to that first phone call, Brent had remembered the Russian's offer.

Over the years, the two men had kept in touch, often discussing how the world was changing around them. Kristoff valued the friendship that had developed between them and when Brent had called seeking his assistance, he had not hesitated.

"He must be a good man, this submariner of yours," the Russian noted, his thoughts returning to the present.

"The best, Kristoff," Brent answered, "the best."

* * *

Yelizovo Hospital, Kamchatka Peninsula, Russia

Having carefully sidestepped most of the questions thrown at him by the delegation of Chinese officials, Darren had feigned discomfort and as promised, the doctor had immediately called an end to the meeting. Ordering a wheelchair for the Canadian, Doctor Chou asked Nurse Su to bring Darren back to his room where she helped him into bed and ensured that he was comfortable. Still pretending to be in agony when he moved, Darren had moaned a few times for good measure as he settled himself in.

"Do you need something for pain," the nurse asked, a genuine tone of concern in her voice.

"No, no thank you Miss Su. I think I will be okay if I can just lay back and rest."

The last thing he wanted was any more drugs injected into him.

"It late anyway. You sleep now." She carefully brought the blankets up around his shoulders and smiled as she added, "I be nearby if you need me."

"Thank you. I appreciate your taking care of me like this."

"Pleasure is mine Mr. Cole." With that she bowed and left the room, closing the door quietly behind her.

Relaxing into the soft pillows, Darren contemplated the meeting. He knew they were leading him with simple question to put him at ease. The Chinese had gone all out to make sure he felt safe and his 'in pain' test had shown they would be patient with him. Good, he thought. It would buy him time and right now, time was important. They were good—very good, but a small mistake by the so called Canadian Embassy Official's while describing one of his army mate's funeral had been their undoing.

In what he now realized had been a strange twist of fate, he and one of the soldiers had spoken at length around the campfire about the different customs regarding burials. Corporal Aabid was Muslim and he had explained to Darren during their rather macabre conversation, the rituals observed by his faith and how his parents had scrimped for years to purchase a small plot where they would all be buried together. Darren had been surprised to learn that devout Muslims only allowed the men of the family to attend the burial, so the funeral described by the 'official' with all of their families present was definitely out of the question for the corporal. There had been other things; notably the lack of typical hospital sounds occurring around him, and that followed by the funeral slip made it clear that things were not as they seemed.

In spite of the obvious care taken in the ruse, they had made the amateur mistake of being too detailed with their stories and that had been their downfall. Cole knew someone must be out there looking for him and he had to buy more time. He also knew he had to be careful. This was in fact a more dangerous interrogation method than Ugly Russian's. There, the pain had kept him alert and on his toes, but now, being fawned over by everyone, he realized it would be much easier to slip up.

If only there was a way to get a message out of here, he thought before closing his eyes and trying to sleep. He realized that would be impossible and that stalling the Chinese as long as possible was his only hope.

* * *

Hotel Yelizovo, Kamchatka Peninsula, Russia

Someone pounding at his door woke Stu from a fitful sleep. Slowly rolling over, he shielded his eyes from the morning sun streaming in through the window and grunted at the time displayed on his watch. Padding over to the door in his bare feet, he opened it a crack. Liza stood outside the room, bringing a smile to the SEAL's face as he stepped back to let her enter.

"Hurry and get ready! We have received information!" Without waiting for a response, she turned and continued up the corridor to Cookie's room.

"Yes!" Stu pumped his fist into the air and headed to the bathroom for a quick 'shit, shower and shave' as he called it. Twenty minutes later, he joined the rest of the group in the restaurant downstairs. There were other people sharing the cafeteria with them this morning and he surmised that most of them were probably grabbing a quick breakfast before heading to work at the submarine base. The SEAL seated himself at the table as Cookie poured himself a cup of coffee.

"So," Stu asked, reaching for a cup and filling it from the second pot of coffee sitting on the table. "What have you got?"

"He is at abandoned hospital, less than a kilometre from here," John answered quietly. "I suspect they are trying to fool him into thinking he has been rescued."

"Ah, 'good cop—bad cop'," Cookie sneered.

"Yes, exactly!" John was a fan of old American movies and TV shows.

"So, what's our plan?"

"The information just came from our operatives. There is an agent inside and they were able to communicate it to Canada."

"To Canada?" Stu asked.

"Yes." John replied, "It is a Canadian agent."

"Oh?" Stu turned to Cookie. "You have agents?"

"You don't think we trust the stuff you guys give us without double checking, do you?" Cookie ducked the playful jab thrown at him and continued. "So it's an abandoned hospital. Getting inside shouldn't be any more difficult than the last building."

"Unfortunately," Alexski noted. "There is a problem."

"Always is," Stu remarked.

"We do not know who operative is."

"We can find out?" Asimov asked.

"We do not have to," Yelizaveta interrupted.

"No?"

"No. Whoever it is, they know the situation and would be expecting us to try and free Cole. It is up to them to be ready and protect themselves."

"Cold." Cookie breathed.

"Yes Cookie. But it is the life w … they know."

The submariner saw a look of pain in her eyes that had not been there before. Or, perhaps it always had been and he just hadn't noticed.

"Hell of a way to make a living," he said, staring into his coffee and realizing she had done just that herself. Looking up and once again admiring her beauty, he wondered how many people she had killed, before quickly pushing the thought from his mind.

* * *

HMCS Victoria, Pacific Ocean, West of San Francisco

"See that faint, broken line? That's him."

"Not much of a signature," remarked the leading seaman sitting alongside Petty Officer Alexander Yokov at *HMCS Victoria's* sonar console. After some much needed sleep, the petty officer was back at his post.

"No, that's one quiet boat for a nuc," Yokov agreed. "Captain, distance to contact is unchanged."

"Good," replied Commander Rene Bourgeois, ducking around a fixture protruding from the submarine's overhead. *Victoria's* crew had been tracking the elusive submarine contact for hours and they continued to marvel at how quietly it moved through the water. During one self-test, the Canadian submarine's own noise had almost blanketed the contact's sound and *Victoria* was one of the quietest boats in the Pacific Ocean.

If this was not one of the new *Virginias*, it was either a brand new class which had somehow been designed, built and launched without anyone knowing about it, or a current design which had been so heavily modified; the computer was unable to recognize it.

Knowing the information could be important, Rene ordered a short burst message sent to Esquimalt via signal buoy. It would contain the information they had so far, along with a recording of the contact's signature. This would ensure the navy had the information should something go wrong and they were unable to deliver it themselves.

* * *

K-335, Pacific Ocean, West of San Francisco

Aboard *K-335*, the sonar operators had just cleared their baffles once again and found nothing in the area other than a single far away surface contact. The boat's captain nervously looked at his watch and wondered when the message from Chinese Naval Headquarters giving them the location of the US Navy battle group, and more importantly, the tactic to break through the aircraft carrier's protective screen of warships, would arrive. Zhong Xiao Chong stepped into a small alcove off the main control room and looked down at the men manning the boat's communications equipment.

"Anything?"

"No, captain. Nothing yet." The man who had spoken looked across at his shipmate and smiled. The captain was getting impatient. That much was obvious.

"Nothing," the captain echoed quietly, before returning to his perch behind the submarine's engineering station. He looked at his watch again. Something must have gone wrong, he thought. They had assured him the information would arrive by the end of the day yesterday. He exhaled loudly, immediately regretting the lapse. He did not want to appear impatient to the crew who would exaggerate their suspicions into a rumour that could spread throughout the boat in minutes.

Not far from where *K-335's* captain was damning himself, Rene Bourgeois was also becoming more impatient but in his case, it was with his quarry's apparent lack of direction. He had seen this before while tailing an American *Ohio*. That was expected with Boomers however, as they just seemed to sail around aimlessly within their patrol box while waiting for orders to destroy the world. But this had to be an attack boat in front of him and those guys were usually going to or from some area where they would probably be doing naughty things. They never just 'hung out', although that appeared to be exactly what this one was up to.

* * *

Yelizovo Hospital, Kamchatka Peninsula, Russia

Darren awoke the next morning feeling more alive than he had since his capture. Stealing a look at the clock on the wall, he noted with satisfaction that it showed 5:57am. He had always automatically awakened close to oh six hundred and this was a sign his body and mind were slowly returning to normal.

Looking around the room, he noticed that Nurse Su was not in her usual chair. Perhaps she hadn't really spent every night by his bed and had simply showed up before he had awoken those previous mornings.

As if in answer the door swung open and she entered the room. Seeing him awake, she smiled and greeted him cheerfully.

"Good morning, Mr. Cole! It good to see you up early!"

"Thank you, Miss Su. I am feeling mu ..." Catching himself, he continued, "...a little better today." He noted a look of understanding cross her face before she replied.

"That is good. Do not be in rush. You heal just fine."

"I suppose they will want to speak with me again today."

"Yes," she replied, looking away.

"I hope I'm up to it," Darren observed. "I'm looking forward to going home."

She looked down at him, and without uttering another word, left the room. The petty officer watched as she left, and could not help but harbour a strange feeling that she was hiding something. Not just what everyone else in this hospital was hiding, but something more—a Russian agent perhaps? That would make sense. They would have infiltrated Chinese security, but if so, who was actually behind his kidnapping? Lying back on the pillow, he pondered his next move. Darren felt certain that he could pull off another delay by feigning a bout of severe discomfort during the questioning, but he also knew that ploy would not work forever.

Staring at the door, the submariner realized that he would eventually have to go outside his room and check the level of security on the other side, and this was as good a time as any. Slowly slipping from the bed, he moved across the room and placed his ear against the wooden door. No sound came from the other side. Any hospital he'd ever been in previously was always a pretty noisy place early in the day, with carts of breakfast food being wheeled up and down the hallways and endless beeps and announcements coming from the public address speakers. This was clearly anything but a working hospital. The only problem was, he'd been wheeled in on a stretcher, but what could he do to make sure he didn't leave the building that way too?

Darren carefully pulled the handle down, and gently opening the door, looked down the hall. There was no one in sight and he quietly stepped out of the room. A nurse's station was visible to his right, so he slowly moved in the opposite direction. Peering into the first room he came upon, he noted that it was completely empty. No beds or chairs. Nudging the door open a little further, he stepped inside, looking back out the crack in the door to see if anyone appeared in the corridor outside. After a couple of minutes with no sign of movement, he slipped out into the hallway again. The next room he came upon was empty as well except for a few pieces of two by four lumber leaning against one wall.

Obviously not a busy place, the submariner thought as he continued to move slowly down the corridor. Seeing that the hallway turned to the right about twenty feet ahead, he crossed over to hug the opposite wall. Taking a quick look around the corner, he saw the space ended a few feet away in a pair of large doors secured by a padlocked chain wrapped around the push bars. Examining the lock and seeing no way past it, Darren tried to look through the door's large reinforced windows into the space beyond. It was dark but just enough light shone through from behind him, to show the hallway on the other side was a shambles. Faded, peeling paint covered the walls and a few broken light fixtures hung from the ceiling. Only a few sections of stained ceiling tiles remained and beyond the carnage he could see only blackness. Turning to retrace his steps, Darren found Nurse Su standing in front of him, an angry expression clouding her face.

"Mr. Cole! You must not leave room!" she whispered harshly. "Come! Quickly!"

Darren followed her back to his room where he expected she would report him to the doctor and the hospital security staff.

"Stay here," she commanded before turning to leave. Looking back at him as she turned to leave, she added, "They come speak with you shortly."

He stared as the door closed behind her. Pondering what he'd seen, he realized his earlier intuition had been correct. Whatever this place used to be, it was now an elaborate ruse for his benefit. Cole knew from his visit to the room where he had spoken with the Chinese Officials, what lay to the right outside his door. His escape route was going to have to be in that direction.

Pulling the chair around, he sat down and closed his eyes. The submariner looked forward to the meeting today and the opportunity it would give to explore his options for getting out of this place. He knew there would be increased security once Nurse Su reported his actions. Hopefully, he thought, that would only make his escape more difficult, but not impossible.

* * *

Hotel Yelizovo, Kamchatka Peninsula, Russia

"So, what are our options?" Cookie asked, looking at the blueprints spread out in front of him.

An hour earlier, someone had arrived at the hotel carrying a satchel containing the original floor plans to the hospital Petty Officer Cole was being held in. Alexski had spoken briefly with the man before returning to the restaurant where Cookie, Stu, and the Russians were eating breakfast. While remarking on how fortunate they were that the FSB was able to track down and deliver the old blueprints so quickly, Alexski carefully removed the sheets of paper from the case, giving consideration to their fragile condition. The plans were faded, torn and stained, but the building's layout was still legible.

"It is unfortunate that they are using second floor. That will complicate matters," John observed. "There are two entrances for that floor, but according to the inside source, one of them is secured and would be too difficult to penetrate."

"That leaves the front door," Stu observed.

"Yes," John continued. "The main entrance is here and it should only be guarded from inside, as the building is abandoned and must appear that way. They may have someone watching from outside with radio communication to those inside."

"We will drive around building and look for that before we go in," Alexski noted before adding, "Only one question—when?"

"At first light. We really shouldn't wait any longer or it might be too late," Cookie warned.

"Yes," Asimov acknowledged. "I agree."

They crowded around the plans and made notes from the drawings while discussing a way to enter the building and more importantly, the quickest way to exit it. Provisions were also discussed for the possible condition they might find Cole in. Hopefully he would be able to walk on his own but the possibility existed that he could be unconscious—or worse. That event was also discussed and it had been decided that if at all possible, his body would be returned home.

After almost two hours of intense planning, Yelizaveta looked up and asked if they needed to see anything further, and with everyone satisfied they had the information they needed, she carefully folded the blueprints and returned them to their case.

"These must be returned now or they might be missed," she warned. "I will deliver them back to our FSB contact and afterwards we will go over the plan again, without the blueprints to guide us."

Cookie watched her walk away, his mind wandering.

"Hey bubble head!" Stu joked. "You'll need those eyes back in your head for later."

"Yeah."

"No, she is not," said John.

"Not what?" Cookie asked.

"Married."

"Oh."

"I thought I would save you the trouble of asking."

"Yeah," Cookie remarked absentmindedly, his mind wandering again. "Thanks."

"Geeze, what was that you said a couple of days ago? She's ex KGB Stu. It would never be allowed Stu …," the SEAL teased, mimicking Cookie's voice.

The submariner shoved him and they threw a few playful punches back and forth.

"You two are always like this?" Alexski asked, frowning.

"Hell no!" Stu replied. "We're not usually this serious."

* * *

Cole Residence, Halifax, Nova Scotia

Her scream reverberated around the room. The nightmare had come to her again and she was finding it more and more difficult to shake off the after effects of the dream. Heather wondered anew if she would ever see Darren again, but the same feeling of peace that had given her strength since his disappearance from the Canadian north filled her heart once more. She knew he was alive. Not necessarily safe, but definitely alive. Looking at the clock, she saw that it was just past midnight. A knock at her bedroom door made her jump.

"Heather?" George Carroll asked quietly from the hallway outside her room. "Are you okay?"

"Yes, Daddy. Come in."

Opening the door, he stepped inside. It hurt him to see his daughter going through this trauma night after night. Used to having tremendous power at his disposal, here he was helpless to do anything for his own child. His daughter was sitting up in bed and he could see her eyes were still red from crying herself to sleep earlier in the evening.

They had spoken frankly about Darren's chances of making it back, and the retired CNO had shared what he knew from similar events he had experienced in the past. In his heart, George believed that the people working on this case would be successful. It was the only thing he could believe for Heather's sake. On the other hand, he had to be up front with her about her husband's chances of returning alive in order to prepare her for what might happen.

"The same dream?"

"Yes," she replied, her lips still trembling. She had been having the recurring dream for a few nights now and although it made no sense to her, it seemed so real. So much so that once she awoke, all of the details were crystal clear in her memory, except for one. Darren was in mortal danger and there was another woman in the dream but frustratingly, she could never remember why the woman was there once she woke up.

"It's just the stress honey. You are going through a lot right now and your mind is playing tricks on you."

"I know, but the dream seems so real. I never had them until the night before last."

"Wait until we get him home, Heather. They'll go away then."

"Oh, Daddy," she hugged him. "When will he be coming home?"

"Hopefully, soon. O'Hanlon has half the world out after him. He'll get him back."

"I know he will. I can feel it."

Admiral Carroll hugged his daughter tightly, while in his mind he tried to convince himself that Darren would be back safely. As each day passed however, he knew the odds of that happening were becoming less likely. Looking down at her, he could see she had fallen asleep again. The girl was totally exhausted but refused any medication to help her sleep so she could be awake when word came about her husband. She's a good wife, he thought. Cole is one lucky sailor.

* * *

Yelizovo Hospital, Kamchatka Peninsula, Russia

"Are you sure you feel up to speaking with us, Mr. Cole?"

They were slick, thought Darren. The only thing they hadn't done so far to make him think he was a free man was to take him for a tour of Tiananmen Square.

"I think so, sir. Thank you very much for asking." Darren's plan was to be respectable with the men in order to appear that he harboured no suspicions.

"Very good. Please let us know if you feel uncomfortable. Now, Mr. Cole, we presume the Russians were after knowledge concerning your submarine service. There is very little we do not know about that." The representative of the Chinese government smiled, hoping to convince the Canadian that this was indeed the truth. "We assume the same is true of the Russians however," he noted before continuing. "Our concern is that they were after information from you to use against us. I am sure you are aware that we have not been on good terms with the Russians recently."

"I have heard …"

"Mr. Cole," the Canadian diplomat interrupted as Darren began to speak, "the Russians have been posturing a lot lately and we fear they may be trying to regain some of the stature they had in the days of the Soviet Union." He paused to let that scenario sink in. "This would mean they see China's emergence as a superpower to be a viable threat to them."

"I can see how that would happen," Darren agreed. "Especially with the new weapons they possess and being so close geographically."

"Exactly, Mr. Cole. That," explained one of the Chinese officials, "is why we are concerned about what they wanted to know. Because we are such good friends with your country, your government has allowed you to co-operate as much as possible with us, and for that we are very grateful."

"The first thing they wanted to know was about our torpedoes," Cole explained. "They were interested in what version of the Mk-48 we were using. I suspect they wanted to know if we had ADCAPS, or just the regular fish."

"Fish?"

"Oh, that's what we call the torpedoes sometimes."

Petty Officer Cole then went on to give a long explanation on the differences between the two types of MK-48 torpedoes. The officials hung on to his every word as he disclosed almost verbatim the information anyone would have been able to read in the latest volume of Jane's Fighting Ships.

Guess they don't read much, Darren thought, while carrying on with his explanation regarding the differences, and how the Royal Canadian Navy submarines were only equipped with the older version. They didn't bat an eye, and he could tell they hadn't caught the lie.

"And these 'regular' models are not as powerful?" the older official asked.

"They are similar. Just not as fast and a little less range," Cole replied.

"That information wouldn't help them. There must be something else they wanted to know."

The government official had thrown the comment out there to see if Darren would offer anything. While waiting for a response, he was startled when the submariner grabbed his side and nearly fell forward from the chair he was seated in.

"Mr. Cole! Are you alright?" The doctor was at his side in seconds.

"Wow," Darren stammered, trying to stand up. "Something just seemed like it was …" He grabbed at his side again and suddenly fell to the floor.

"Nurse! Come quickly!"

Nurse Su rushed over and cradled Darren's head in her arms while feeling for his pulse.

"His pulse very weak, Doctor."

"I am sorry, gentleman," Doctor Chou announced sternly. "That will have to be all for today."

"We understand, doctor. Be sure to take good care of this man," the younger official ordered. "Please call later and let us know how he is doing."

Darren had to suppress a smile. He had a moment of concern at Nurse Su's comment regarding his pulse. Maybe he really hadn't fully recovered from his time with Ugly Russian.

Two orderlies pushing a gurney rushed into the room and carefully picked up the petty officer, laying him gently upon it.

"Be careful with him," the doctor ordered. "Take him back to his room. Nurse Su; please stay with him."

"Yes, doctor," she responded with a slight bow.

Darren lay still as they wheeled the gurney down the hall. On the way to the meeting he had taken in the surroundings and noticed the layout was the same as in the opposite direction from his ward, with the exception of the padlocked doors. At this end of the hallway, the doors were held open and the corridor beyond was clean and brightly lit. Noting the location of the nurse's station on this end of the hallway, Darren screwed his eyes shut, trying to look as though he was in pain as the orderlies brought him into his room. Making a few moaning noises as they carefully lifted him over and onto the bed, Cole lay still and didn't open his eyes.

"They gone, Mr. Cole."

He opened his eyes to see Nurse Su looking down at him.

"You must rest now." She smiled at him, and winked.

Seeing the wink, Darren gave her a puzzled look.

"Rest," she repeated, before seating herself in the chair by his bed and picking up a magazine.

* * *

MARLANT, CFB Halifax, Nova Scotia

Although it was now well after midnight, lights still streamed from the windows of Admiral Brent O'Hanlon's office. Jody had long since gone home and Brent was at his desk, running the events of the past few days over in his mind, trying to think of anything they might have overlooked in regards to his missing petty officer. He considered Darren and all the other ranks 'his' men, and like an over-protective father, hell's fury would come to anyone who messed with them.

Across the room, General of the Russian Army, Kristoff Nikolev relaxed quietly in one of the over-stuffed chairs, nursing a small glass of Scotch served earlier by O'Hanlon. Next to him, George Carroll, the retired Chief of Naval Operation for the United States Navy, sipped on a steaming mug of black coffee, lost in his own thoughts of how his daughter would react to … No, he thought. That would have to wait until this mess played out. Carroll had arrived back at MARLANT an hour earlier; having waited at his daughter's apartment to ensure Heather was going to stay asleep.

"I think we have covered everything, my friend," Kristoff noted.

"Yes, I think you're right." Brent replied, saying a silent prayer that he was.

"Petty Officer Cole; does he have other family?"

"No, Kristoff," George replied. "He was abandoned by his mother as an infant. Sad. Someone out there gave up the chance to have a son they would have been extremely proud of."

Kristoff shook his head, remembering his own mother and the sacrifices she had made while bringing him up during the tough times then in the Soviet Union.

The three old friends began rehashing the situation. Not the rescue mission itself. That was now out of their hands; but rather the big picture. What did the Chinese hope to gain by attacking a United States warship? Once the dust had settled, they would definitely be in a position of greater power in the Pacific, but it was an act of war and surely they did not think anyone was going to buy the 'rogue Russian submarine' idea for very long.

One of the walls of O'Hanlon's office had been turned into an impromptu white board, covered with writing, after the photographs and pirate flag previously hanging there had been removed and carefully set aside in one corner of the room. The information was broken into two columns—the left one labelled 'Facts' and the right one 'Suppositions'. The 'Suppositions' list was much longer.

"The only thing Cole has to offer is the tactics they used when *Corner Brook* broke through the Brit carrier force," offered O'Hanlon. "Other than that, the knowledge he has applies strictly to the *Victorias* and I can't see the Chinese wanting that."

"No," agreed the Russian. "They must want the tactics, but would they really dare attack an American aircraft carrier? That would be suicide," he added, answering his own question.

"Yes," interjected Carroll. "But if they get the tactics out of Cole, they might get lucky and hit the carrier, and for China right now, that would be quite a feather in their cap. Then," he added, "with all the political finger-pointing that would follow, the press would eventually lose interest and the story would become a political football to toss around whenever some politician feels the need.

"It would be a mess," Kristoff noted. "Especially if Mother Russia ends up taking the blame."

The three men were silent for a few moments; each examining the ramifications of the attack if it were successful. The carrier battle groups had been touted for decades as the most secure military formation in existence and the loss of even one of the huge ships would be a disaster, not only in lives lost, but it would also open the door for a few other unfriendly countries that might be eager to try and replicate the act.

Research was quickly being conducted on which Chinese submarine captain would have the knowledge and experience to pull off such an attack, even with the tactics devised by *Corner Brook's* combat team. O'Hanlon knew it was doubtful they would have that answer before it was too late.

"If they get Cole out, hopefully we won't have to worry about this at all," Brent offered before turning to Kristoff and adding, "Then we can just turn our assets lose to track your submarine down."

"That will not be easy, Brent. *K-335* is used to test our newest equipment," Nikolev noted. "With all the money the scientists have because of our new found oil wealth, they had what you call, 'a blank cheque' to design the best submarine possible."

"Someone will find them, Kristoff. It's not that big an ocean, but just in case, our friends to the south are pulling all the Pacific carrier groups into port except for one. *Enterprise's* group sailed from San Diego yesterday morning."

"It is such big risk."

"Yes, and she's one hell of a big bait," Brent noted smiling. "But they have a couple of 'ringers' joining up with them."

* * *

USS Enterprise, Pacific Ocean, West of San Francisco

"Rough Rider, this is Charlie Gulf Alpha Lima plus one, requesting permission to enter the group."

"Roger, Charlie Gulf Alpha Lima. Permission is granted and the admiral sends welcome."

HMCS Calgary and Vancouver had caught up to the carrier battle group and were steaming ten knots faster than the US ships. Roaring past the 'Tail end Charlies' of *Enterprise's* screen, the Canadian frigates moved swiftly through the formation, taking up station five hundred yards off either beam of the huge warship.

On the carrier's bridge, Admiral Clark Thomas and Captain Nelson Craig looked across at *Calgary* in the early light of dawn as she slowed to match the carrier's speed. Both men had reached the pinnacle of their careers and were grateful to have been selected for this mission, although both would also admit that the thought of finishing their careers by losing a navy icon like *Enterprise* was not an appealing thought. They also shared a deep gratitude for the new addition to the battle group. The Canadians were known worldwide to be second to none when it came to killing submarines.

"Glad we have them along, admiral."

"Me too, Nelson. Me too …"

* * *

Hotel Yelizovo, Kamchatka Peninsula, Russia

A third of a world away from where the *Enterprise* battle group cruised in formation, Cookie and Asimov were leaving the hotel. Climbing into the battered old army truck and pulling out of the parking lot, Asimov manoeuvred the vehicle down the street towards the abandoned hospital where they were to reconnoitre the area around the building. Not seeing anything suspicious or seemingly out of place, they drove by the old hospital's entrance once for a quick look, feeling any more than that would possibly arouse suspicion.

"A few trips around the neighbourhood before we head back?" Cookie asked.

"Yes, I know the area well," the Russian replied. "I was stationed here a little more than five years ago. Much nicer back then."

"Tell me, Asimov. How did you guys get so good at English?"

"It is required Spetsnaz training. We must be able to read and write the language as well."

"I can see where that might come in handy."

"Very much, my friend. One never knows when he will be thrown into mission with Canadian who cannot speak Russian." Asimov laughed at his own joke.

"Good point, and …" Cookie cut himself off as he spotted something between the buildings they were passing on the right. "Isn't that the hospital building on the next block?"

"Yes, that is it."

"Check out that antenna on the roof."

The structure had been hidden from their view while driving by the building, but now, from a couple of blocks away, the antenna was clearly visible. Asimov slowed and pulled the truck over to the edge of the road, being careful to avoid the remnants of the curb that jutted out like a miniature tank trap. Looking past Cookie out the passenger window, he could see a metal framework rising from the old building's roof. "That is new design. It is a very low frequency antenna for special commando units."

"Why would they have it there?"

"It is for communication with submarine which is below the surface."

"Okay, I get it now. Whatever information they get from Cole, they plan to transmit right away."

"You have idea what they want to know?"

"No, but hopefully we'll get Cole out of there in one piece before they find out. This plan," he noted, "had better work."

Asimov looked at him. "Hopefully it will, my friend. We should go back now and let others know about this and try to get rest before we come back in the morning."

The two men took one last circuit around the blocks surrounding the hospital, trying to avoid taking the same route more than twice. No one had appeared to be hanging around the building's entrance when they had driven by and the whole area looked as though it had been neglected for many years.

When they arrived back to the hotel, they found the rest of the team in John's room going over the next day's plans one last time. Joining the group, Cookie and Asimov shared their experience scoping out the hospital, as well as the discovery of the antennae on the building's roof, before going over their parts in the upcoming mission. After ensuring that everyone knew not only their own tasks, but those of the rest of the team as well, they all returned to their rooms to try and get some sleep. For the most part however, they all lay in their beds staring blankly at the ceiling while going over the plan in their minds before finally succumbing to exhaustion.

* * *

Yelizovo Hospital, Kamchatka Peninsula, Russia

"Thank you, Nurse Su."

"You welcome, Mr. Cole." She smiled warmly at him while placing a tray of food on the table next to his bed.

Darren sipped a spoonful of the soup. Odd thing to serve for breakfast he though before wondering again why this woman seemed to be helping him. He finally dismissed it as her being sympathetic because of all he'd gone through, or perhaps she was another part of the plan. Maybe whoever she was working for hoped he might confide in her, or they were soon going to kill him and she felt badly about that—though not half as bad as he would.

"What is this?"

"Chicken soup, with fish add to it."

"Ah, that's what it is," the Canadian acknowledged. "I remember eating something like this back home." He paused. Odd that a woman in China would use the same recipe as his aunt who claimed it was an old Acadian dish.

"It is old Chinese recipe." Seeing him contemplating this, Nurse Su attempted to change the subject. "What is it like where you from?"

"It's a nice province on the east coast of Canada called Nova Scotia. You would like it. The weather is pretty good," he continued. "Never too hot or too cold."

"It sound nice."

"It is," Cole whispered, a sad expression crossing his face. "I can't wait to go home."

"I'm sure you go soon, Darren." It was the first time she had called him anything besides 'Mr. Cole'.

"I hope so," he replied looking down at the bowl in his hands. "Sometimes I wonder if they've forgotten about me back home."

"They haven't."

The words had been spoken with a firmness that caused him to look up at her. Their eyes met and he saw a sincerity in them, and something else …

"I must go," she said, averting her gaze. "Rest, Mr. Cole. They may be here any moment."

"Who may be …?"

She ignored him and left the room.

* * *

Prime Minister's Office, Ottawa, Ontario

At 5:30am, some of Ottawa's politicians were still asleep, although a few of the harder working ones were already awake and heading to the Hill as the sun began to rise for another day. Two of those were seated across from each other in a pair of over-stuffed chairs in the Prime Minister's Office. Canada's leader listened as his Minister of National Defence voiced her concerns at the goings on halfway around the globe. The tension in the room was palpable as they discussed the previous day's events while awaiting information on what was currently transpiring in Russia.

"I know what you're saying," the Prime Minister replied to a remark from his Defence Minister, pausing to take a long drink of coffee from the Montreal Canadiens cup he held. "We don't have much choice though. CSIS claims their asset is well placed and that they have their most experienced people working on this file."

"Yes, but …"

The senior minister raised his hand. "Caroline, it will be okay. I know you're concerned about Cole, and I respect you for that. So am I." He paused for a moment before continuing. "You wouldn't be my Defence Minister if I thought you'd feel any other way about one of your people."

"Thank you, Prime Minister. I just wish there was something my people could do."

"You already have Barnes out there, and the people with him are among the best in the business."

Caroline Wheeler, Canada's Minister of National Defence knew he was right. The people working this mission were second to none, and although she had survived more than her fair share of close calls in combat situations, she now had to allow the people in place to do their job.

"I know what else you're anxious about," the Prime Minister continued, "and don't worry. I know Bourgeois personally and he will not lose that Russian submarine."

The message received earlier at CFB Esquimalt from *HMCS Victoria* regarding the submarine they were following, had been forwarded directly to Ottawa where navy officials quickly put two and two together and notified the Minister of National Defence.

"It's not so much the Russian boat I'm worried about losing," she replied.

"Yeah," the Prime Minister sighed. "Let's hope he has the same luck Simpson did in the Med. We'll soon have to read Rene in on the current situation. Speaking of sharing, how are the press taking their muzzle order?"

"They understand. They don't like it, but they understand."

"They're good people and they know what's at stake here."

"Yes …"

Although she didn't like it, Caroline knew they had to trust the media on this one. The 'official' story, for now, was that a freak storm had swept in up north and the soldiers from Greenwood had been caught in the open with no shelter. The fact that a submariner had been with them had not been disclosed. The men's immediate families had been briefed that there was more to what they were hearing in the media and they would be the first to learn what had happened as soon as the information could be shared. The families were not particularly happy with that arrangement, but they had learned long before that the security of the country came before their personal needs.

Caroline had sworn she would be there when the wives and children were told what had really happened. The soldiers had been killed on her watch and the pain she felt over their loss continued to eat at her. When the truth came out, those families would know that the deaths of their loved ones had not been and vain, and hopefully, had been well and truly avenged.

Sadly, she knew, the media would soon forget them and move along to some other story. Afghanistan had completely fallen off their radar now that the Canadian's roles there had reverted to training. The Defence Minister wished they could have been with her the last time she had visited that war torn country. While on an inspection of the training base, a little girl had come up to her and proudly presented a tiny bouquet of flowers and a note she had printed herself. The flowers were beautiful, but the woman who had calmly wrestled a Royal Canadian Air Force Hercules through the night skies of Iraq while anti-aircraft shells tore into its fuselage, had been unable to fight back the tears when she'd read the words carefully scrawled on the piece of paper; 'Thank You Canada'. Ten years earlier, the Afghani girl would have never been allowed to see the inside of a classroom let alone become literate. Smiling at the memory, she brought her thoughts back to the present.

"Anything on the diplomatic front from China?" she asked.

"No, nothing," the Prime Minister replied. "We don't want to go after them until we have insurmountable proof as to what happened." He closed his eyes for a moment, recalling the events of the past four days, which felt like weeks. The stress was catching up with him and he could feel his body protesting its lack of sleep and nourishment.

He remembered when Caroline had shown up at his office, just as he had packed his briefcase and was about to head home for the day. Surely, he thought, that hadn't only been four days ago?

"You'll want to stay, I'm afraid", she had announced walking right by him into the office. "There has been trouble up north and I have a brief from CSIS that you need to hear now."

He had noted the expression of concern on her face and knew he would not be going home any time soon.

"Sure. Another Arctic oil protest gone bad?"

"No, but you'll wish that's all it was."

As the Minister of Defence filled him in on what had happened to the troops in the Arctic, the missing submariner, and the information CSIS had picked up, he had felt a deep sense of loss as he had every time he was notified that one of his people had been killed. Whether by an IED on a peace keeping mission, or an accident here in Canada, the pain he felt was always the same

Dropping into a chair in front of his desk, any thoughts of a pleasant evening at home with his wife and children had vanished. Of course CSIS could be wrong, but his heart told him that was not the case.

"I'm sorry to bring such bad news," said Caroline after briefing him.

"Damn them to hell!" the Prime Minister had exclaimed. He'd felt rage rising within himself and took a deep breath before apologizing for his outburst.

"Not at all, Prime Minister. I know you care about our people as much as I do."

The Prime Minister had stood and walked behind his desk. Pressing a button on the phone, he'd spoken into the intercom. "Betty? Get Admiral O'Hanlon on the phone. What's that? Well call him at home or have the MPs find him. I need to speak with him right now and ..."

A knock at the door startled him back to the present. The assistant staff had not arrived on the Hill yet, and Caroline rose to answer it. She was surprised to see a young man standing there who appeared equally shocked that the Minister of Defence has answered the door.

"Message from CSIS, ma'am."

"Thank you."

Taking the envelope, she closed the door and returned to her chair. Reading the message inside, she handed it over to the Prime Minister who scanned the two sentences typed at the top of the note before placing it on his desk.

"So they're going in. God be with them." He slowly stood and turned to put another pot of coffee on, adding an extra teaspoon to the basket this time. I'll have to grab a quick nap later, he thought to himself as he reached below the cabinet for the sugar bowl he kept stashed out of sight. He'd need the real thing this morning. Artificial sweetener just wasn't going to cut it.

* * *

Hotel Yelizovo, Kamchatka Peninsula, Russia

As the Prime Minister read the note, Cookie was smiling at the reflection he saw in the bedroom mirror. The Russian naval uniform he wore fit perfectly and the submarine badge of the *Voyenno-Morskoy Flot Rossii* fastened to the tunic made it even more fitting. It was the vice admiral's rank insignia that left him worried. The Russians were obviously keeping some aspects of the operation to themselves as someone had arrived in the middle of the night with uniforms and more surprisingly an official Russian Navy staff car.

John knocked and entered the room. "It is perfect!" he exclaimed. "You look more like an admiral than anyone I know and with this rank, you will not be expected to speak."

"Yeah," Cookie noted. "All the admirals I know are famous for their quiet manners." He smiled at the thought of O'Hanlon holding his tongue about anything. It had been decided that Cookie would have to play a part in the frontal assault on the hospital building as it would be crucial for Cole to recognize him right away to ensure there would be no hesitation on his part during the rescue.

"Do not talk. Just grunt. I've heard you grunt before. You will do fine."

Cookie looked at himself in the mirror again and wrinkled his face into a fierce scowl before uttering a ferocious sounding grunt.

"Cookie!" Yelizaveta was staring at him from the doorway, a look of pure shock on her face. "You sounded exactly like my father!"

"I hope that's a good thing, Liza," the submariner replied, winking at her, and smiling when she blushed in response.

"John," she asked. "Do you have what you need?"

He was adjusting his own uniform adorned with the insignia of captain 2nd rank. As with Cookie's, it fit perfectly, and after smoothing out the tunic, he adjusted the belt holster which held a 9mm Yarygin MP-443. Cookie carried the same sidearm and was now examining the handgun. It did not function as smoothly as the Berretta 92F he used as his own personal sidearm back in Canada (to the chagrin of the powers that be), but it wasn't all that bad either.

"Yes. The papers are perfect and whoever looks at them should have no problem believing that we have arrived to examine the structure. Cookie?" he asked. "What do you think?"

"Geeze; sucker hold 17 rounds. That's more than my 92F does! Oh, sorry; it's perfect. I'd love to take this uniform back home with me though. O'Hanlon would throw a fit if I came aboard wearing it!" He chuckled at the scene. "I'm all set. The plan is sweet and simple. We show up—we're surprised to find someone there—mutter about typical government screw ups to the bad guys, and they hopefully feel relieved as we apologize and turn to leave."

John continued, "Then you guys come storming in the side windows and at that point we turn to take out whoever came to the door."

"Yes," she replied. "Then, as Cookie said yesterday, we 'play it by ear'."

Cookie looked at Yelizaveta and smiled. Hearing her quote him felt good; a feeling he hadn't experienced in a long time. Not since … "So," he asked, pushing the memory from his mind, "time for a quick coffee?"

"Good idea," she replied, wondering at the distant look in Cookie's eyes. "Then we go."

In the restaurant downstairs, Cookie had an opportunity to try out his disguise when a pair of young Russian sailors entered the room boisterously shouting before stopping dead in their tracks at the sight of an admiral having coffee with his aide. Cookie looked up at them and grunted his obvious disapproval, as his 'aide' rushed over and admonished them for not acting properly in public. Returning to his chair, John glared at the two sailors over his cup of coffee.

The remainder of the group had already left in the truck, planning on making a couple of trips around the hospital's neighbourhood to take one last look around for anything that might pose a threat to them. After giving them enough time to make sure everything was clear, Cookie and John would drive to the hospital in the Russian Navy staff car.

Driving the old truck past the front of the hospital building, Stu kept his eyes peeled for anything out of the ordinary, but nothing seemed to be out of place. Turning down a side street a block away from the building, he parked along the curb and turned the motor off, glancing down at the MAC-10 sitting on the console between the front seats. If they had spotted anything suspicious, he would have parked the truck directly across the street from the hospital building's entrance as a prearranged warning for John and Cookie.

Looking up the street from the truck's cab, Stu and Asimov watched for the staff car to drive through the intersection ahead. That would give them two minutes to start the truck and make their way to a street next to the hospital around the corner from the main entrance. There they would enter the old building through one of the side windows.

"Hope they didn't get lost," Stu commented, gripping the steering wheel tightly.

"Yes, me too," Asimov replied before adding, "Or lose car."

* * *

USS Enterprise, Pacific Ocean, West of San Francisco

"Clunker One, Climax tower, you are cleared to land on Spot 3"

The faded grey Sikorsky CH-148 Cyclone swung in from just above the *USS Enterprise's* port side and slide over the deck until it was directly above the circle surrounding a faded and tire scuffed '3' on the aircraft carriers flight deck. The helicopter's pilot skilfully reduced power until the large craft dropped gently to the deck. Checking that all the engine's parameters were reading okay before shutting them down, he returned the thumbs up from the officer behind him who was already on his feet and heading for the side door.

"Damn fine landing, Leon!"

"Thanks, skipper! Can't let these carrier people think they're the only ones who know how it's done!"

Slapping the pilot's back, Commander Chris Donnelly stood in the Cyclone's doorway a moment, taking in the huge flight deck which seemed to stretch out forever in either direction. Removing the flight helmet he wore and straightening out his uniform, he thanked the chopper's crew again before slapping on an *HMCS Vancouver* ball cap and jumping down from the helicopter.

The moment his feet hit the carrier's deck, a bell rang out over the ship's public address system and *"HMCS Vancouver,* arriving!" blared from loudspeakers all over the carrier's island structure.

"Nice touch," Chris remarked, shaking hands with a lieutenant who had rushed over to him.

"Welcome aboard captain! I'm Lieutenant Clancy." the officer yelled over the roar of an E-2C Hawkeye taxiing by uncomfortably close. "This way please, sir!"

"Thank you, lieutenant. Right behind you!"

They both crouched slightly as they moved away from the helicopter, mostly from force of habit, as the Cyclone's rotor blades were well above their heads. Chris followed the officer to an opening in the side of the carrier's island where, once inside the structure, they climbed a pair of ladders to *Enterprise's* bridge. Entering the wide space, Chris was momentarily taken aback by the huge digital displays that seemed to cover every vertical part of the space.

"Far cry from old *Coral Sea*, isn't she?"

"Nelson!" Chris walked over to the aircraft carrier's captain and warmly shook his hand. "I hear you need some help making sure this giant tub toy doesn't get sunk!"

"Yup, so we called for the best," he replied with an evil grin, "but all we got was you and those two sorry sons a' bitch excuses for frigates you drug along with you!"

The bridge crew looked on in shock. The two old friends had just broken rules covering everything from sailor superstition to naval etiquette.

"Come on, Chris. The admiral's looking forward to meeting you."

They exited the bridge and walked through a short passageway to another ladder which took them to the upper bridge, and from there, into the admiral's cabin. Damn thing's bigger than *Vancouver's* operations room, Chris thought, gazing around at the space.

"Commander Donnelly! Good to meet you finally!" Admiral Thomas roared as he stepped around his desk to shake hands. "Nelson's been telling me some pretty weird sea stories about you."

"Good to meet you too, Admiral Thomas, and for the record sir, none of what he's told you is true, especially the part about my sinking any French boats!"

"I believe you," Thomas laughed, and then turning serious, remarked, "Looks like you might have to sink a Russian one though."

"So I've heard."

The three officers sat down and discussed the tactical situation while an aide arrived and served coffee to everyone. They harboured no misgivings that the Russian boat was at the top of the heap when it came to capabilities, and that her crew was probably the best in the Chinese Navy, along with a few Russian sailors who had joined up as part of the operation.

"Hard to believe they managed to rip off that boat, though," Nelson remarked, reaching for his cup of coffee.

"No kidding," Chris replied. "You have to know a lot of Rubles changed hands somewhere along the way."

"Well, our screen is as good as it's going to get," the admiral interjected. "So we'll just see what happens if they try to break through. With the modifications to the disposition and you Canucks at the sharp end, I don't give them much of a chance."

"Hopefully we won't have to find out, sir."

* * *

Yelizovo Hospital, Kamchatka Peninsula, Russia

Almost a third of the way around the globe, Stu was fidgeting in the truck's front seat. Patience was not one of his virtues and he was just about to suggest that something may have gone wrong when the staff car slowly crossed the intersection ahead of them before disappearing from sight. Starting the truck, Stu slipped the transmission into gear and slowly pulled away from the curb, driving towards the building and the boarded up side window they had previously decided would be the best way to enter the hospital.

Around the corner, John brought the staff car to a stop directly in front of the hospital's entrance and rushed around to open the rear passenger door for his 'admiral'. Coming to attention as Cookie stepped out, he smartly closed the door and made a show of glancing at the clipboard in his hand as they casually walked up the broken concrete sidewalk to the building's entrance.

They were both momentarily startled by the sound of a car coming to a stop on the street behind them before the driver gunned the vehicle's engine and raced off, making a hard right turn at the next corner. Regaining their composure, they continued walking towards the entrance, but not before Cookie had caught a good look at the car, a nondescript four door sedan with a bespectacled man wearing a suit sitting in the back seat. Odd, he'd thought, wondering if the incident had anything to do with their mission.

Around the corner, Stu had to swerve the truck hard into the curb as the car came directly at him before careening away and speeding down the street.

"That is probably not good," Asimov remarked, watching the car disappear in his side view mirror.

Oblivious to what was happening just outside, Darren was getting dressed in clothing Nurse Su had brought in earlier. They did not fit well and he realized that giving her his usual sizes had been a mistake. The shirt fit loosely and the pants would practically need braces to hold them up. He had obviously lost a lot of weight since his ordeal had begun, but the clothes, even as ill-fitting as they were, certainly felt a lot better than the hospital gowns he had been wearing since his arrival. Tightening the belt to the last hole, and looking at himself in the mirror fastened to the wall by his bed, he saw Nurse Su walk into the room and admire him from behind for a moment before speaking.

"Officials be here soon," she announced. "Are you feeling okay to speaking with them today?"

"Yes, Miss Su. Thanks. I'll be fine."

One floor below, the operative covering the building's front entrance was surprised when upon hearing a car pull up and looking out the door's window, he saw an admiral and his aide exiting a navy staff car instead of the interrogation team he had been expecting. There was no time to warn anyone on the floor above as the aide strolled briskly to the door and opened it before standing aside to let the admiral enter. Not knowing what else to do, the Chinese agent who was wearing a Russian Army lieutenant's uniform and who had been chosen for this post because of his Slavic features and fluent Russian, stepped through the door and came to rigid attention.

"Oh, I am sorry, lieutenant," John offered in Russian, returning the man's salute and glancing down at his clipboard. "I was told there was no one here. The admiral is just inspecting the older base buildings to determine which ones should be taken down and which ones are worth saving."

"We are just here doing an inspection of our own for the base safety department," the agent answered smoothly, hoping his voice did not give away the fear he could taste welling up inside his throat.

"Admiral, I am sorry," John explained. "It appears there is already an inspection underway. Do you wish …"

The admiral grunted, clearly upset at finding someone else there. He gave John a displeased look and turned away, heading back towards the staff car.

"Er, I guess we will come back at some other time, lieutenant. As usual, things are messed up at headquarters," John sighed convincingly. He could see the guard was buying it. "How much longer do you think you will need here?" he added.

"I am …" A muffled explosion from somewhere inside the building caused the agent to turn around, at which point he felt a sharp blow to the back of his head before dropping to the ground unconscious.

"Move!" John yelled at Cookie, who had already turned back to the door while cocking the MP-443. They rushed through the entrance, momentarily stunned by the bright, clean hospital interior before them. Having viewed the building's dilapidated exterior, they had not expected to find the interior so perfectly restored.

"Stay left," John whispered loudly as they made their way down a short corridor. A nurse's station jutted out on the right and they ducked below the counter before jumping up in unison, guns aimed at what turned out to be an empty space. Ahead they heard two muffled shots and then silence.

"Let's go. We have to find the stairs," Cookie directed. With the explosion and gunshots, he knew the Chinese would be aware that unwanted guests had arrived.

Around the next turn on their right, a door marked with a logo indicating stairs was half open and John threw himself through the opening and lay down, sighting up the stairwell as Cookie hopped over him and quietly made his way up the steps two at a time. Reaching the top, he found a closed door with a small window mounted in it. The submariner glanced through the glass, seeing a corridor stretching off in both directions.

"Damn!" he hissed. "We're in the middle of the hallway!"

The building's plans had shown the stairs leading out to the north end of the corridor allowing them to make their way in one direction only. Now they would have to split up, cutting their firepower in half.

"Okay, you go left and I'll go right," John ordered.

"This never works in the movies," Cookie replied, slowly pushing the door open and crouching along the near wall.

John followed him through the opening and moved to the opposite wall. They slowly began to make their way in opposite directions, stopping occasionally to listen for any sound that might warn them of impending danger.

Down the corridor and around a corner from where Cookie was slowly inching along, the rest of the team had just entered through a door at the top of a flight of stairs from the space below. A dead guard lay crumpled at the bottom of the steps, taken out by Yelizaveta as they had entered the stairwell. He had been on his way down to investigate the explosion and had run headlong into her, hesitating long enough for her to fire a round squarely into his forehead.

Asimov peered down the brightly lit hallway. No one was in sight and he crouched down to present as small a target as possible as he moved, signalling the others to follow. Yelizaveta crept slowly along the opposite wall with Alexski right behind her.

Stu remained behind on the ground floor, securing their escape route and the truck which had been left parked on the street with the motor running. He hated to miss the action but appreciated that someone had to stay behind and another person upstairs who was unable to speak Russian would be one too many. He hoped Cookie would be okay, dreading the thought of returning to face O'Hanlon with bad news about both Cole AND his favourite bubblehead.

One floor above, Cookie was approaching a corner in the hallway when he heard someone coming up behind him. Throwing himself to the middle of the aisle, he quickly brought his gun to bear before realizing it was John making his way towards him.

"Dead end," whispered the Russian.

Cookie nodded and they slowly moved ahead until they reached the point where the hallway turned a corner. Peering carefully into the next corridor, John made out Yelizaveta at the opposite end of the long space. She signalled that all was clear behind her and he and Cookie waited at the corner as the other team approached a series of doors along the opposite wall.

"Must be wards," the petty officer whispered to John, pointing to the doors.

John nodded, assuming the same spaces were repeated along the near wall as well. From his vantage, he would see if anyone came out of any of the rooms and would have a clear shot down the middle of the hallway at them.

Asimov reached the first ward and ducking low, slid into the room. It was completely empty. Signalling all clear out the doorway, he made his way along the corridor again until he was just outside the door to the next room. Reaching for the door, he gave it a slight push and quickly pulled his hand away. He looked over at Yelizaveta and signalled that it was locked. Waiting as they cleared the rooms on their side of the corridor, he leaned closer to the door, listening for any sound from the other side but heard nothing.

"What do you think?" Alexski asked, slowly moving behind him.

"No sound. I will kick the door in from the bottom—you two go in on either side."

Yelizaveta nodded and stood aside as Asimov positioned himself a few yards away. Cookie and John, weapons ready, crouched further down the corridor to take down anyone who might make it out past the other three.

Signalling he would move on 'three', Asimov counted down with his fingers and leapt up, pushing against the opposite wall and threw himself feet first at the door which burst from its hinges and flew across the ward.

Yelizaveta and Alexski rushed in, crouching down on either side of the opening and sweeping the room with their weapons. No one was visible and Alexski was about to shout clear when he sensed something beneath the lone bed in the room.

"Look out!" he shouted in Russian, dropping to his knees and bringing his gun to bear.

"Wait!" A shout emerged in English from the darkened space.

"Come out slowly! Hands first!" Yelizaveta commanded. Cookie and John now stood outside the doorway, adding theirs to the other three guns all pointing at the floor around the bed.

"I am Canadian." A voice beneath the bed announced loudly.

"Damn it, Cole," Cookie laughed. "Aren't you a little old to be hiding under the bed?"

"COOKIE!" The submariner poked his head out and the expression on his face went from shock to a huge grin. "You are seriously a sight for sore eyes!"

Asimov reached down and helped Darren to his feet.

"Can you walk?"

"No problem. I'm fine," Cole replied, reaching back beneath the bed.

They all stood in silence as he helped Nurse Su to her feet.

"So, Cole," Cookie smirked, giving Nurse Su the once over. "I see they've been pretty rough on you."

"You have no idea. This is Nurse Su. She has been taking care of me since I was brought here."

"Nurse Su, I am Cookie and this is ..."

"No names," Alexski interrupted him.

"That's okay," the Chinese woman said in perfect English. "Xue Lee," she announced, offering her hand to the Russian. "Canadian Security Intelligence Service"

Cookies jaw dropped. A muted 'damn' was all he could manage.

Darren just stared at her, unable to speak at all.

"Okay," John ordered. "Let's save the pleasantries for later. We have to get out of here now!"

They rushed down the corridor and quickly descended the stairs into the room where Stu stood aside the blown in window. He started to say something upon seeing Darren but stopped, knowing this was not the time.

"I think some friends of yours dropped by earlier Cole," Cookie noted. "Some suits in a car made out of here like a bat out of hell when they saw us coming to the entrance."

"My interrogators," Darren replied. "They …"

"Will be back," Xue interjected. "They will have orders to kill you if they don't get the information they need, and they are ruthless!"

Jumping to the grass outside, Stu ran to the truck, throwing the doors open.

"Quite the getaway car, pal," Darren observed climbing in.

"All they had left on the lot!" Stu tossed back. "I got a great deal on it though—really low mileage—only driven by a little old Russian …!" The rest was muffled by the slamming doors.

Cookie and John raced along the side of the building and quickly climbed into the staff car before roaring up the street in the opposite direction they had come from. Peering in the mirror, John could see the truck racing to catch up behind them and in minutes they were back on the highway in the opposite direction from the hotel.

"Not going back?" Cookie asked.

"No, it will be too dangerous. We have a safer place."

"Ah."

As they drove, all signs of civilization disappeared and they were soon traveling through hills covered in thick forest along a highway that appeared deserted except for the odd vehicle going in the opposite direction. A short time later, Cookie looked out to the left and spotted a huge satellite dish with more of them becoming visible as they drove along.

"What's that over there?" he asked John.

"That is a cosmonaut communication base," he replied. "It is one of our main centres for space communications."

"Huh," Cookie remarked, impressed with the size of the huge base and its numerous antennas all pointing skyward. "Secret stuff?"

"Not so much anymore. We work closely with NASA now."

An hour later they were driving along the coast of Krasheninnikova Bay and off in the distance across a short stretch of water, Cookie noticed what appeared to be a navy base. Seeing the dark silhouettes of submarines berthed alongside the piers, he looked over at John and asked, "Er, where are we going?"

"I thought you would be at home at submarine base."

"After today, I'll feel right at home anywhere," Cookie replied. "How close are we going to pass by the base?"

He saw the answer as they swerved around the next corner and splayed out before them was the heavily guarded main entrance to the Rybachiy Naval Complex, the largest submarine base in Russia.

"Oh shit, John. Are you sure about this?"

"Trust me," the Russian smiled. "Besides, remember that you are admiral. No one will dare say anything to you."

In the truck following behind them, Cole was staring wide-eyed at the huge sign alongside the gate ahead of them. He recognized the submarine insignia of the Russian Navy and felt a wave of fear wash over him as he remembered his last encounter with a Russian submarine.

Huge concrete pillars protected the entrance along with half a dozen armed guards standing behind them. An officer walked towards the gate, holding up a hand for them to stop as they approached.

"Stu?"

"It's okay, man. They know we're coming—I hope."

"But ..." Darren was not at all sure it was okay.

"Hey, don't fret. Wait 'till you find out who our new playmates here are."

* * *

MARLANT, CFB Halifax, Nova Scotia

Although it would be a couple more hours before the sun rose into the skies over Halifax, lights shining from two windows at MARLANT showed someone had arrived to work very early, or had never left the previous evening. Admirals O'Hanlon and Carroll, along with General Nikolev, sat quietly in Brent's office waiting for further word on the operation taking place on the opposite side of the globe. When the phone on O'Hanlon's desk rang, the three men stood as one, staring at the device for a moment before Brent reached over and punched the speakerphone button before bellowing his name. The call came from the communications building a few blocks away and the person on the other end of the line began with, "We have him and …" The rest of the sentence was drowned out as the men shouted and clapped each other on the back.

The information had come from the commanding officer of the Russian submarine base who had been advised that the rescue team would be arriving shortly, and Brent couldn't help but ponder that for a moment. It was amazing how much the world had changed in the past twenty years. After the cheering had subsided, Brent learned that Cookie and Darren were expected to arrive at the base any time now and further information would be forwarded once the submariners were debriefed.

Hollering 'thanks' at the phone, Brent pushed the disconnect button and picking up the receiver, called Petty Officer Jody Fletcher to share the good news with him. O'Hanlon ordered him to get up and go to the mess for a bottle of champagne, with instructions to 'shoot someone if you have to, but don't come back without it!' Hanging up and looking over at George, he noted, "You'd better call Heather and let her know."

"Thanks, Brent." The retired CNO of the Unites States Navy was not surprised when she answered shortly after the first ring. Telling her right away that Darren was safe, he went on to explain that her husband would be coming home as soon as he was checked over by the base surgeon in Russia. Heather bounced between tears, and shouts of joy, and was about to head for the base when she realized that as soon as he could, Darren would call her at the apartment.

"I'll wait here, daddy. I know he'll call as soon as he can."

"Okay, Heather. You call me back as soon as he does and let me know how he's doing," George asked, and then pausing as she spoke, concluded with, "Yes, I'll call your mother right now. Love you!" he called into the phone. "That is one happy little girl," he beamed, reaching over to dial his own home number.

"While you call your wife, Kristoff and I are going to go down for some air and meet Jody at the gate."

"Thanks."

As they left, closing the door behind them, George sank into Brent's chair. He had dreaded the mission ending in failure and watching what that would do to Heather. Saying a quick prayer of thanks, he listened as the connection was made and wasn't surprised when, as his daughter had, his wife answered on the first ring.

"You haven't been getting your beauty sleep tonight, have you?" he chuckled into the phone.

"Oh, George! He's safe!"

"He's safe. The Russians have him." Carroll paused at that. Comparatively safe at the Rybachiy Submarine Complex at least, he thought. How safe was that?

"Do you know when he'll be home?"

"I'm not sure yet, Deb. They will want to debrief him, which is understandable, but Admiral Andreev has assured us it will not take long."

"As long as our little 'advertising executive' is safe. That's all that matters."

"Yes," George laughed, recalling the first time they had met Darren. "It is."

At the main entrance to the CFB Halifax dockyard meanwhile, O'Hanlon and Nikolev had startled one of the guards at the main entrance who had nearly keeled over upon seeing a Russian general and Admiral O'Hanlon standing behind him.

"Sir ... s?"

"It's okay son," Brent smiled at the leading seaman manning the gate. "We're just making sure there are no delays when Fletcher arrives. He will be carrying top secret documents and don't let me hear that you did more than wave him through!"

"Yes ... sir," the young man answered, not sure which officer to salute.

* * *

Rybachiy Nuclear Submarine Complex, Russia

John slowly pulled up to the main gate of the Russian submarine base and brought the staff car to a stop, handing a note to the sailor who approached the vehicle, while three other guards aimed their AK-74s at the car. Blockhouses on either side of the road ahead concealed more firepower should the vehicle attempt to proceed any further without clearance.

The officer read the note and glancing over to the passenger side, came to rapt attention, saluting Cookie, before waving the car through and signalling to an unseen person in one of the squat brick buildings ahead. When Stu pulled the truck up to the gate a few moments after the staff car had driven through, he smiled down at the sentry who sneered up at him and waved the truck through the gate. Driving half a kilometre down the road, John pulled up next to a building festooned with antennas and turned the engine off. Asking Cookie to remain with the car, he got out and walked over to the building. Pressing a button next to a door which was the only opening in the large expanse of concrete wall forming the front of the structure, he stood aside and waited.

Momentarily an officer came out, greeting John warmly before following him back to the car. Looking as the man approached, Cookie recognized the same admiral's rank insignia on the uniform the man was wearing, as he had on his. *That one is the 'Real McCoy' though,* the submariner thought, opening his door and stepping out. Not sure what else to do, Cookie came to attention, saluted and waited for the admiral to acknowledge him.

"John! What is the meaning of this!?" The officer's face showed a look of deep concern. "We may have to have this man shot! He cannot be here dressed in this uniform!"

Cookie's knees nearly buckled before the man broke into laughter at the expression of angst on the Canadian's face.

"Welcome to Rybachiy, Petty Officer Barnes! John here," the admiral laughed, "said I should just grunt, but that did not seem very officer like. I do not know where he gets his ideas."

The two men shook hands as Stu pulled up alongside them in the old army truck and they all piled out.

Seeing Xue, the admiral did a double take and asked, "Prisoner?"

"No, Admiral," Asimov replied. "She's one of us—well, one of them anyway," he added, pointing to Darren and Cookie. "A Canadian spy."

"Ahhh, they are much prettier than ours, with the obvious exception of course of Liza here," he announced giving Yelizaveta a hug. "How is your father, Liza?"

"He is well admiral, and I know I speak for him when I express our deepest gratitude for your assistance."

"That is what friends are for, are they not?"

"Yes, very much so," she replied, blushing slightly from the admiring look Cookie was giving her.

"And you must be Petty Officer Cole," the admiral embraced the submariner in a huge bear hug, his burley arms enveloping Darren. "I am Admiral Dimetry Andreev. Welcome to the Rybachiy Submarine Complex.

"Thank you, sir. I appreciate your help."

"Not necessary, my young friend, but there is someone who wishes to speak with you. I hope you do not mind," he smiled, "but I took the liberty of calling her when I was informed that you had arrived at the base entrance." Handing Darren a cell phone, the admiral gestured everyone else aside.

Darren brought the phone up to his ear. "Hello?"

"DARREN! I love you!"

"I love you too, hon. Oh god, I needed to hear your voice again."

Across the parking lot, the admiral and the rest of the group looked over and watched as Darren sat down on the grass next to the road, oblivious of his surroundings, while talking with his wife.

"Do we have transportation back home?" Stu asked.

"Yes," replied Admiral Andreev. "John and the rest have an aircraft waiting to take them back to Moscow tomorrow. John, FSB would like to debrief you on what took place. I have informed Moscow of your actions, and congratulations have arrived from your superiors for a job well done."

"Almost, well done. Some of them did get away," John noted unhappily.

"Oh, I am sorry. In the excitement of your arrival, I forgot to tell you. There was a strange and terrible automobile accident near here earlier today. One of the base armoured personnel carriers ran into a civilian car. Sadly," he added with a smile, "there was only one survivor."

John gave him a knowing nod, wondering if the sadness was that there had been only one survivor, or that there had been any.

Darren joined them and handed the cell phone to the admiral, thanking him.

"You are welcome. I understand how important it is that we let our wives know what is going on, and yours made it clear that she was to be called immediately. She is a lot like her father that one."

"She is that, sir." Darren replied. He wondered if everyone above the level of petty officer knew everyone else no matter what navy they served in, or if it was just the people he knew.

"Come, my friends. I am sure you are all hungry and wish for a chance to wash up. We have clothing ready for you, especially for Petty Officer Barnes here," Andreev joked. "I do not want any of my men having a heart attack when they see this 'grunting' admiral coming at them."

They all laughed at Cookie's expense, making him blush. He blushed even more when Yelizaveta took his arm and led him to the building's entrance.

"Come with me, my soon to be demoted admiral," she purred. "I wish to enjoy being in the company of such a handsome senior officer while it lasts."

Cookie placed a hand on her arm and escorted her up the few steps of the building, holding the door open and bowing as she stepped inside.

"After you, my gracious lady."

The admiral had seen to it that all the stops had been pulled out for the group, and they found an assortment of comfortable clothing and toiletries carefully laid out in rooms that had been prepared for them ahead of time. Andreev returned to his office, knowing his guests would be enjoying a long, hot shower.

Especially Cole. Thinking of what the submariner had experienced, he knew it would all hit him later, probably tonight as he lay in bed waiting to fall asleep. The admiral hoped the huge supper being prepared, along with a generous supply of good Russian vodka, would blur his memory and that he might have a good night's sleep before the first bouts of 'survivor syndrome' crept into the submariner's mind. Andreev knew the fact that Cole alone had survived in northern Canada would haunt the young man for the rest of his life.

Admiral Dimetry Andreev had lived through his own experience of survivor's guilt over thirty years earlier when the TU-95D Bear he was a crew member on crashed with only one other survivor besides himself. It had been the Royal Canadian Navy who had rescued him that day and he had longed for the opportunity that would allow him to repay that debt.

"Admiral, we are ready."

His aide motioned him to a doorway across the hall from his office. Peering inside, the admiral gave a satisfied nod.

"Yes, this will do fine," he announced, surveying the huge mess hall which had been decorated in a festive manner. In the centre of the room, a long table was resplendent in a starched white tablecloth; each place setting ringed with silverware dating back to the Russian Revolution. Crystal wine glasses trimmed in gold stood by each plate opposite glass teacups in sterling silver cup holders. "Well done, senior lieutenant."

The officer saluted and left to check on the meal which was being prepared by one of Moscow's most renowned chefs who was still trying to recover from his early morning flight to the base in a twin seat SU-35 fighter aircraft. The fighter squadron's commander had at first denied the admiral's request for use of the aircraft and its pilot for what he had called 'a frivolous mission', but a phone call from the Kremlin shortly afterward had changed his mind.

Andreev's thoughts returned to that day so long ago, when the icy waters of the north Atlantic had almost lulled him into a final sleep. Yes, he surmised, Petty Officer Cole would have some rough days ahead, but tonight, the young submariner will not have time to think about what had happened over the past week. He would see to that. Looking around the room one more time, he returned to the foyer where John had just arrived, looking relaxed after his shower and wearing a casual shirt and pants.

"Thank you again, admiral, especially for the clothes."

"You are welcome, John. Now where is the rest of your travelling circus? Surely they must be hungry!"

"They are almost ready, sir. The CSIS agent had to leave however. A message came through to expedite her return to Canada."

"That is too bad," Andreev noted. "She is going to miss a very good meal."

Half an hour later, they were already starting in on the second course of the lavish meal which had been prepared for them. Cookie had just returned from the kitchen where he had been 'interrogating' the chef about how he had prepared the meal's scallops, with the help of Alexski acting as interpreter.

"Okay," he explained to Yelizaveta who was seated beside him. "At some point during the cold war when we thought you were after our military secrets, your guys stole some great recipes for cooking scallops. There is no way someone who was not born in Newfoundland came up with this recipe!"

"Cookie!" she laughed heartily. "You are so paranoid, and besides," she lowered her voice to a husky whisper, speaking right into his ear so he felt her hot breath with every word, "there is no secret I could not get from you, given enough time."

Sitting across from the couple and seeing Cookie's face turn scarlet, Stu smiled at his friend. "Geeze, Barnes! Better cut back on the vodka! You're lookin' a might flush there!"

"Yeah," Cookie stumbled, "It's pretty powerful stuff." Beneath the table, he felt Yelizaveta's hand take his and squeeze it. "Mighty powerful," he repeated, blushing again.

"I have to apologize for these two, admiral," Darren joked, gesturing at Stu and Cookie. "They don't get out much."

"It is okay, my friend! Tonight, we enjoy ourselves, and while I am still able to stand, I propose a toast."

They all stood, a wobbly Asimov being helped to his feet by Alexski.

"A toast to Canada, truly a great and proud country. Also, a toast to her navy, one of the finest in the world!"

Shouts of 'Here, here!' and the clinking of glasses filled the room.

"I return the toast, admiral," Darren responded raising his glass. "To Mother Russia! The Northern Bear! May she always prosper and may her people live long!"

"Oh god," Stu whispered loudly over to Cookie. "He thinks he's a Vulcan now."

"Just got it backwards is all," laughed the submariner before he raised his own glass. "I also respond with a toast! To hell with Canada and to hell with Russia! I toast these scallops and the rest of this meal!"

Everyone in the room broke into laughter and when the noise finally died down, a group of sailors wearing dress whites appeared carrying desert. Looking down at the ornate plate placed in front of him, Stu wrinkled his nose at the unidentifiable but colourful food sitting upon it. Slowly taking a small spoonful of whatever it was, he brought it to his mouth.

"Damn!" he exclaimed. "Whatever this ugly lookin' stuff is, it's some good!"

As the food disappeared, and the vodka continued to flow freely, Alexski struggled to his feet and excused himself when his pager went off.

"Hell, Alex!" Asimov grumbled. "Can't you leave work for one night?"

"Not this time," the ex-Spetsnaz replied, a stern expression crossing his face.

Admiral Andreev, who no amount of vodka seemed to affect, was sitting next to Darren and in spite of his attempts to steer the topic in another direction, found himself listening intently as the young man described what he had gone through.

The admiral had been incensed to discover that the man who had first tortured the Canadian, was Russian, and in his mind, he was already drafting the letter that would be sent to the FSB first thing the next morning. They would make sure no other 'Ugly Russians' had their expertise for sale over the internet or anywhere else.

Darren reminisced about his training up north and how the soldiers from Greenwood had taught him so much about survival in the wilderness. Andreev was cautious when the subject strayed to the Russian submarine. One of his closest friends was already in prison over the incident. He felt bad for the officer, but although the man was not directly responsible, the submarine's security had been partially his responsibility. Sad; he had such a beautiful family.

"I hope they find those damn ...," his voice cracked. "Whoever they were ..." Suddenly, the faces of the soldiers who had been with him appeared in his mind's eye. The realization that they were all dead, primarily because of him, smashed through the vodka induced haze and hit him hard. Cole looked down and wiped away the tears which fight as he might, stubbornly formed in his eyes. Andreev put a huge arm around the young man's shoulders and it was then that he slipped.

"They already have. One of your boats …" He cut himself off, but it was too late.

"One of our boats what?"

Darren was looking him straight in the eye; the effects of the Vodka suddenly gone as a tear slowly fell down his cheek.

Admiral Andreev knew he could just lie, but he also knew that what this man had gone through would haunt him forever. Unless, he thought, Cole was allowed some kind of retribution.

"Your submarine, *Victoria*, is following them."

"What!?"

"They have been trailing a contact for a few days now but had not been able to identify it. Your people contacted us to check on the possibility that it might be our missing boat." There was no point holding anything back from the submariner now. "We matched its signature."

Darren was about to say something when a Russian officer came over and whispered something in the admiral's ear. His expression changed from sullen to overtly happy. "Come with me my friend," the admiral motioned for Darren to follow him. "You will want to see this."

Alexski stood waiting for them outside the mess hall and he led Darren and the admiral down a long corridor to a locked door. Knocking, the commando stepped aside to let them in first. Darren was taken aback to see the 'Charges d'affaires' he had met at the hospital sitting in one corner of the room. A look of panic crossed the man's eyes when he saw Darren enter.

"Well, Mr. Westmorland. How have you been keeping yourself," Cole asked, his voice slurred by the vodka.

"He has been better," Alexski replied, before the man could speak. "He's told us everything we need to know however, so he shall live. Admiral, I have the code and frequency to contact the submarine with."

"What?" Admiral Andreev was stunned by the news. This man was the only survivor of the group who had held Cole captive and it was remarkable luck that he possessed the information they so desperately needed. The admiral was surprised the man had told them anything. He looked as though no amount of interrogation technique had been used on him—his clothing was not even wrinkled.

Guessing what the admiral was thinking, Alexski walked over and handed him something. "I only had to show him this," the ex-Spetsnaz explained. "Along with one of the Vienna sausages from your fine meal."

Examining the torture instrument Alexski had secretly taken from Ugly Russian's work bench, Andreev shook his head. Turning to Darren, he handed the instrument to him. "I think you should keep this. You are a brave young man Petty Officer Cole. I would be honoured to have you serve under me in the Russian Navy."

Darren took the instrument in his hands, causing the events of the past two weeks to briefly flash through his mind once again. He looked down at Westmorland and moved closer to him. Seeing the man flinch, he smiled down at him. "Don't worry, you useless piece of shit. We don't play the same games you do."

"Admiral, with your permission," Alexski asked, "I will send the necessary message to the stolen submarine. We have worked out coordinates which will send them in the general direction they would be expecting, but not close enough to the aircraft carrier for them to be a threat." He had been fully briefed on what was transpiring before his 'chat' with Westmorland.

"Very good, Alexski. Are they expected to acknowledge us?"

"No," he replied. "The plan is to send the message three times with ten minutes between transmissions."

"Let me know when it is sent. You will rejoin the party then, and Alex, that is an order!"

"Yes, sir," the Spetsnaz replied. "As soon as I make sure our guest here is looked after."

"Be sure that he is comfortable. I want him in good shape when we deliver him to his controllers. I am sure they will be excited to learn how useful he was to us …" He paused, "after we deal with our submarine, of course."

Returning to the mess hall turned banquet area, Darren and the admiral walked in just as Stu was making a toast to improved world relations in Cookie and Yelizaveta's direction. Seeing the admiral and Cole entering, he tried to turn to them with his glass but tripped over a table leg and went crashing to the floor.

"Sad," Cookie uttered, watching the SEAL slowly get back to his feet. "You'd never last in Newfoundland, my son. Not if you can't hold your liquor any better'n that."

"Well that's 'cause they don't go from milk to Scratch where I come from," he retorted, grimacing as he climbed from the floor, limping back into his chair.

"That's Screech my boy! Screech!"

Everyone laughed as they returned to the dessert. Taking a spoonful of his and swallowing slowly while deep in thought, Darren looked over to the admiral.

"Sir?"

Andreev turned to him slowly, knowing what was coming.

"I need to get aboard *Victoria*."

* * *

HMCS Victoria, Pacific Ocean, West of Seattle, Washington

Driven by the huge propeller turning over lazily at her stern, *HMCS Victoria's* hull slid silently through the water.

"Coming around ... okay. On original course. Same speed."

The master seaman seated at the sonar console looked over his shoulder, and Rene nodded in acknowledgement. The announcement, as with all verbal communication throughout the submarine, was curt but not loud. An observer would find the short snippets of conversation bewildering, as the crew went about their business. The uninitiated would not be able to discern who the snippets were directed at, let alone understand them. As Rene liked to point out to newer members of his crew, it was all about maintaining situational awareness.

"Hold course and speed."

Victoria's commanding officer was not enjoying this game of cat and mouse. Half an hour earlier, a communication had arrived via low frequency radio, but instead of the usual 'come up to periscope depth for a message', the four letter code group had only notified them to be ready to receive emergency traffic in the near future.

"That's weird," Commander Rene Bourgeois had noted, while passing the note to his executive officer. He was, however, relieved they did not have to leave the mysterious boat they had been tailing for so long, although a sickly feeling in his gut told him that this chase would not end with the usual sonar lashing and everyone happily returning home.

"You know, I have a bad feeling about this," Lieutenant Killiam, the boat's XO noted.

"Yeah," Rene replied. "I do too."

* * *

K-335, Pacific Ocean, West of Seattle, Washington

Just over a thousand yards ahead of *HMCS Victoria*, the captain of *K-335* was pondering a mystery of his own. The information he desperately needed to complete his mission was long overdue and he was concerned that it might not be coming at all. Looking up at the clock on the forward bulkhead, Zhong Xiao Chong noted the message was now over thirty hours late. He hid his growing anxiety from the crew; not even sharing the doubts that permeated his thoughts with the boat's executive officer. The lack of contact was making him nervous. If word did not arrive soon—any word—he would have to make his next move. The problem, he realized, was that he had no idea what that could be.

"We can always bring the submarine back to the Russians and see what they would pay for it," he had joked earlier with one of the crew in an attempt to defuse the stress that penetrated every nook and cranny of the boat. At that time, when the message had only been an hour late, it had seemed funny, and the men in the control room had broken into laughter. Now his mind contemplated even that possibility. He knew the Russians would be glad to have their boat back, and more so, might even handsomely reward him. The crew would be another matter, but the men had known the dangers when they volunteered, and this was no 'Hunt for Red October' movie. The crew would probably all be eliminated after the mission was completed, no matter what happened.

Glancing over the shoulder of the man at the helm, Chong noted their depth and course. They were currently on a bearing that would take them a few hundred miles off the west coast of the United States where they would hopefully intercept an aircraft carrier battle group, as the Americans called them, and sink the carrier. He still harboured a few misgivings about the mission, but having studied the capabilities of the submarine he now commanded, and more importantly, how an undisclosed source would supply them with information allowing him to break through the escorts surrounding the carrier, the veteran Chinese naval officer realized there was a better than even chance the mission would succeed. With its success would come glory beyond his imagination, not just for him personally, but for China itself, as an emerging world leader. This act would once and for all move the balance of power in the Pacific Rim from the West, who had held it for far too long, and assuming the information he needed arrived … a movement to his left jarred his mind back to the present as the radio operator rushed at him clutching a folded, piece of paper in his hand.

"Sir! We must prepare for a message!"

A stern look from the captain calmed the man down, and he came to attention, caught his breath, and handed the note to his captain.

"I am sorry, sir. We have received a message to come to periscope depth."

"That is better, thank you." Taking the note, Chong forced himself to unfold it slowly, wanting to appear calm to the rest of the men in the control room. "Helm, bring us up to periscope depth. Slowly," he ordered, as nonchalantly as he would a cup of coffee. Then turning back to the radio operator, he touched his shoulder. "Be prepared to receive the message the moment the antennae is clear. We must do so quickly so as not to be spotted."

"Yes, sir!"

The *Akula II*, although one of Russia's most advanced attack submarines, possessed one design flaw. The location of her after vent had been moved to allow for a change in size to the boat's reactor shielding, and that had resulted in an increase in noise levels when ballast was being blown from the stern tanks. Follow on construction had corrected the problem in later boats of the class, but on this unit, in spite of all the advancements added to the design since her launch, that issue had been deemed too costly to rectify.

* * *

HMCS Victoria, Pacific Ocean, West of Seattle, Washington

HMCS Victoria's sonar easily picked up the sound of *K-335's* ballast tanks blowing.

"Target is blowing ballast. He's coming up."

"Slow to ten—hold depth."

While *K-335* slowly continued towards the surface, Rene decided to keep *Victoria* at her present depth. There was always a risk when blowing water from the ballast tanks that a stray noise would give away their position and he wanted to remain the 'cat' in this game.

"Target maintaining depth," Leading Seaman Stewart who had the sonar watch announced. He could no longer detect any sound from the other boat as its hull reacted to changes in water pressure, and the newest member of the submarine's crew was anxious to show off his skills on the boat's sensitive listening devices. "Estimate contact at periscope depth."

"He might have gone up to send or receive a message," *Victoria's* XO suggested.

"Maybe."

Bourgeois was puzzled by the 'mouse's' actions. Submarine commanders seldom communicated with anybody outside their boat during a patrol. His thoughts were interrupted by the sonar operator.

"Target is diving again. He was level for less than a minute. Must have been a satellite burst transmission," Stewart surmised.

"And a short one at that," Rene noted. "Is he still holding course?"

"Yes … NO! Just changed, he's coming left to one six zero degrees."

"Helm, come left ten slowly to one six zero degrees on my mark."

Rene counted down the seconds to allow time for *Victoria* to enter the other boat's baffles. Situational awareness had always been his strongest asset.

"Mark!"

"On course one six zero, sir. Maintaining depth and speed."

"So my friend, where are you taking us?" Rene asked out loud.

"To periscope depth, I'm afraid," Lieutenant Mark Killiam interjected. "Just came in; we have to come up for a message."

"Okay, up ten to eighteen metres," *Victoria's* CO ordered. "Sonar, try not to lose him."

"Aye, sir," Stewart acknowledged.

"Comms? Make it quick," Bourgeois ordered. If the message had anything to do with their staying at sea, he would have to request a supply meet. They had not planned on being out this long and although *Victoria* had plenty of fuel remaining, the food stores were starting to run low. Hopefully a friendly AOR in the vicinity would be able to provision them, or it would be time to start restricting rations until they returned to Esquimalt. That wouldn't go over well, he knew, although some of the crew could stand to drop a few pounds.

"Yes, sir. Will do."

The helmsman brought the submarine up smoothly as the water in *Victoria's* ballast tanks was blown out with a gentle hiss of compressed air. In a few minutes, the comms mast poked above the ocean's surface and although the radar absorbent coverings on the mast would make it hard to detect by any passing ship or aircraft, this was when a submarine was most vulnerable. A rogue wave could cause her to breach, exposing the upper hull if the helmsman was not paying strict attention to the boat's attitude.

"Have it sir," Mark called out from the communications console. "Message received and acknowledged."

"Helm, down fifteen to one hundred and fifty metres—same course."

The executive officer handed the printout to Commander Bourgeois who read it through twice before handing it back.

"Well, I didn't see this coming."

The message briefly explained the situation with the hijacked submarine and the Chinese involvement, along with the possibility they would be ordered to sink it. The note also included a time and position for an UnRep with a US Navy replenishment ship. The message ended with notice that they were to await confirmation of the attack order, but if attacked, *Victoria* was free to retaliate.

* * *

MARLANT, CFB Halifax, Nova Scotia

At MARLANT headquarters in Halifax, Brent was gazing at a spreadsheet he had just pulled from his printer. "No," he replied to a question from George, while examining the page in his hand for the information he required, "They'll need more food pretty soon. Damn! I'd give last year's pay for *Vic* to be a nuc right about now. Those things can carry enough food to last a couple of months."

"Yes, but the Chinese would have heard her by now if she was," remarked Carroll from across the room. "It's because she's NOT a nuc that *Victoria's* crew have been able to tail that boat this long."

"You're right there," Brent replied, highlighting something on the piece of paper and sliding it into his 'out' box. "According to the latest position reports, *USNS Rappahannock* is in the vicinity and they can rendezvous with our boat in about five hours. That info was sent out to *Victoria*. *Rappahannock* won't be able to slow down much or change course though. The carrier escort is expecting her to feed them too, and we don't want to advertise that someone else in the area needs replenishment. Bourgeois will have to make sure he's moving right along the same track when the oiler appears on scene."

"That's going to be a neat trick," Carroll noted, picturing the submarine and replenishment ship timing their rendezvous that tightly.

"Maybe so, but if the Chinese captain detects any change in course or speed from the replenishment ship, he's going to assume it has something to do with him."

"Maybe if we could create a diversion …"

"No, too risky. We don't need anything else to complicate this mess."

"Sir?" Jody poked his head around the door. "I have Admiral Andreev on the line for you."

"Put him through!"

That was strange, thought O'Hanlon. They had just spoken a couple of hours ago. He picked up the receiver and hollered, "Geeze Dimetry! You must have a good long distance plan!" He listened for a long time as the Russian spoke and Admiral Carroll noted the expression on Brent's face changing rapidly from cordial to angry. "Yes they're setting up for an UnRep, but no, Dimetry, that's impossible!" Another pause ensued as Brent listened further and pondered how the Russian knew about the replenishment already. Then the admiral's face contorted as he exclaimed into the receiver, "He's only made three jumps! I don't think the middle of the Pacific Ocean onto a moving ship's helo pad is a good place to try a third one." The expression on the admiral's face grew angrier as he listened to the retort from the other end of the line. "No," O'Hanlon bellowed again. "If something goes wrong out there, he's dead!"

George had a feeling they were discussing his son-in-law, and he had a pretty good idea what Darren was asking for. Surely, he thought, Brent will quash that idea dead in its tracks. His thoughts turned to fear however, as he noted Brent's facial expression soften to one of reluctant acceptance.

"Hold on, you can tell him yourself. If he goes along with it, you have my blessing." O'Hanlon turned, handing the handset over to George.

Taking the receiver in his hands, Carroll threw a puzzled glance at Brent who simply shrugged his shoulders without saying anything. "Admiral, how are you?" he asked.

"I am well Admiral Carroll," Dimetry replied. "I need to tell you a story before I make a personal request." As George listened, Admiral Andreev told the retired Chief of Naval Operations how he had been a crewmember aboard a TU-95D Bear reconnaissance bomber shortly after joining the Soviet Air Force. He went on to describe an incident in 1966 when his aircraft had collided with a Royal Canadian Air Force Argus long range patrol aircraft, leaving only two Soviet survivors; himself and the radio operator, both freezing to death in the north Atlantic.

Carroll listened intently, hearing the pain in the Russian's voice as he described how survivor's guilt over the loss of his fellow crewmembers had followed him throughout the rest of his life, and how he continually relived the moments before the crash, wondering what he could have done differently. "I am sorry, admiral," George sympathized. "It must be a terrible burden."

"It is," the Russian replied sadly. "When a person goes through something like this and there is no closure, the guilt follows you forever."

"This is why you feel Petty Officer Cole must go to the submarine." It was a statement, not a question.

Dimetry smiled. He'd known that Admiral Carroll would understand. How odd, he thought. As antagonists, they had fought a long and bitter Cold War for many years, and now here they were, carefully discussing the fate of a single man. "Yes, Admiral," he replied. "I feel it is very important."

Carroll was silent for a few moments. He knew Andreev was right, and he knew Darren enough to realize that the submariner would blame himself for the deaths of the men who had been with him. He felt a slight shudder run down his spine at the thought of how Cole must feel. Throughout his ordeal, he had probably given little thought to that aspect, but now that he was safe, Darren would continually replay what had happened and what he might have done to change the outcome.

"It is, Dimetry," Carroll practically whispered. "Please tell him that I wish him luck."

"I will admiral. I must go now to arrange an aircraft."

"Thank you, and please keep us informed."

"I will George. It is good to speak with you."

The line went dead.

"I'm a dead man, Brent."

"Huh?"

"Twice, actually. Heather will kill me first, the moment I tell her that Cole is not on a plane headed back here."

"And the other death?" Brent asked, knowing the answer.

"If anything happens to him, my wife will kill me all over again."

"The burdens of command, my son," O'Hanlon quipped, his eyes crinkling as his face broke into a huge grin and he reached for one of the two bottles of champagne his aide had delivered.

* * *

Yelizovo, Russian Air Force Base

Petty Officer Darren Cole was by no means a short man and he had worked out prior to his trip up north, so even after his recent experience, he still had a 'bit 'o meat' on his bones now, as Heather put it, but the Russian commando towering over him in the shade of a huge aircraft hangar, made it seem as though he was the proverbial ninety pound weakling. The Canadians and Russians had arrived at the nearby Yelizovo airbase a few hours earlier, where the base commander had given them a brief tour culminating in a close look at one of the Mikoyan MiG-31s parked along the ramp.

"Now listen carefully," the giant of a man was telling the submariner. "You will only have one chance to get this right! This is your main release. It is the same as on the chutes you have used before. THIS is the backup release," he pointed out in perfect English. "It is NOT in the same place as you are used to."

Darren was thinking it was a good thing the Russian did not realize that he wasn't used to any parachute as he followed the commando's moves on the chute he was wearing. It did feel lighter, and seemed to fit better than the one he had used at Gagetown, although he had been assured that the canopy was 'almost' the same size and shape as the Canadian chutes, and would fly about the same.

"Maybe you guys use thinner lines," he tried to joke to Alexski who was watching them from a few yards away as the instructor helped him adjust the parachute's straps.

"Perhaps, but no one has ever complained," the Russian replied with a straight face. "Just do not miss ship when you land."

"They said if I do, there will be a boat in the water to fish me out right away. I'm not too worried."

"You will be fine, my friend and besides," Alexski paused, becoming serious, "you must finish mission for us."

Before Darren could reply, Alexski grabbed him in a huge bear hug, slapping his back before turning away and heading back into the hangar. The instructor checked the straps of Cole's chute one last time, insuring they were all tight and correctly positioned. Finally, he looked down at the submariner and held out his hand.

"Good luck, petty officer, and do not lose my parachute!"

"I'll send it back," Darren promised, taking the instructor's hand and feeling the massive strength in it as they shook. "Thank you."

As the two men parted, a truck pulled up next to them and Admiral Andreev, Cookie, Stu and Yelizaveta hopped out.

"So my young friend, you survived instructions."

"Yes, admiral. He was extremely thorough."

"He is our chief instructor with Spetsnaz. If he had said you could not go, even I could not challenge that. I apologize that I could not introduce him properly to you, but they are careful about use of names."

The sound of an approaching aircraft caught everyone's attention and they all turned to glance down the runway. In the distance, seeming to hang in midair without moving, an AN-124 Ruslan slowly grew in size before settling down onto the runway.

"Man, that's one big bird," Cookie remarked watching the transport turn onto a taxiway and lumber towards them before turning back towards the runway and coming to a stop.

The ramp at the rear of the aircraft's colossal fuselage opened and a crewmember standing on the platform waved them over.

"Go, and be careful!" Admiral Andreev called out over the whine of the engines, while pointing them to the cavernous opening at the back of the plane.

The group headed towards the ramp before Darren stopped and turned back.

"Thank you, admiral," Cole hollered, while coming to attention and saluting.

"No need," the Russian officer yelled back, returning the salute. "Give my best to Brent when you see him again."

They shook hands and Darren rushed to catch up with Cookie, Stu and Yelizaveta who were just climbing up the ramp into the gaping maw of the Ruslan's cargo bay. Once inside the massive aircraft, they were directed to a ladder attached to the forward bulkhead. Climbing towards a hatch high above, Cookie entered the space behind the cockpit where one of the flight crew pointed to drop down seats along the port side of the space and a Russian Air Force officer helped them strap in.

"We are taking off right away," he announced, helping Cookie adjust the belts around his waist. "This section of the aircraft is heated well so you will not be uncomfortable."

"Thanks," the submariner replied, feeling constrained in the metal seat which was a bit narrow for his large frame. It's going to be a long flight, he thought.

"Hey," Stu called over after fastening his own belts, "at least they didn't make me take my shoes off this time."

"Maybe I should have looked into jumping with you so I wouldn't have to fly so far with this guy," Cookie remarked to Darren who was wrestling with his seatbelt, trying to get it to fit over the parachute he wore.

"See! That's what I get! Zero respect!" The SEAL's pained expression made them all laugh which stopped when the whine from the engines suddenly increased.

As the aircraft began to taxi back onto the runway, Darren stretched to peer out one of the small windows behind him, catching a glimpse of Admiral Andreev waving up at them. Cole waved back through the small portal, vowing to keep in touch with the Russian who had been instrumental in organizing his rescue.

Straightening around in his seat, Darren looked over to Cookie and gave him a thumb's up. Although the aircraft was much quieter than the Hercules he'd last flown in, it was still difficult to talk over the whine of the turbofans as they spooled up to lift the colossal transport off the ground. A short time later, they had reached cruising altitude and the pilot throttled the engines back, making normal conversation possible again as the aircraft flew west.

"Where did Xue get to?" Cookie asked while unfastening his seat belt. He noticed her absence since the group had arrived at the Russian submarine base.

"I don't know," Cole replied. "She came by to say she had to leave before supper and was gone. I expect she had to get right back to Ottawa for debriefing."

"Makes sense."

"I told her to make sure she comes to Halifax for a visit sometime. I know Heather will want to meet her." Darren smiled as he thought of his wife. Although he knew she would eventually understand, he wondered how his father-in-law had broken the news about the change in plans.

* * *

Cole Apartment, Halifax, Nova Scotia

"I'll kill him!"

"I don't know honey. He survived my SEALs AND the Chinese," George joked. He was trying to bring a little levity to the atmosphere at Darren and Heather's apartment. After taking a taxi over to explain what had happened, not daring to tell her what was going on over the phone, Heather had exploded. Upon learning that not only was Darren not on his way home, but that he was instead heading right back into the fray, she had started to pace between the living room and kitchen. Carroll had wisely left out the part about parachuting down to the replenishment ship, and thankfully Heather hadn't asked how her husband was going to get aboard *Victoria*.

"Oh daddy ..." She rushed into his arms and held her father tightly. "What is he thinking?!"

"Come sit, Heather. I need to tell you about something that happened to a Russian friend of mine about fifty years ago. I think," or so he hoped, "it will explain why Darren has to do this."

A short time later, Heather was wiping tears from her eyes as she hugged her father again. "I understand daddy. I really do." Then she added with a smile, "I still might have to kill him though."

"God knows your mother threatened to do that to me more than once," George replied, hugging his daughter even tighter. "I knew as long as she wanted to kill me now and then, she still loved me."

* * *

Prime Minister's Office, Ottawa, Ontario

Killing was also being discussed in the Prime Minister's Office, but in a much more serious tone. Caroline Wheeler, Canada's Minister of National Defence, and the Prime Minister had just returned to the his office after a long, and at times emotional meeting with the Cabinet and Chief of the Defence Staff, where the Canadian leader had explained the situation and his plans. Also present at the meeting, having been invited due to the highly sensitive nature of the issue, had been the leaders of Canada's other two major political parties. Both of them had immediately shoved politics aside and agreed with the Prime Minister that action had to be taken; assuring him that he would have the full cooperation of their parties. Someone had mentioned the absence of the leader of Canada's fourth political party which had brought a chuckle from a couple of people, momentarily breaking the tension in the room which had become so thick that even the proverbial 'knife' may have been unable to cut it.

Now, three hours later and mentally exhausted from the planning sessions, the Prime Minister handed his defence minister a cup of coffee from the pot behind his desk

"I don't want to give the idea that I'm thinking of backing down from the agreed action, Caroline, but can you think of any other possible alternatives; perhaps some action we haven't explored?"

"No, Prime Minister. There really are no other alternatives," she replied. "We have to sink the submarine if for no other reason than to show the world that terrorism on this level will not be tolerated by anyone. Ever."

"Do we have any idea of the crew's makeup yet?"

"Not for certain, but CSIS is pretty confident they are mostly Chinese, along with some disgruntled Russians from the submarine's original crew."

"Well, at least we know the Russian Government is behind us," the Prime Minister noted. "Their President has made it clear that we have his blessings in sinking the submarine. They know there is little chance they would ever get it back from the Chinese anyway so I expect they would rather see it sunk than remain in Chinese hands."

"*Victoria* is setting up her rendezvous with the replenishment ship to take on more food and when she surfaces will be the best time to send Rene the operational order. He'll be able to confirm the message immediately while on the surface."

"Tell me, Caroline," he continued, "do you think our men will have any problems carrying out their orders?"

The Prime Minister was certain they wouldn't, but he had to ask.

"No, Prime Minister," the MOD replied firmly. "None."

"Okay, send the order to Rene. Tell him he has clearance to sink the Russian submarine."

"Yes, sir."

"And Caroline?"

"Sir?"

"This isn't going to be like the mission with *HMCS Corner Brook*. I want every reporter within five hundred miles of British Columbia meeting *Victoria* when she pulls in," the Prime Minister ordered. "I don't want any member of the crew to ever doubt that what they did was the right thing to do, and that the whole country supported them in doing it."

"Yes, Prime Minister." Caroline Wheeler stood and turned to leave, but stopped and turned back. "Thank you, David. That will mean a lot to the community."

"You're welcome, Caroline. I know how hard it was for you to bite your tongue after *Corner Brook's* mission." He stopped, deep in thought for a moment before adding. "I'd love to be on the pier when they pull in, but I don't want this to look like a political 'photo-op'. I'll have to think of something else."

She managed a tired smile and nodded before leaving the office. Outside in the hallway, the Minister of Defence could barely contain herself. When she arrived at her own office, she arranged a quick conference call with MARPAC and MARLANT to inform her admirals of the Prime Minister's order. Hearing Brent's usual gruff greeting as he joined the call, she could not help but tease him.

"Good to hear your voice Admiral O'Hanlon. I know you still consider all the boats to be your own personal property so I thought I'd better ask your permission before giving Admiral Leger orders for *Victoria*."

The two naval officers laughed heartily before Brent finally stopped and replied, "No, I'm over that stage now, Minister. I have learned to share my toys, albeit reluctantly."

"Don't believe him for a second!" Admiral Leger exclaimed from his office in Esquimalt, the west coast headquarters of the Royal Canadian Navy. "I have to fight tooth and nail to get anything sent out from Halifax! You'd think there were three boats there instead of here!"

"You call me if he gives you a hard time, Ray. I know how to handle Mr. O'Hanlon." Caroline quipped.

Going over her conversation with the Prime Minister, she explained how it had been decided that *Victoria* was to sink the stolen submarine at the first opportunity. Caroline heard Brent whisper 'Damn!' over the line and couldn't help but wonder if it was a shocked reaction to the news, or a regret that his east coast boat wasn't going to be involved—with him aboard.

"And Brent, I know you're not totally out of the picture. I heard your favourite 'spy' is on his way to join *Victoria*.

"Er ... yes."

Brent had a moment of hesitation as he wondered if his decision to allow Cole's joining the boat should have been cleared higher up the chain of command first.

"Don't worry, O'Hanlon," the Defence Minister interjected, sensing his concern. "I would have done the same thing. After what Cole's been through, this will be good therapy for him, and on that note, there's more."

Caroline shared her orders in regards to having the media meet *Victoria* upon her return to Esquimalt.

"I want this event to make *HMS Conqueror's* return to Britain look boring by comparison," she ordered, referring to the Royal Navy submarine that had sunk the Argentine Navy cruiser *ARA General Belgrano* during the Falklands war.

"That's excellent!" Admiral Leger exclaimed into the phone. He appreciated how many successful missions his submariners took part in, only to have them hushed up. The only time the boats made the news, he often lamented, was when something aboard one of them broke.

"Okay, gentleman, I'm going to leave the call now as I am sure you two have things to talk over. If you run into any snags," she cautioned, "call me immediately."

Ending the call at her end, Caroline sank back into her chair. It was suddenly completely quiet in the room as she pondered how *Victoria's* crew would react to the order. They will be fine, she told herself. There really is no choice. What had happened could not be left unanswered and the men aboard the submarine knew that.

She also realized that having Petty Officer Cole aboard might be just the motivation they would need. Submariners, she had learned, were as much a brotherhood as the army; perhaps more so.

* * *

O'Hare International Airport, Chicago, Illinois

Watching the last of the passengers who had shared her late night flight from Toronto leave the terminal building, Xue Lee relaxed at one of the small tables outside the Terminal 2 coffee shop at Chicago's O'Hare International Airport. Earlier that evening, the Air Canada flight originating in Vancouver, had made a short stopover in the 'Big Smoke', allowing her a chance to send a quick text to CSIS for an update on the contact she was to meet at O'Hare along with her ROE for the trip. Xue had thought it odd, while thumbing the data into her Blackberry; this was the first time she had discussed Rules of Engagement for a trip into the United States. Thankfully, she was not suffering from jetlag, in spite of her recent overseas flight to Canada from Russia, as with most international agents, she had trained her body to sleep when it needed to, regardless of the time of day.

Glancing down towards the mostly deserted main foyer of the terminal building, she took a long sip of coffee while scanning the headlines in the previous day's Chicago Tribune. Xue loved reading newspapers—any newspaper. It was an old habit she had learned from her father. The CSIS agent had come to appreciate the relaxing combination of a morning paper and a good cup of coffee as the perfect way to begin the day.

Her parents had immigrated to Canada from China just before she was born, settling in western Ontario where her mother operated a small book store. Her father, an English language teacher back home, now taught history at the nearby high school. The newly arrived couple had found it strange at first, living in a huge country whose entire population was only a third of the size of Guangdong Province, where they had resided back home in China.

Xue's parents had a great appreciation for the value a good education would be to her, and they had been excited upon learning of her plans to take advantage of above average marks in high school to attend medical school and become a doctor. They had been distressed later however, when she had explained that the medical courses were boring her to death and that she had accepted a recruiter's offer to join CSIS, the Canadian Security Intelligence Service.

Xue smiled at the memory. It had been the right decision. Flipping to the business section, she read the latest news concerning the economy. It must have been a slow news day, she thought. The stories were mostly updates on previous financial events that had taken place in the 'Windy City' and around the world.

Finishing the last of her coffee, she folded the newspaper, and walked over to the counter, setting the empty cup down there so the lone server working the graveyard shift wouldn't have to bother going over to pick it up. Sitting down on one of the counter's barstools, she glanced around the concourse, still holding the newspaper. That was a prearranged signal for her contact. Only a few people remained now, probably like her, waiting for someone to come and pick them up. With luck, the person she was to meet would arrive soon.

"Luck," she whispered aloud.

Luck had played an uncomfortably large part in her current assignment and hopefully that luck would not run out any time soon. 'Lady Luck' had first reared her seductive head when an urgent message had arrived through her controller in China, informing the CSIS agent operating undercover as a member of MSS, China's security agency, that she was needed for an operation originating in Shanghai. If all went according to plan, the message noted that she would be leaving there as part of a medical team to an undisclosed location.

"What is the operation?" she had messaged her controller, a woman she'd never met.

"Do not ask," had been the expected, curt reply.

Fortune smiled upon her again, when after arriving in Shanghai, Xue had learned she would be accompanying a group of Ministry of State Security agents to Russia. She had only been told by one of the Chinese agents that the mission was classified and MSS had been forced to carry it out in Russia in case anything went wrong. It was imperative, she'd been told, that neither China, nor its State Security operatives be linked in any way to the operation.

Four days later the Canadian operative had found herself in an abandoned Russian military hospital, parts of which had been cleaned up and painted. Those areas now looked as though they had never closed. The operation's leader had brought them all into one of the wards where he explained what was about to happen. A captured Canadian submariner was being brought in and to ensure the success of an important mission, it was crucial that knowledge he held be retrieved quickly.

Xue had stifled a gasp when the she heard 'Canadian'. What would China want with a Canadian sailor, the CSIS agent had wondered? One thing was certain; her main objective, after somehow getting information of this operation to her contact, would be to make certain that this man survived whatever was about to happen.

When they brought Cole in a few days later, she had been shocked at his condition. Whoever had worked him over obviously knew what they were doing as none of the young man's injuries, although serious, were life threatening. Nursing him back to health, she had been tempted many times to divulge her true identity to the man but in his medicated and weakened state that might have proven dangerous.

"Luck," she whispered, spinning around in her seat to drop a dollar bill next to the empty cup as a tip. "Please be a lady tonight."

"That's a pretty generous tip for a cup of coffee."

Turning abruptly, she saw a man and woman approaching her. "It was a really good cup of coffee," she replied before adding, "I hope it doesn't rain tonight. I forgot to roll my car windows all the way up."

"You must be Agent Lee," the man laughed, recognizing the prearranged signal. "I don't think you'll have to worry about rain tonight, what with the full moon shining out there.

His eyes reflected his laughter. Slightly shorter than the woman, he possessed no distinguishing features; a valuable asset for an agent who might need to blend in somewhere and not be noticed.

"Special Agent Todd Connors; NCIS, and this is Special Agent Carol Henning," he announced offering his hand.

"Pleased to meet you guys," Xue replied, shaking hands with both agents.

"Another team is tailing our boy," noted Carol. She was tall and nicely proportioned, Lee noted. The suit she wore did little hide her muscles, or the large automatic in a shoulder holster under her right arm. Unlike her partner, she would easily stand out in a large crowd – more so because of the shock of bright red hair and the countless freckles dotting her face.

"You're a south paw."

"Good catch," Carol noted with a smirk.

"Thanks."

"How was the flight in?" Todd asked, as they walked through the concourse.

"Quick. It didn't seem like we had taxied for take-off before we were on approach to land."

"We're right here," he pointed to an official looking car sitting at the curb in the red zone.

Xue tossed her bag onto the car's back seat before sliding in after it. As they pulled away, she noticed an intricate communications panel built into the dash to the right of the driver where the navigation system would normally reside.

"Quite the setup."

"It's brand new," Carol replied, while flipping a switch on the device causing a large LCD panel to light up, displaying a number of icons. "We can talk with any NCIS agent anywhere on the continent and it piggy backs on the cell phone networks without skipping a beat, even while jumping carriers."

"Impressive."

Xue wasn't really impressed. CSIS had a similar system, only one third the size of this one, and portable. It also wasn't only restricted to cell phone frequencies as a few ham-fisted agents had embarrassingly discovered.

"So, fill me in on how you came across our buddy."

"Well," Todd began, while smoothly merging into the traffic on Interstate 294, "It was really pure, dumb luck."

In the darkness he could not see the grin on Xue's face. She had been about to comment, but decided against it.

"A Marine Gunny on TDY to your army base in Gagetown, New Brunswick called into our field office in Portsmouth, New Hampshire saying that he'd overheard one of the other jarheads talking to someone on his cell phone about a snatch. He kept listening and picked up a few words but the one that stood out in his mind was 'submariner'."

"Oh?"

"It gets better," Carol noted.

"So, when this Gunny calls, he tells one of the agents there about this phone call he's overheard. Meanwhile, the agent in New Hampshire is literally holding in his hand, a report from you guys about your missing man." Todd paused to let that sink in. "So meanwhile, his Marine unit is now back here at Great Lakes and we've been watching the guy, but haven't seen anything suspicious."

Agent Henning reached between the seats and handed a tan coloured folder to the CSIS agent. "Here's his file."

Scanning through the pages, the first thing Xue noted was that the Marine was Asian. Brian Pulsifer? Adopted perhaps? She pondered whether the face staring back at her from the photo might be a Chinese agent. The man was 28 and had a clean record with nothing outstanding in the file, not even any minor infractions. That was suspicious in itself. Most Marines managed to get into trouble at some point in their careers, but this one was flying well under the radar. She noted his height: 6'2". Odd for someone of his, and Xue's, race. She could not think of anyone in her family taller than her 5'8".

"Big fellow."

"Yeah. Mean, too," Carol noted. "The latest incident report's not in the file because it only happened last week, but he was involved in a fight with a couple of sailors and put both of them in the hospital."

"And he's not in custody?"

"No," Todd answered while smoothly turning into a parking area in front of a non-descript building. "We didn't want to take any chances on spooking him so we had the swabbies tell him that they denied the fight had taken place, claiming they couldn't risk the attention because of an earlier fight they'd been part of."

"Fortunately, our suspect bought it," added Carol.

An hour and a half later, pulling into a reserved space close to the building and turning the ignition off, Todd turned to Xue and cheerfully announced, "Welcome to Naval Criminal Investigative Services, Central Field Office, Agent Lee"

"Nice digs," Lee noted, glancing at the extensive landscaping that surrounded the parking lot. The area was well lit by a seemingly endless number of LED light fixtures carefully placed amongst the trees.

"They're not bad, but sadly, it's about to close. There just isn't enough activity in this part of the US to warrant having an independent field office up here."

Leaving the car, she and Carol followed Todd to a side entrance where he scanned his ID and signed Xue in at the security desk. Entering an empty office, the three sat down and discussed their plans for the upcoming arrest.

"He'll try to run," Xue surmised, "and if he's cornered, he will fight."

"We thought as much ourselves," Carol responded. "I've got half a dozen other agents who will be working with us and a few more on standby just in case."

"Sounds good."

The CSIS agent looked over the suspect's file once again. She noted he had been born in San Francisco, California, and wondered if his parents were still alive. If he was a bona fide Chinese operative, the odds were pretty good that his parents were as well. Probably deep cover plants from the Cold War. Mentioning her suspicion to the NCIS agents, they agreed and Todd made a quick call to the Los Angeles NCIS office to alert them. That part of the investigation would have to wait until this operation was completed, but NCIS LA could at least get a head start on the paperwork. In the meantime, Xue brought them up to speed on the operation in Russia.

"Damn!" Todd exclaimed. "They've got balls to have tried to pull that off right under the Kremlin's nose!"

"They do at that, and now it's time to hit the street," announced Carol. "Our boy likes to have an early breakfast at one of the local eateries and if he's true to form, he will just be arriving there about now. I think it will be best to take him down when he's feeling full. Hope you were able to grab some sleep on your flight down, Agent Lee."

"I did."

Todd handed her a Beretta 92F and a belt clip holster. Xue could tell by the handgun's weight that the weapon held a full magazine of fifteen rounds.

"Just in case."

"Hopefully I won't need this," the CSIS agent remarked. She preferred a smaller, lighter automatic. If you ever needed more than ten rounds in their line of work, she had noted to one of her colleagues, you wouldn't be around long.

"Yeah, and hopefully the massive breakfast he seems to prefer will slow him down a little," Carol noted, grinning widely.

Leaving the NCIS building, they drove a short distance to a divided street where most of the fast food companies had set up shop. Sprinkled amongst the familiar locations, a few actual sit-down restaurants had opened, hoping, no doubt, to pick up the burger crowd over flow.

Todd pulled into one of the parking lots alongside a restaurant whose signage proclaimed that they served 'The Best Meal You've Had Since Leaving Momma!' Driving behind the building, he backed into a spot giving them a clear view up the side of the restaurant towards the main entrance. Setting the transmission to 'park', he turned off the motor and settled down into his seat.

"That's his wheels," Todd noted, pointing to a blue Honda Civic. The car had been tricked out and sat a good two inches closer to the ground than the day it had left the factory. The compact also sported a custom paint job and wheels that reflected every nuance of the rising sun.

"I'll go have a look and check that he's alone," said Carol, zipping up the leather jacket she wore. It would not do for their suspect to look over and notice the gun hanging from her shoulder holster. Walking nonchalantly along the side of the building, she casually glanced inside the windows and immediately picked him out sitting alone at a booth in the back corner facing the door. Smart move, she thought. They planned on waiting until he left, so his view of anyone entering the establishment would not save him this morning. Returning to the car, she slid back into the passenger seat and reported her observations.

"Did you notice if he'd been served?"

"Yeah, he was just finishing up so he should be coming out any time now."

"Let's get into position," Todd ordered. Expecting that Pulsifer would leave by the main entrance closest to his car, he and Carol planned to act as a couple on their way into the restaurant in order to get as close to the Marine as possible before taking him down. Xue would cover the opposite entrance in the unlikely event he exited from that side of the building. If that happened, she would simply follow him until he went around the back of the building towards Todd and Carol. In the adjoining parking lot, another pair of NCIS agents waited patiently in their car in case they were needed.

A few minutes later, Carol saw the glass door open and their suspect walk out.

"There he is," she whispered without looking directly at him. Pulsifer was walking slowly to his car while folding his wallet closed. Reaching behind to slide it into his back pocket, he noticed the couple walking towards him, sharing a hearty laugh about something.

"No! She didn't!" Todd roared as he and Carol came within ten feet of the man.

"Yes! She really did!"

Something in their conversation wasn't natural and Pulsifer picked up on it. He immediately quickened his pace towards the car and away from the two agents.

They turned in unison, reaching for their weapons.

"Federal Agents! Hold it right there Pulsifer!" Carol screamed at him.

With an incredible burst of speed, the man leapt over the hood of the nearest car in the parking lot and tore around the back of the building—running head on into Agent Lee who had started to run around the building at the sound of Carol's shout. As the two collided, Pulsifer glowered down at her stepping back a couple of feet.

"She said, hold it right there!" Xue screamed out, reaching behind her waist for the Beretta. The agent saw the Marine's muscles tense and a huge hand beginning to lunge for her. She would not have enough time to bring the weapon to bear.

Pulsifer's only thought was to destroy this small person before him, but in his rage, he failed to note the woman shift her body weight over to one leg. Nor did he see the foot which moved with blinding speed towards his crotch.

Todd and Carol came running around the corner to find the man lying on the ground in the fetal position, a low moaning sound coming from his mouth.

"Ouch." Todd couldn't help but smile.

"The bigger they are …" Xue nodded.

"Okay Pulsifer, let's get going," Connors ordered, helping the man to his feet. The injured man almost made it before falling back down to his knees and throwing up. With no hint of sympathy in his voice, Todd added, "You are under arrest for accessory to murder, kidnapping, and espionage … oh, and puking in public. That's disgusting."

He went on to read Pulsifer his rights while cuffing the man's hands behind his back. Carol returned to the car and called off the other units waiting to assist them, while Xue and Todd helped their prisoner into the back seat, where he collapsed in severe pain.

"Hell, you're mighty accurate with your feet Agent Lee."

"I find men respect you much more when you take them down this way," she noted. "It kind of removes any feelings of dominance they might be harbouring."

"Hmm, I'll have to keep that in mind." Carol winked at Todd. The two had been dating for some time to the chagrin of their director, who chose to feign ignorance as they were two of the best agents he had.

"So, Mister Pulsifer," Xue looked him straight in the eye as they pulled out of the parking space. "You will be returning to Canada sooner than you expected."

Whatever answer he had in mind was interrupted by a loud moan as the car lurched through a pothole while leaving the parking lot, sending a shock of pain through the Marine's body.

"Sorry!" Todd called back, not meaning it.

* * *

Beijing, China

China's President was not happy. The news presented to him half an hour ago by a nervous advisor, regarding contact being lost with the operatives in Russia, could mean only one thing: someone had leaked information to the Russians. When that person was found, he or she would pay a dear price for their indiscretion. What happened to them did not concern him right now however. What did, was a large and powerful loose end which had to be eliminated quickly. He had summoned Admiral Dai to his office and the naval officer was now standing at attention in front of his desk.

"Are you sure Kuo will succeed, Admiral Dai?"

"Yes my President."

"I wish I could share your confidence," the President responded; his voice barely a whisper.

"Lieutenant Commander Kuo will catch the Russian submarine and sink it before the Americans find them. We were able to intercept the signal that was sent to the *Akula* by the enemy agents so we know exactly where they will be."

"I still do not understand how the Russians discovered where our agents were," China's leader lamented once again. His frustration was made deeper still by the apparent lack of anyone to hold responsible for the mission's failure. It was unlikely any of the operatives in Russia were still alive, he realized, enjoying the small feeling of relief that knowledge brought him. They would have been severely dealt with by the FSB.

"Our people will find out who it was, my President."

The admiral doubted that would happen. No officer of the People's Liberation Army Navy would ever betray his country. Perhaps it was just one of those events where someone in the right place at the right time … No, he stopped himself in mid-thought. It had to have been one of the political connections to the President, and that would make any kind of investigation impossible.

Hopefully, he pondered, with no one else to point a finger at, he would not be made a scapegoat. His uncle should be able to protect him, unless of course it was at the cost of his own standing in the party. If that should happen, Dai knew he wouldn't live to see the end of the week.

The Chinese President's mind meanwhile, switched to how he would deal with Canada. Although not a nation he feared in any way, if the Canadian Prime Minister was to find out that China had been part of what happened in their north, he would probably protest through the United Nations. Although the accusations would be easily denied, they would leave a dark cloud over relations with the country who had become one of China's favoured trading partners. The Chinese security service should have tried to find an American with the information they needed but it had all seemed so easy once his advisors had shown him the article on how a Canadian submarine had hunted down a British aircraft carrier without being detected. Too easy, he now realized.

"I should not worry so much," he said, looking out the window.

"I am sorry?" asked the admiral, who was lost in his own thoughts.

"My own concern. You may go."

"Yes my President."

As Admiral Dai left the Presidential Office Building, he slipped on a pair of sunglasses to shield his eyes from the unusually bright, morning sun. He was concerned, but not overly, with the new direction the operation had taken. When he returned to his office, the admiral made a phone call and ordered a message sent by the navy's very low frequency transmitter—to no particular station—just a single character, repeated three times.

* * *

Prime Minister's Office, Ottawa, Ontario

Half a world away, the Prime Minister of Canada was having a late evening meeting in his office, with one of his top security advisors.

"No, Prime Minister. We haven't noted anything unusual in our everyday communications with China."

"Good, John. Let me know if you smell anything," the Prime Minister ordered. "Oh, and John, is the Chinese Ambassador still in his residence?"

"Yes, sir. We have people watching the building and they will contact us if he leaves, or if anyone outside the usual visitors drop by."

"Okay, I expect things will start happening shortly and I don't want our side to be the one letting anything slip."

"Yes, Prime Minister."

"Thanks, John. That's all."

With that, the advisor left the office, leaving the Prime Minster to return to his desk. Looking at the growing pile of paperwork for a moment, the Canadian leader wondered if major world events in the past had been worked out between countries simply because their leaders realized they had to be, or they would have never caught up on their paper work.

* * *

Russian Air Force AN-24, West of Seattle, Washington

There was surprisingly little turbulence inside the AN-24's massive cargo hold as the loading ramp slowly opened, revealing a panoramic view of the Pacific Ocean far below. The pilot descended to five thousand feet while pulling the throttles back, slowing the giant aircraft to a crawl compared to the speed at which they had flown across the ocean.

Darren avoided looking down and instead gazed directly aft through the gaping hole at the clear blue sky beyond. His relief that the weather was perfect for his jump was tempered with regret that a cyclone hadn't moved in, forcing him to reconsider his plan.

Standing next to Cole in the middle of the AN-124 Ruslan's hold, Cookie was shouting something in the submariner's ear, but with the whistling sound of the aircraft's slipstream echoing through the hold and the tight-fitting helmet he wore, Darren was unable to make him out. Giving up, cookie shook his hand and gave him a quick pat on the back before returning to his seat.

One of the Russian crew walked over to Cole, and after getting his attention, pointed to a light fixture next to the ramp mechanism, that was glowing a dull red.

"When light turns blue, you go!" he yelled into Darren's ear, after shoving a gloved hand between Cole's helmet and the side of his head.

Replying with a nod and thumbs up, Darren slowly walked towards the opening, not taking his eye off the light. Seconds later, the light turned blue and without hesitation, he took a deep breath, walked onto the ramp and stepped off.

The first thing that struck him was how quiet everything seemed compared to his earlier experience jumping from an RCAF Hercules. He'd barely had time to contemplate the differences between the two aircraft any further, when he was hit by the blast and deafening whine of the jet engines as he fell into the aircraft's slipstream, his body tumbling around in the air like a rag doll. Quickly regaining his composure, Darren stretched out his arms and legs as he had been taught and smoothly brought the gyrations under control while counting the seconds of his free fall.

Looking down, he spotted a ship's wake in the water far below. The AOR steaming at the head of the white line seemed impossibly small, but he did note that it was growing larger by the second. Shaping his body to bring his decent into a slightly forward motion towards the replenishment ship's bow, the submariner quickly calculated the distance to the deck and where he should be when he opened the chute. Fortunately, a report from the ship had indicated the surface winds were negligible meaning he only had to account for the ship and his movement which was proving to be difficult enough. Grabbing the ring a few seconds later, Darren yanked the cord out and was rewarded by a quiet whooshing sound from behind as first the pilot and then the main chute billowed out above him.

'Nice,' he thought, admiring the morning sun's effect on the intricate camouflage pattern printed on the canopy above his head. There had been less of a jolt and much less noise compared to the Canadian Army chute he had jumped with, and he bet this one wouldn't be making its way back to Russia until the army guys had a good look at it. Steering the chute with handles attached to a set of cables hanging down from the lines on either side of his head, Cole brought himself around to line up with the helicopter landing pad on the ships stern. Out of the corner of one eye, he made out a Zodiac zipping along after the ship; no doubt standing by in case they needed to fish him out of the ocean.

Giving the handle clutched in his right hand a firm tug, the submariner set himself up for what he thought would be a perfect landing when a large swell brought the ship's stern up, causing him to crash hard onto the deck. Sailors immediately came running from the edges of the landing pad and quickly flattened the chute so he would not be carried overboard if a gust of wind came up. Stunned for a moment, Darren felt hands grab his body and slowly help him to a sitting position and though still dazed from the hard landing, he heard someone asking if he was okay. Taking a moment to move his arms and legs and finding them responding as they should, he replied that he thought so and carefully stood, which brought a cheer from the men standing around him.

"Welcome aboard *Rappahannock*, Petty Officer Cole!"

The announcement had come from a speaker on the hangar bulkhead behind him.

"Unfortunately, there is no time for pleasantries," the disembodied voice continued. "Clear the pad for helo landing!"

"This way, chief!" a sailor shouted, pointing to a short ladder leading down from the landing pad to the ship's port side.

As Darren approached the edge of the landing area, he spotted *HMCS Victoria* steaming alongside the tanker and his face broke out in a huge grin. A fueling hose stretched down to the submarine while a few sailors stood by a hatch on the boat's deck, and he jumped up and waved to them. The grin was suddenly replaced with a grimace, as a sharp pain shot up his left leg. Obviously, he thought, that landing had been a bit too hard.

Turning around to lower himself gingerly down the ladder, he watched as members of *Rappahannock's* crew pushed a small pallet out from an opening in the ship's superstructure onto the flight deck. He was about to ask what they were doing when the roar of turbines washed over him as an SH-60 Seahawk swooped down the ship's starboard side before coming around to hover above the deck. Within seconds, a cable lowered from the helicopter had been attached to the pallet, and the helicopter lifted off and flew towards *Victoria*, where it slowly descended over the bow of the submarine.

As soon as the pallet touched the submarine's deck, the boat's crew rushed forward and formed a human chain, transferring the cargo down through the forward hatch where more sailors passed it along the passageway to various storage spaces.

Having watched Darren's abrupt landing, and noting the slight limp as he made his way down the ladder, Rene called down from his perch on *Victoria's* bridge for his medical officer to stand by to look at Cole's leg as soon as he was aboard.

HMCS Victoria's commanding officer was still dumbfounded over the message he had received upon surfacing, informing him of Cole's transfer from the American ship to his boat. Observing as the sailors aboard *Rappahannock* tied a life jacket around the petty officer before sending him down the ship's boarding ladder to a waiting Zodiac, Rene acknowledged a message from below that the stores transfer would be completed in ten minutes.

Jumping into the Zodiac, and hiding the jolt of pain in his leg, Darren hung on as the sailor manning the boat's wheel threw it over hard after slapping the throttles forward, and headed towards the submarine. In a matter of seconds, Cole was being helped up to *Victoria's* deck.

"Welcome aboard, Cole!"

Darren turned and looked up to the top of the sail. Saluting, his face a huge grin, he called up to the submarine's commanding officer.

"Thank you, sir! I appreciate the lift!"

"Get below! Doc is waiting for you!"

"I'm fine sir! I'll just ..."

"Head below and see doc!" Rene finished Cole's sentence, pointing to the aft hatch.

Making his way around the sail and to the opening in the deck, Darren waved over towards the tanker's bridge before the man next to him patted his arm while pointing to the hatch and beckoning for him to hurry.

"We have to get back down chief! We've been tailing another boat and …"

"I know!" Darren replied, shouting to be heard over the roar of the helicopter as it lifted the now empty pallet and headed back to the replenishment ship. "We need to catch that bastard!"

* * *

Type 041 SSK, PLA Navy, West of Seattle, Washington

Chief Petty Officer Darren Cole was not the only one desperate to catch up with the Russian boat. On the opposite bearing from *Victoria's* position to the Russian submarine, another 'steel shark' moved silently through the water. Aboard the Chinese SSK, code named *Yuan* by NATO, and Type 041 by the People's Liberation Army Navy, the boat's captain was discussing their new orders with his executive officer. The coded message received earlier from naval headquarters had momentarily shocked the captain, but he'd quickly recovered and ordered the boat's second in command to his cabin where they had discussed the ongoing situation. Now they met again, planning the attack which would kill some of their countrymen.

"We should be within range in two hours, sir," the executive officer announced while discreetly closing the thin door behind him.

"Good. And the crew?"

"I have not heard any concerns. They understand how important this mission is."

A few of the *Yuan's* sailors had close friends aboard the Russian submarine, but they knew that something must have gone terribly wrong for the situation to have come to this. They would do their duty, even if that duty was to kill their friends.

"Good. Let us hope everything goes well."

"I am sure it will, my captain. The other submarine will not hear us coming and will not expect what is about to happen."

He had made the usual switch by naval officers; referring to his boat and crew as one, but always only to the boat when speaking of an adversary.

An hour later, approaching the general area where the Russian submarine was expected to be waiting for its target, the Chinese boat's sonar failed to detect the equally quiet Canadian submarine which crossed the *Yuan's* path at a slightly deeper depth.

* * *

HMCS Victoria, Pacific Ocean, West of Seattle, Washington

"Anything?"

"Nothing yet, sir," replied *Victoria's* sonar operator, thinking to himself, as all sonar operators had, *if I had a dollar for every time someone asked me that.*

Having replenished their food stores and picked up an unexpected new crew member, Rene had quickly ordered *HMCS Victoria* to the last known depth of the Russian boat they had been tailing. He was hoping to continue the game of cat and mouse where it had left off before the message ordering him to rendezvous with the oiler had arrived.

In the submarine's torpedo space, Petty Officer Cole was going over the load out with *Victoria's* weapons officer.

"Have you had these on *Corner Brook* yet, Cole?"

"Yeah, we took them on last month," Darren replied while fastening one of the inspection hatches back into place on the Mk-48 Advanced Capacity torpedo he had been examining. "Sweet little fish."

"Very," replied Lieutenant Kirk MacIntosh, *Victoria's* weapons officer.

"I guess we'll find out what these babies can do."

"Yeah, Cole. Guess we might at that," Kirk replied, his voice not hiding the trepidation he felt about their mission.

The mood aboard the Canadian submarine was electric, tempered with a tiny tinge of fear as the crew went about their duties with an extra degree of thoroughness. Knowing they would soon be going into action, no one wanted to let their shipmates down by missing any detail no matter how small. None of *Victoria's* crew had ever expected to see the day when they would fire a live torpedo at another boat.

In the control room, Yokov was staring intently at the sonar display in front of him. One spot in particular on the slowly moving 'waterfall' seemed to be forming into a more solid line and the audio equivalent was just barely breaking through the background clutter of sound outside the submarine.

"Sir?"

"Got him?"

"Oh yeah."

"Bearing?"

"Dead ahead. Right where he should be."

"Helm, slow to ten knots."

"Ten knots, aye, sir."

* * *

K-335, Pacific Ocean, West of Seattle, Washington

Less than two thousand yards ahead of the Canadian submarine, *K-335* continued to slowly follow an oval shaped course while her captain anxiously counted down the time to when his sonar operator should pick up the first sounds from the American carrier's outer screen. The Russian boat's executive officer was keeping the longer legs of their course 'side on' to the direction the battle group was expected to appear from in order to maximise the towed array's sensitivity on that bearing.

The boat's Chinese captain was unaware that the co-ordinates he had received from his base, and that his sonar operators were focused on, were thirty degrees north of the actual route the US carrier battle group was approaching from. He also did not realize that the fleet steaming down on him had a pretty good idea where he was, which was about to be confirmed by an SQQ-53E DIFAR sonobuoy dropped a short distance away by *HMCS Vancouver's* Cyclone helicopter flying well ahead of the frigate.

As the beige, forty inch long plastic tube bobbed on the surface, a long hi-tensile cable stretched down deep into the water from an opening at the bottom of the sonobuoy. Hanging from the end of the cable, a microphone encased in a watertight covering was picking up the minutest sounds from the surrounding ocean. The audio it picked up was processed by the buoy and converted into an RF signal transmitted up to the Cyclone's radio receivers which simultaneously sent the information to the helicopter's computers, as well as transmitting them back to *Vancouver*, where the information was displayed on the frigate's tactical screens.

"Got him!" the operator strapped in front of the helicopter's sonar display announced. "Submerged contact!" He relayed the contact's coordinates to the cockpit while plotting the most direct course to the submarine based on the its speed and direction of travel. A few seconds later, the information had been shared with all the ships of the escort screen, and as planned, the *USS Rodney M. Davis*, well out ahead of the rest of the battle group, increased speed and changed her course so she would approach the Russian boat from the direction their crew would be expecting the battle group to appear.

Davis' captain was enjoying the game of cat and mouse and he had sent the *Oliver Hazard Perry* class frigate's crew to action stations, hoping that an opportunity might present itself for his ship to be in on the kill. He knew his command had been picked because of a mechanical issue that made her the noisiest ship in the battle group. The Chinese sonar operator would have no trouble hearing her, and in case something went horribly wrong with the plan, *Davis* was also the oldest, and therefore the most expendable unit of the group.

Looking over to his XO, who was scanning the sea through a pair of binoculars, Commander Vincent Franks waved the officer over.

"They should have us shortly, Les."

"Yes, sir. We're making enough racket to be heard all over the pacific. I bet the SOSUS guys back home are wondering what we're up to."

"I don't doubt they are, XO," agreed *Davis'* captain. "You might want to launch the helo now, just in case. They would be expecting us to have it operating this far out on the screen," he added. The ship's SH-60F, borrowed from the *Enterprise* air group and armed with a pair of MK-54s had been sitting on the helicopter pad with the engines idling. The frigates usual 60B had been swapped out for the dipping sonar equipped 'Oceanhawk' for this mission.

"Aye, sir. I'll call down and have the '60 kicked off."

Franks turned back to the display screens arrayed in front of him, paying special attention to the sonar repeater on his left. A submariner himself, he was watching for the telltale lines that would show something man made amongst the rest of the 'noise' filling the screen. Not that we won't practically be on top of it by the time we hear the sub with all the noise we're making ourselves, he thought.

Meanwhile, *K-335's* sonar operator was straining to pick up a sound he had earlier classified as a ship's screw seconds before it had disappeared. The low level swishing had broken through the background noise in his headset and had barley registered on the display in front of him; the ship emitting the noises either heading off in another direction or perhaps slowing down. Regardless, it might have been one of the aircraft carrier's escorts so he turned and waved towards the captain to get his attention.

"What do you have?" Chong asked, stepping towards the operator.

"It is gone now, but I am sure I had a ship traveling at high speed."

"Bearing?"

"One nine three, sir."

Liu Chong nodded. That was the general direction the communication from China had said the American carrier would be coming from. It must be one of the escorts from the outer screen. Probably the lead ship, the one their instructions had warned about.

This screen plan had one ship miles ahead of the actual fleet whose mission was to flush out any submarines along their path. What was different with this new pattern was that the first ship was only a decoy and there was in fact a second lead ship watching to see if they could catch anyone trying to avoid the first one. Most submariners would feel safe once the lead escort had passed and would drop their guard slightly as they focused on the main target.

"Yes," the Chinese captain said out loud for the benefit of the men nearby. "I know who you are and we will be careful to slip by you AND your friend who follows."

The control room crew looked at him, and one of the officers nodded, a smile forming on his lips. He too had been apprehensive about this mission earlier but with the knowledge they now possessed, he was confident they would not only sink the American aircraft carrier but would also safely escape after doing so.

Reaching for the microphone hanging from the bulkhead next to him, Chong looked into the eyes of every man in the control room before pressing the transmit button.

Speaking in a calm almost casual voice, he commanded the weapons crew to arm all tubes. In the confines of the weapons space in the submarine's forward compartment, the men cheered quietly before going through the process of loading the heavy TT-5 torpedoes into the torpedo tubes. Once that task had been completed, they would prepare the smaller Type 53 torpedoes sitting in their racks in case an escorting submarine confronted them. As one of the sailors closed and locked down the last tube hatch, he kissed his fingers and patted the door.

"You will kill Americans," he quietly whispered.

* * *

HMCS Victoria, Pacific Ocean, West of Seattle, Washington

Petty Officer Darren Cole was performing a similar ceremony as he fastened tube number four's hatch over a Mark 48 ADCAP and tested the wire connections to ensure the torpedo could receive data from *Victoria*.

"Don't let me down baby," he whispered, patting the hatch. For a brief moment, he pictured *HMCS Corner Brook's* old Mark-48s upon which a crewmember had penned women's names. That episode had resulted in a fleet wide memo warning of dire consequences should someone write upon or do anything other than standard maintenance to the navy's torpedoes.

"All tubes ready, sir," he announced, initialling the check sheet fastened to the bulkhead on his left.

"Thanks, Cole," MacIntosh replied while reaching for the intercom. "Control room—weapons. All tubes loaded and ready."

"All tubes loaded and ready, aye" echoed a voice from the speaker above him.

"That should be about it for us, petty officer. I don't expect we'll have time for reloads if anything goes amiss."

"Yeah," Darren replied, pondering his decision to come aboard. Then he recalled the troops who had been with him in northern Canada on the survival training course and he turned back to the circuit tester to ensure once again that all six torpedoes were hooked up properly.

"So how's married life treating you?" MacIntosh asked, seeing the look of sadness on Cole's face and wanting to drag him back from whatever dark place his mind had wondered to.

"Great, sir!" The change in Cole's expression was instant. "Heather is the perfect wife and I am one lucky sailor to have her."

"That's good to hear. We were worried that considering who her father was, she might try to pull rank on you."

"Yeah," Darren laughed. "She does that anyway though, and I don't think it has anything to do with who her father is."

* * *

MARLANT, CFB Halifax, Nova Scotia

"Heather!" Petty Officer Jody Fletcher exclaimed as Mrs. Cole entered the office. "I'm so glad to hear Darren's okay!"

"Thanks, Jody," she replied, a huge grin covering her face. "So am I!"

"Your dad's already here," the petty officer informed her as he knocked and opened the door to Brent's office. "Go right in."

"Thanks."

Admiral O'Hanlon came around his desk and greeted Darren's wife with a warm hug. "I'm sorry I haven't seen you before this, Heather. As you can imagine, things are pretty hectic around here right now."

"I understand Admiral O'Hanlon," she replied. "I felt better knowing you were looking after things. Hi daddy," she added going over and hugging her father. At that point she noticed another man standing in the opposite corner of the room. She had no idea what his rank was but from the amount of metal hanging from his uniform it had to be pretty high. The stranger smiled and came over to her.

"Heather, this is General of the Russian Army, Kristoff Nikolev," Brent announced, introducing the officer to her. "We could not have rescued Darren without his help. Kristoff, this is Heather, Darren's wife."

George had already told her how this man had brought in help from the highest levels of the Kremlin, and that he had moved heaven and earth to make things happen on the other side of the Pacific.

"I am honoured to meet you, sir. Thank you so …" Heather began stretching out her hand. Kristoff ignored the hand and embraced her in a huge bear hug.

"This is how we greet friends in Russia," he laughed. "And thanks are not necessary, Mrs. Cole. It is the least I could do for a friend of Brent's."

Brent pulled a chair over for Heather and she sat down. Reaching behind his desk he offered her a glass half filled with a dark liquid. "The champagne is long gone but we have lots of Crown Royal; our navy runs on it," he explained with a mischievous grin.

"So my father has told me," she replied, reaching for the glass.

"Heather, Darren is safely aboard *Victoria*," Brent continued. "His jump went perfectly," he presumed, not having heard anything to the contrary, "and they are now searching for another submarine. We have discussed the situation and decided that you should be brought up to speed on everything."

Brent went over what had taken place since her husband had been kidnapped from the Arctic and although he did not go into exact details about the torture Darren had endured, the admiral did point out that it had been severe. Twenty-five minutes later, Brent concluded with how a deep cover CSIS agent had managed to co-ordinate the rescue from within the Chinese group at incredible risk to herself. Had she been found out, he explained, her fate would have been horrible beyond imagination.

"I have to meet her," Heather announced, wiping tears from her eyes. They had started falling down her cheeks as Brent had delicately explained some of what Darren had gone through with the Russian interrogator.

"She's still working on the op somewhere else, but I am sure we can arrange for you two to meet once her mission is completed." He jotted a quick note on his blotter to remind himself to call CSIS later.

* * *

NCIS Central Field Office, Naval Station Great Lakes

The interrogation rooms inside the NCIS Great Lakes building were surprisingly small, designed that way to ensure the personal space of the person being questioned was nil. A sturdy wooden table stood in the middle of the room, leaving barely enough space for a person to sit down on either side of it without their chair hitting the wall behind them. Todd, Carol and Xue stood on one side of the table with the door behind them, while Brian Pulsifer sat in a metal chair across the table, trying, but failing to fight the feeling of claustrophobia that threatened to envelope him. The temperature in the room was purposely kept warm, with no visible source of ventilation to add to the 'closeness' of the space. The classic one-way mirror had long been replaced by multiple high definition pinhole cameras, strategically placed and nearly impossible to spot unless a person knew exactly where they were. They were all connected to a bank of monitors in an adjacent space where everything taking place in the interrogation room could be viewed and recorded.

"Pulsifer, tell me who your contact is," Xue demanded in a surprisingly loud voice for her stature, "or I won't be able to help you. It's simple really. You make me happy with your answers and I might drag your sorry ass back to Canada with me, but if you piss me off, I'll leave you here. If that happens, I'm sure my colleagues will have you on a plane to Guantanamo faster than you can say water-boarding."

Before questioning the man, the three agents had decided that immediately playing the 'Cuba' card would be the best route to take in light of the time constraint on them. Up to now, Pulsifer had been trying hard to act tough, but the threat had the desired effect and Lee could see a growing fear in his eyes as his mind weighed the two options.

"Look, Brian. We know that all you did was supply information to somebody," said Carol, a look of concern on her face. It had been decided that she would be the 'good cop'. "It's that person we want. Tell her what she needs to know and we can process your ass out of here."

"I don't know his name. He's somewhere on the west coast … I think," Pulsifer began, the toughness completely gone from his voice now. "I only have a phone number."

"Write it down, please," Xue commanded, sliding a piece of paper and stubby pencil towards him.

As he wrote the number down, she read it from across the table. The area code, 236, Xue noted, was for British Columbia. She would call Ottawa with the information as soon as they finished here.

"Do you have anything else to add?" She looked at him sternly before adding, "Remember, your co-operation and honesty will determine whether you go to Canada or on an all-expenses paid Cuban holiday."

"No. No, that's all. Someone called me and said they had a way for me to make some easy money and no one would get hurt and …" The enormity of his situation finally struck home and he broke down, his body heaving as he sobbed. "I'm sorry … oh god … wait … I heard something in the background during the call. A name I think … Dai."

"I'll go check this out," said Xue.

"Okay," Todd replied. "We'll take him into custody until transfer arrangements are made."

Xue left the interrogation room and went back to the main office where she sat at an empty desk, picked up a phone and asked for a secure outside line. Dialling the CSIS Director's number in Ottawa, she went over the events of the past twenty-four hours with him, ending with a request for information on the phone number Pulsifer had shared as well as the name 'Dai'.

"Let me check on the name, Xue. Oh, and good work," he added. "They went ape shit up here over what happened across the water."

"It was pretty wild there for a bit but it worked out perfectly in the end. How is our sailor doing?"

"Back out sailing again."

"What!?"

"Hey! We already have a hit on the phone number. It's real," the Director announced, ignoring her question. "I'll see what we can find out regarding that name and let you know when you get back. Bringing me a souvenir?"

"Yes, a nice big one that I know you're going to love."

The director laughed. "Okay, Xue. Pack it well so it doesn't get broken on the flight."

"I will, sir." She smiled, remembering Pulsifer's painful groin injury and how the cramped airline seat would compound that. Hopefully, she thought, there would be lots of turbulence on the flight back to Canada. "See you in a day or two."

* * *

CFB Comox, British Columbia

"Comox Tower, this is Russian Military nine two seven heavy. We are six miles south east of field, requesting landing instructions." The heavily accented voice caused everyone in the control tower to look up at the pair of speakers mounted to a support beam above their heads.

"Russian Military nine two seven, roger. Comox altimeter is two niner niner three and the winds are calm."

"Thank you Comox tower."

"Er, Russian Military nine two seven heavy, will you be requiring any special ground equipment?"

"Negative, Comox Tower. We have everything we need, thank you. We have field in sight."

"Russian Military nine two seven, roger. You are cleared to land runway three zero. Check the gear."

"Comox Tower, our gear is down and locked. Nine two seven."

Inside the control tower, a dozen pairs of eyes strained through binoculars to catch a glimpse of the huge visitor. A mysterious phone call had come in a few hours earlier, informing the tower crew of the Russian Air Force aircraft's arrival time and the previous shift had remained in the tower to witness the huge plane's landing.

"There he is," one of the controllers called out, pointing to the south before adding, "Big mother."

They all watched the aircraft grow larger as it approached the runway, amazed at how it seemed to float gently in the air at an impossibly slow speed which was an illusion caused by the AN-124's massive size. The Ruslan settled to the runway with only a tiny puff of smoke escaping from its tires, and rapidly slowed down.

"Russian Military nine two seven, if you are able, turn left on taxiway Charlie—contact ground on two five zero point three."

"Two five zero point three, roger, this is nine two seven," the pilot confirmed before adding, "Thank you sir."

Spotting a sign far below on the runway's edge displaying a yellow 'C', the Ruslan's pilot began the slow turn which would bring the aircraft onto the taxiway. An SUV with 'Follow Me' painted across the back doors pulled out in front of the Ruslan and headed towards the ramp, with the driver noting that although he could see little more than the AN-124's double nose landing gear in his side view mirrors, the aircraft's immense shadow stretched out far ahead of him on the concrete.

"Comox ground, Russian Air Force nine two seven is here on taxiway Charlie."

"Nine two seven, ground. Welcome to Comox. Please follow the truck to the ramp and you will be directed where to park once you arrive there."

"Nine two seven."

Minutes later, the aircraft's flight engineer powered down the engines and started filling in his log, listing a few discrepancies which had appeared during the flight across the Pacific Ocean. There was a tap on the cockpit door and the co-pilot slid it open, revealing Cookie standing there with his hand thrust out.

"Thank you for the lift, gentlemen. We really appreciate it."

"You are welcome," the engineer replied. "It is our pleasure."

"Are you staying long?" Cookie asked. "I'd love to buy you a beer."

"No, we are going to fuel aircraft and head back," the pilot answered, his voice reflecting the disappointment at not being able to accept the offer. "But thank you."

After thanking the flight crew one more time, Cookie joined Yelizaveta and Stu in the aft compartment where they descended the narrow ladder leading down to the cargo deck. Upon reaching the loading ramp, Cookie turned to take Yelizaveta's arm as she stepped onto the tarmac, throwing her balance off and causing her to trip and fall into his arms. They stayed that way for a few seconds before she stepped back, absentmindedly brushing the uniform shirt she had changed into at the submarine base.

"You are a gentleman …" she managed to get out, not sure what to say next.

"Thank you Liza. I …" The rest was drowned out as a camouflaged G-Wagon pulled up to them and screeched to a stop.

"Hey! One of you Cookie?" yelled the driver through an open window.

"Yeah."

"I'm Sergeant Cullen! Get in! I have to deliver you guys to Admiral Leger down at Esquimalt right now!"

Cookie opened the passenger door for Yelizaveta and waited as she climbed in before closing it behind her. Taking one more glance back at the giant aircraft, the submariner slid into the back seat opposite Stu, who was fastening his seat belt.

"First time I've been in a G-Wagon," the SEAL noted. "Pretty impressive ride."

"Sure is," chirped the driver. "We can run circles around the Yanks in their Hummers with this thing," he noted with a chuckle, unaware of his passenger's nationality.

As if to prove the point, he stomped the gas pedal and the Mercedes leapt forward, tearing across the tarmac towards the main gate. Yelizaveta hung on for dear life as the driver tore down the road, ripping past the slower traffic, most of which indicated their displeasure at the military vehicle by honking their horns and directing the universal one finger salute in its direction. In the back, Stu and Cookie exchanged the same glances they had aboard the old Twin Otter back in Russia.

What seemed like an impossibly short time later, the sailor slammed the G-Wagon to a stop at the main entry to the Esquimalt naval base and after a brief exchange with the sentry, was waved through the gate, where upon he ignored all the posted speed limits and skidded around a few buildings before screeching to a halt in front of the command building.

"Damn," Cookie exclaimed. "I need to get me one of these!"

"The civilian model's pretty expensive," noted the driver while nervously glancing in his mirror at a Military Police car pulling up behind them.

"Naw, I'd want a bare bones one like this. Not some sissy truck," the submariner replied before adding, "Thanks for the lift!"

"Any time!" the sailor replied before greeting the MP who appeared at his window with a cheery, "Hi! Sorry Lewinski. They're special delivery for Admiral Leger. Orders were to ignore everything and get their ass … er … them here fast."

Hopping out of the truck, and ignoring the Military Police officer tearing a strip off Sergeant Cullen, Cookie, Yelizaveta and Stu sprinted up the building's stairs. They had just reached the double glass doors when one of them swung open and Admiral Ray Leger stepped out.

"Cookie! Damn it's good to see you again!"

The petty officer came to attention and was about to salute before catching himself.

"Sorry, sir. Forgot what I was wearing there for a minute."

"That's alright petty officer. You look good in Russian Army garb," Leger noted while shaking his hand. "It's almost slimming on you," he added with a hearty laugh.

"Thanks!" Cookie replied. "Admiral Raymond Leger, may I present Miss Yelizaveta Nikolev."

"Welcome to Canada, Miss Nikolev. I trust this sorry excuse for a sailor has been behaving himself?"

"He has been a perfect gentleman, admiral."

Leger noticed her hand touch Cookie's arm as she spoke. Perhaps Russian-Canadian relations are about to improve, he thought with a smile.

"That's good to hear. Your father will be arriving in a few hours. He's on the way here with some people from the east coast."

"And this ugly creature is …" Cookie began.

"Ensign Stu Cunningham!" Leger smiled, reaching out a hand to the SEAL. "I can't tell you how much we appreciate your help. You can be assured that I will be speaking with your commanding officer personally about this. Unfortunately, as I'm sure you're used to, nothing official can be recorded."

"My pleasure, sir." Stu had wondered on the long flight back how he was going to explain the past few days to the boss and was pleased that now he wouldn't have to.

"Is Admiral O'Hanlon coming in from Halifax as well, sir?" Cookie inquired.

"He certainly is. So are Admiral Carroll and his daughter."

"Excellent!" Cookie exclaimed. "Cole will be pleased as shit to … err, sorry sir."

"Not a problem, petty officer. Come up to my office. I have so many questions for all of you that I don't know where to begin."

Walking through the foyer and down a short hallway, they rounded a corner where Leger's aide jumped up from behind his desk, quickly stood to attention and opened the ornate door to the admiral's office for them. Stepping around his desk, Admiral Leger motioned Cookie and Yelizaveta to the chairs on the opposite side of the large piece of oak furniture while bringing his own chair around for Stu. The three men remained standing until Yelizaveta had seated herself and then they sat down—the admiral sitting on a corner of his desk.

"So," the admiral began. "Before you tell me anything else, how is Cole doing?"

"He'll be fine, sir." Cookie responded, noting the concern in Leger's voice. "His going aboard *Victoria* will be just the tonic he needs to start healing."

"Good. We were all very concerned. From what we heard from Admiral Andreev, it was no picnic for him."

Over the next hour, they covered the details of what had taken place, and finally, Admiral Leger stood and motioned his visitors to the outer office.

"I have to go up to Comox and pick up everyone," he noted. "Barnes, why don't you guys head down to the gym and freshen up?"

"Yes, sir,"

"Thank you, admiral," Stu began, "I wasn't sure how much longer I was going to be able to stand Cookie's sme ..." A hard punch to his shoulder from Cookie sent him and the submariner careening down the hall and through the office doors.

"I'm sorry you've had to put up with those two, Miss Nikolev."

"It has not been too difficult, and please, call me Liza."

Outside the building, the admiral's Toyota Highlander was waiting and they waved as Leger climbed into the vehicle before his driver hit the gas and tore off towards the base entrance.

"They sure do drive like lunatics around here," Stu observed, watching the SUV careen around a corner.

* * *

HMCS Victoria, Pacific Ocean, West of Seattle, Washington

"Target aspect changing slowly. Coming right. New heading zero nine zero. He's closing the oval," Yokov reported from *HMCS Victoria's* sonar console.

"Right fifteen to zero nine zero and maintain speed," Rene ordered quietly. "We'll stay off to his starboard this time and remain inside the oval."

They had been following the Russian submarine closely as the other boat's captain cruised along the boundaries of a twenty-five hundred yard long oval. If the Canadian skipper had not known the nationality of his prey before, he would have certainly known it now. The odd pattern used to clear their baffles was an idiosyncrasy of the Chinese PLA Navy. The manoeuvre was now being tested by NATO as well, after its captains had discovered that the circular course previously employed by most nation's submariners meant that the towed array was never in a straight line and although the narrow 'oval' left the submarine with a temporary blind spot in two directions on every second clearance of baffles, the improved sonar coverage with their 'tail' trailing straight behind on the long, straight legs more than made up the difference.

Rene contemplated the mixture of Russian and Chinese sailors he was facing. Both countries had developed underwater tactics that crossed the lines of safety, and he prayed they would be able to quickly dispatch the other boat and not have to fight against the near suicidal contrivances the combination of both navies might place in front of him.

Victoria's commanding officer pondered taking a shot now but he knew they had to wait for the *USS Davis* to get closer. The American frigate was going to be the submarine's 'back up' in case anything went amiss with the attack. Rene and the crew however, were starting to get antsy with the game of cat and mouse, primarily because they all knew *Victoria* could very quickly become the mouse if their presence was detected.

"Active sonar!" Yokov called out quietly while punching buttons on the keypad in front of him. A few seconds later, 'AN/AQS-13F' flashed on the upper right of the screen.

"That will be *Davis'* helo," Rene observed. "Update solution on target."

"Solution locked, sir," replied the weapons officer. "We have … TORPEDO! Torpedo in the water! Dead ahead!"

Every eye in the control centre turned to Yokov.

"It's not from the helo or the other boat," the petty officer continued, answering everyone's question. "Aspect changing!"

Rene was standing over him, staring at the thin line representing the torpedo's sound signature moving slowly across the screen. He felt a wave of relief at the realization that the moving line on the display meant the torpedo was not heading at them. His agile mind quickly calculated its course and realized where it was heading.

Yokov's fingers were flying over his keyboard as he queried the computer for the torpedo's identity.

"Can't compute the range. It's close. Heading for our contact. Wait! Got it! It's …"

The rest of the sentence was drowned out in a muffled explosion heard and felt throughout *Victoria's* hull. Moments later the submarine was shoved sideways as though a giant hand had grabbed the boat and pushed it aside, sending everyone and everything not fastened down flying to the deck.

As he lifted himself back into his seat in front of the sonar console, Yokov looked around for a moment to see where his commanding officer had ended up. Rene was slowly trying to stand from where he had been thrown on top of the sailor manning the helm.

"Sorry, son. I …" *Victoria's* commander was cut short by the sharp pain of his head striking the overhead. "DAMN!"

"S'ok, sir. I'm fine."

"Yokov?"

"The other boat's breaking up sir."

The control room was silent. Everyone stopped picking up the various items which had flown around the space and stood still. Each of them envisioning what they thought the end of the other submariner's lives would have been like as the pressure hull imploded around them.

"All stop—quiet boat," Rene ordered. Reaching for the intercom, he requested a damage report from the boat's other compartments and was informed that other than a few cuts and scrapes amongst the crew, everything was fine.

"Computer says it was a YU-4," Yokov noted as soon as Rene had turned from the intercom.

"Chinese?"

"Yes, sir. Not hearing anything out there now."

"It had to come from somewhere, Yokov. Keep looking."

* * *

USS Rodney M. Davis, Pacific Ocean, West of Seattle, Washington

The explosion had been picked up by the sonar operators aboard the *USS Rodney M. Davis,* and momentary panic ensued as a report arrived from the ship's Oceanhawk that a Chinese torpedo signature had been detected just before the Russian submarine disappeared.

"XO! Get the helo crew to comb the torpedo's track! Tell them to find the bastard who fired it!"

"Yes, sir!"

The executive officer only had to step through a thin blackout curtain to reach *Davis'* combat information centre where he ordered instructions sent to the SH-60 crew to search the area down the track that the torpedo had come from. The frigate's sonar team had not heard anything until just before the torpedo had hit its target, and a passive search had been useless in the turbulence left behind by the warhead's explosion, and the sounds of *K-335's* hull breaking up.

The SH-60's pilot swooped down over the water in the general direction he had been ordered to search while the techs behind him dropped active sonar buoys, hoping to shake loose whoever was hiding below the surface.

* * *

USS Enterprise, Pacific Ocean, West of Portland, Oregon

The tactical information and sonar recordings from the helicopter and ship based sonars had been instantly transmitted via satellite back to *Enterprise* where the information had stunned her captain and Admiral Thomas.

"Someone has changed the rules of this game, Nelson. Better get our Canadian friends heading out there fast to see what they can find," ordered the admiral.

"On the way, admiral."

Stepping off the bridge, Captain Nelson Craig ducked into the carrier's command center where he had one of the communication specialist contact the two Canadian frigates still holding their positions on either side of the huge ship.

"Tell them the data they need is on its way, and that they are detached to head over smartly to assist *Davis*."

"Aye, sir. Sending now," replied the petty officer, his fingers a blur as they moved over the keyboard in front of him. Seconds later, an acknowledgement came back from *HMCS Vancouver*, followed almost immediately by *HMCS Ottawa's* confirmation.

"Both ships confirm message received, sir."

"Thank you, petty officer, and anything from those three ships is priority one for me."

"Aye, sir."

Satisfied the Canadian frigates would now be headed for whatever was lurking out there, Craig walked over to the plot board, actually a large transparent panel, which showed every unit of the battle group as well as combatants in the surrounding area. Grease pencil and florescent water marker annotations covered almost the entire surface of the panel.

He noted the marker for *HMCS Victoria*, and also the lack of one signifying the Russian submarine's location. The moment it had been positively confirmed as destroyed, the original marker representing *K-335* had been removed as it was no longer relevant to the crewmembers whose duty was to ensure the plot board remained current, and it had been replaced by a square yellow marker with 'SSN Sunk' scribbled on it. The markers for *HMCS Vancouver* and *HMCS Ottawa* had already been moved away from the middle of the board and the small ship silhouettes were now pointing towards the *USS Rodney M. Davis* and *Victoria*.

* * *

HMCS Vancouver, Pacific Ocean, West of Seattle, Washington

"Anything?"

Chris couldn't help himself. He knew he asked the same question more than he should, but it was his way of maintaining perspective.

"Nothing, sir," *Vancouver's* sonar operator replied. "Whoever fired that fish must have been really close to the other boat. The time from sonar acquisition to the explosion was only a few seconds."

"Has to be another SSK. Chinese? There's no way a nuc could have slipped by everybody, but what would be the point in sinking a boat with your own people on board?"

It had been a rhetorical question and Chris did not expect an answer, but received one anyway.

"Sir," began the sonar operator. "What if they had been waiting out here all along, say as insurance in case something went wrong."

"Yeah, they might have intercepted the message we sent to their hijacked boat."

Commander Donnelly walked over to the sonar operator and slapped his shoulder. "Good thinking, son. Care to help me explain all this to MARPAC?"

"Er ... no, sir," the leading seaman replied nervously. "I think that'd be a bit above my pay grade."

"Wish it was above mine too," Chris joked as he ducked into the frigate's secure radio space.

* * *

MARPAC, CFB Esquimalt, British Columbia

The aircraft carrying Admiral Brent O'Hanlon, General of the Russian Army Kristoff Nikolev, the CNO of the US Navy (retired) George Carroll and Heather Cole had landed twenty minutes before the message from *Vancouver* arrived. In order to save time, Admiral Leger had driven his Toyota Highlander out onto the ramp and after a quick exchange of pleasantries, they had all squeezed into the SUV for the drive back to Esquimalt. Shortly thereafter, having just begun to relax in Admiral Leger's office, their chat was interrupted by a quiet knock on the door, followed by the admiral's aide stepping inside.

"Sorry, sir," the petty officer apologized for the intrusion while coming to attention, "this arrived while you were in transit and you need to see it."

"Thanks, son." Admiral Ray Leger read the urgency in the man's face and as the sailor left the room, he unfolded the note and read it over quickly.

"Oh shit," he breathed, handing the note to O'Hanlon.

"Whoa!" Brent exclaimed. "Someone did not like our plan."

O'Hanlon handed the note to Kristoff who grunted disapprovingly before passing it along to George.

"Is Darren alright?" asked Heather, who had been forgotten in the moment.

"He's fine, Heather," George replied quickly, after scanning the message. The retired Chief of Naval Operations was wishing now that he had not caved in to Heather's insistence that she accompany him to Leger's office, although he realized that asking her to stay alone on the base would have been out of the question.

There was an awkward silence as the officers hid their concern over the message, not wanting to frighten Darren's wife any more than she was now. As if on cue, another knock on the door, followed by Cookie, Yelizaveta and Stu entering the room broke the tension.

"Yelizaveta!" General Nikolev rushed over to embrace his daughter. "Papa!"

When they had separated, Kristoff turned to Heather.

"Mrs. Cole, I present my daughter Yelizaveta. She was leader on your husband's rescue mission."

The two women hugged as Heather thanked her over and over again through the tears flowing from her eyes.

"You have a good husband, Mrs. Cole. I ..."

"Thank you, and please, it's Heather. I swear! I'll scream if one more person calls me Mrs. Cole!"

They all laughed at her outburst and for a brief moment, the seriousness of the situation was brushed aside.

"And this must be Petty Officer Barnes. It is good to meet you."

General Nikolev reached for Cookie's hand and buried it in his huge paw while looking the submariner straight in the eye.

"My daughter has told me much about you."

Cookie blushed slightly as he struggled for something to say.

"Oh? Ah, all good ... I hope," he stammered, before pointing to the SEAL and blurting out, "That's Stu!"

"Oh my god!" Brent exclaimed. "Cookie's stuck for words! This is a first!"

They laughed again until Admiral Leger waved his hand to get everyone's attention.

"Cookie, why don't you take Stu, Heather and Yelizaveta and show them around the base?" Leger asked, looking at Cookie and hoping he'd understand that the officers needed to discuss the situation without the extra bodies in the room. "Here," he added, reaching into his pocket and pulling out a set of keys. "Take my car. It's the Highlander parked right outside."

"Good idea, sir," the submariner responded, understanding the 'look', and reaching for the keys. He had noted the tension in the room as they had entered and pocketing the keys, held the door open for the girls before shoving Stu through the opening.

"Guess I'd better get on the horn to the Defence Minister," Ray announced to no one in particular. "She's not going to like this turn of events."

* * *

Minister of National Defence Office, Ottawa, Ontario

"They killed their own people?!"

Canada's Minister of National Defence was stunned by the news that the stolen submarine had been sunk by what was presumed to be a Chinese sub. She had been expecting news of the submarine's sinking, but by *HMCS Victoria*, not some new player in the game. The call with her admiral had been conferenced in by the Prime Minister from his office where he had been directed to join them by an aide.

"Admiral Leger, do we know for certain that it was a Chinese submarine?" he asked.

"Not yet, Prime Minister. We are going with that assumption based on the torpedo signature, but as soon as we find her we should be able to confirm the boat's identity."

"Very well. I will let you all go as I am sure you have better things to do right now than talk on the phone with me," the Prime Minister observed, knowing Leger would appreciate his not interfering in the operation. "Caroline," he continued. "Please come to my office when you hang up. We'll have to work out how we're going to present this new twist to the public when the time comes."

"Yes, Prime Minister," she replied. "Admiral? I'll be waiting to hear from you. Call me with any news."

"I will, ma'am. Thank you."

The line went dead and Caroline laid the headset she had been using down on her desk. Before heading to the Prime Minister's office, she sat for a moment, digesting the new information in her mind. The Chinese must have been planning to sink the stolen submarine all along. The more she pondered the situation, the more sense it made. With the rogue sub gone, there would be no hard evidence that China have been responsible for sinking the American carrier. But why sink it now, and risk someone realizing the Chinese were responsible?

Looking at the file folder sitting on her desk that had just arrived from CSIS, she opened it and gazed at the photograph attached to the single page inside. It showed an older man wearing the uniform of an admiral in the PLA Navy. "Not a bad plan, Dai" she mumbled. "Too bad for you there were witnesses."

* * *

Lightning 302, USS Davis SH-60

AN/SSQ-53E sonobuoys dropped by the *USS Davis'* SH-60 Oceanhawk helicopter bobbed quietly on the ocean's surface, their antennas poking up at the sky. The sonobuoy's complex circuitry, connected to hydrophones hanging far below the plastic tubes, would transmit anything heard up to the helicopter circling above. Most of the buoys had been pre-set to search at four hundred feet by the sensor operator, a petty officer with a great deal of experience hunting submarines. Seated in front of the helo's console behind the flight crew, he suspected the submarine would be trying to sneak away below a thermal layer at a depth of three to four hundred feet. Not completely convinced however, he had launched a couple of the older 53Ds pre-set for ninety feet, just in case.

He needn't have worried.

"Damn, she freakin' quiet," the petty officer whispered as a steady hiss amongst the ocean sounds reached his ears. "November Romeo Mike Delta, this is Lightning three zero two. We have submerged contact. Sending data now."

The day of giving a contact's position report over the radio was long past. A simple push of a button sent all of the information from the sonobuoy over to *Davis* where the data was simultaneously sent to a navy GFO satellite for immediate transmission. Seconds later, it was received by the US and Royal Canadian Navy warships involved in the hunt, where the new information was digested by their commanding officers.

* * *

223

HMCS Vancouver, Pacific Ocean, West of Seattle, Washington

Aboard *HMCS Vancouver*, Commander Chris Donnelly gave orders to bring the ship on a heading for the submarine's location and to send the information over to *HMCS Ottawa* following a few hundred yards astern. Having earlier broken away from the *Enterprise* screen, the Canadian ships would reach the area within a couple of hours although, as Chris had commented to his XO, "Hell knows what we'll do once we get there."

Admiral Clark Thomas, realizing that the original plan was now defunct, ordered the *Enterprise* battle group to come about and head back to San Diego. No longer needed as bait, he did not want to risk the ship being in harm's way any longer than necessary as there appeared to be far too many submarines messing about in this chunk of ocean. *Big E* would make the trip to Norfolk on another day. Besides, he thought, perhaps before then, someone would decide that the ghosts who have walked the passageways of the old girl for decades now, were worth saving.

* * *

HMCS Victoria, Pacific Ocean, West of Seattle, Washington

HMCS Victoria's crew, unaware of what was transpiring on the surface, continued their hunt for the elusive Chinese submarine with the boat's passive sonar.

"Nothing."

"Helm, right …" Rene began before Yokov cut him off.

"Wait! Hold this course."

The control room fell silent as they all waited for the next words from the sonar operator's mouth.

"I think I have him," the petty officer announced quietly.

"Slow to ten knots."

"Ten knots, aye."

Victoria's huge propeller slowed a few revolutions and the sailor 'driving the boat' started earning his keep as the slower speed made it much more difficult to keep the submarine at a constant depth and even keel.

"I have him. Contact is zero three one degrees."

"Helm, come right ten to zero three one. Slowly."

"Zero three one, slowly, aye."

"No range yet, sir," Yokov noted before adding. "Damn, she's hardly making any noise."

"SSK for sure," Rene muttered, while bringing up the digital version of Jane's Fighting Ships on the computer monitor to his right. Typing 'China SSK' into the search bar, the screen immediately showed the *Yuan* Class SSK Type 041, as the Jane's software, like the more cumbersome book version, listed the newest classes first.

"You have any sound data on the new 041 *Yuans*, Yokov?"

His fingers a blur over his keyboard, Alex replied in a few seconds, "No, sir."

"Okay, let's go with the contact being an 041 *Yuan* for now until proven otherwise. Start a file."

"041 *Yuan* it is, sir," the sonar operator confirmed as he labelled the current recording '041 *Yuan* 1'. He hoped it was. No one had a clip of one of the new Chinese boats yet. The rumours that they were deadly quiet seemed to be substantiated now though. Damn thing was quieter than *Victoria*, Yokov whispered to himself, and *Vic* was really freaking quiet!

* * *

Type 041 SSK, PLA Navy, West of Seattle, Washington

Not far away, Shao Xiao Kuo was voicing similar thoughts concerning *Victoria*, which had just appeared on their sonar. Unfortunately for Shao, his sonar operator had long ago misidentified the contact as one of the new class of American SSNs. Like his Canadian counterpart had earlier, he was excited at the prospect of being one of the first to track down one of the lethal *Virginias*.

"You are certain it is a *Virginia*?" The Chinese captain was not totally convinced.

"Yes, sir. It is far too quiet to be one of the older nuclear powered units," the junior lieutenant responded.

He was unaware that the contact was in fact an even quieter Canadian boat, and because of that, he had misjudged the distance between it and the Chinese submarine.

"I have read about them, but I did not expect they would be so quiet compared to our own."

"Do you still have the surface contact?"

"No, it has moved on. We are both below a thermal layer and they would not be able to hear us now. I expect he gave up and left the area."

Kuo pondered his next move. The *Virginia* class boat must have stumbled upon the *Akula*, perhaps as part of the American aircraft carrier's escort. The mission, the commander realized, had quickly become a disaster but perhaps this was a piece of luck for him. They had earlier received the special code ordering them to destroy the Russian submarine immediately which meant Admiral Dai's plan had failed in some way. However, his sinking one of the United States Navy's newest classes of submarines would have almost as great an impact as sinking the carrier itself. There was no time to contact Beijing however, so he would have to make the decision on his own, and quickly. Surely, he thought, if they were willing to sink an aircraft carrier with five thousand people aboard, killing this submarine would not be a problem.

Besides, after the Americans came searching for their missing boat, he surmised, they would also find the wreck of the sunken Russian boat and would assume the two submarines had fought each other to the death. That would ensure the Americans would initially believe the Russians were responsible, but as with previous events from the Cold War, there would always be doubts, especially after a few well-placed leaks made it appear likely that his country was responsible. This would send a message to Washington that the Pacific Ocean was no longer an American 'playground' as they liked to call it.

"Prepare to attack," he ordered, and then added with a smile, "We will make up for the failure of our comrades and return home as heroes."

* * *

USS Rodney M. Davis, Pacific Ocean, West of Seattle, Washington

"Maintain course and speed."

"Maintaining course and speed, aye sir," echoed the *USS Davis'* helmsman.

The frigate was moving through the water at 20 knots in a north westerly direction. The Chinese sonar operator had been right about the American's losing contact, but not as to why they continued on their present course away from the submarine's location.

South of *Davis'* position, *Vancouver* and *Ottawa* were approaching at ten knots to ensure that the same thermal layer protecting the Chinese boat from their towed arrays at the moment would also deflect the sound of the two frigate's screws. The Chinese captain had no way of knowing that in spite of the thermal layer, the men aboard the two Canadian warships knew exactly where he was.

"Lazcom is locked and message from *Victoria* coming in, sir."

"Great!" remarked Chris Donnelly, *Vancouver's* commanding officer. "What have you got?"

"Contact is believed to be a *Yuan* class SSK—one of the 041s. That's brand new, sir," noted the leading seaman at the frigate's Sonar console. "*Vic's* sending up the signature they have so far."

The Lazcom or Laser Communication System had been thoroughly tested over the previous two years and was now installed on all Her

Majesty's Canadian warships. The device enabled surface ships to communicate with a submerged submarine up to a depth of eight hundred feet and also allowed them to exchange small packets of data.

The addition of Lazcom to the new Cyclone helicopter's dipping sonar had also been successfully tested, a procedure which had delayed their delivery with the government taking considerable heat over the issue. The official word had been that there were issues with the aircraft's performance which needed to be addressed. Thankfully, Sikorsky had played along, while their engineers worked feverishly to redesign the dipping sonar to accommodate the extra weight of the communications system.

Commander Chris Donnelly rubbed his chin. If *Vic* had the Chinese boat, they had to assume the opposite was also true. With its mission to destroy the evidence of their failed operation completed, would the Chinese be satisfied and leave the area, or would the *Yuan's* captain want to remove ALL possible witnesses? Chris has no way to know that the Chinese considered the Canadian boat to be far more than merely a witness.

* * *

HMCS Victoria, Pacific Ocean, West of Seattle, Washington

"Contact course change. New heading two seven five."

"He's heading home?" Commander Rene Bourgeois asked no one in particular.

"Let's hope so," muttered *HMCS Victoria's* XO, Lieutenant Mark Killiam.

"Helm, left ten to course zero one zero. Speed ten knots. Let's get out of here," Rene ordered. "Sonar, watch him closely. If he changes direction holler."

"Left ten to zero one zero. Ten knots, aye."

As the huge rudder on *Victoria's* stern swung to the left and the submarine's bow turned towards north and home, the tension in the submarine slowly began to dissipate. Sitting quietly in the mess drinking a cup of coffee, Petty Officer Cole was contemplating the past couple of weeks and how his coming aboard *Victoria* had tuned out to be a waste of time. He could have been home with Heather by now, he thought, and they would be ...

"Cole, thought I'd find you here," Commander Bourgeois remarked as he sat down across from Darren. "Looks like we lucked out, but I'm glad to have you aboard anyway."

"Yeah," Cole replied, trying to smile. "I guess I'm relieved, but in some ways, disappointed too."

"I know what you mean. It would have been great to clean the ocean of that scum, but there's no telling what might have happened."

"Like it did with you and the *USS Carter*?"

"Exactly," *Victoria's* commanding officer smiled at the memory. "Hey, how is Barnes doing? Do you think we'll ever get our favourite chef back aboard?"

"He's doing great, sir. Oh, and I think he's in love."

"What?" Rene shot him an astonished look. "You mean with something other than food?"

"I think so. He met her in …"

The speaker above their heads cut him off.

"Commander Bourgeois to the control room!"

Reaching for the intercom button on the bulkhead next to him, Rene replied that he was on his way. As Darren watched him rush off, something told him they would not be heading back to Canada just yet.

"Commander Bourgeois, Yokov has something." Mark informed the CO as he entered the space.

When Mark called him 'Commander Bourgeois', Rene knew it was serious. Glancing at the sonar display he leaned on Alex's shoulder while trying to discern anything amongst what appeared to be empty background noise.

"Okay petty officer, what have you got?"

"I think he's tailing us, sir."

"The Chinese boat?"

"Yes, sir. I thought I had him for a second, but then he was gone," Alex explained. "Then when we cleared our baffles, I'm sure I heard him again."

"Okay, how long ago did we clear, Mark?"

"Less than ten minutes."

Rene had a bad feeling that the Chinese captain was looking to eradicate them as witnesses, as they had the Russian boat earlier.

"Sound action stations ultra-quiet. Yokov, keep on him. Stewart, contact *Vancouver* and let them know what's going on. Tell them we might be in trouble down here."

"Aye, sir. I have them on Lazcom and sending now."

Hearing the subdued action stations horn and realizing that meant someone else close by, Cole sprinted forward to the weapons space, arriving just in time to hear the order from the control room to check tubes three and four for firing. Lieutenant MacIntosh was just opening the hatch to tube three and was inspecting the guide wire connections with a flashlight. Nodding towards Darren, he ordered him to check on number four. Running a quick test to verify conductivity to the torpedo, Darren closed the tube hatch and patted it affectionately.

"Tube four loaded, checked and set," he announced, sliding the 'Warshot Loaded' placard back into the holder attached to the hatch.

"Tubes three and four loaded, checked and set," MacIntosh announced over the boat's intercom. "Okay, let's get five and six ready to go just in case," he ordered, swinging the hatch to tube number five open and reaching for the ever present flashlight hanging from a clip on his belt.

Working feverishly, the weapons crew checked the remaining four tubes and had them primed and ready to go in record time. In combat, there was little likelihood there would be a need to reload. As the weapons crew darkly noted, if six Mk-48 ADCAPS did not take out the target, it would be because *Victoria* was already on her way to the bottom.

Punching the intercom and letting the control room know that all six tubes were now ready, Kirk turned to the men sharing the weapons space with him and gave them a double thumbs up. Now came the worst part; the waiting.

* * *

HMCS Vancouver, Pacific Ocean, West of Seattle, Washington

Aboard *HMCS Vancouver*, Commander Chris Donnelly could be forgiven for feeling a sense of déjà' vu as the ship smashed down into a trough while the first signs of daylight broke through the solid cloud cover.

"Same situation—different boats."

"Sir?"

"Nothing, Host," Donnelly replied. "Just thinking out loud."

Master Seaman Albert Host smiled and stared at the increasingly rough seas ahead while occasionally glancing down at the monitor indicating *Vancouver's* heading. Making a small correction to hold the frigate's course, he wondered at the commander's comment but soon brushed it aside as he continued to scan the horizon in front of him. In spite of the ship's endless array of radars, sonars and more than a few watch keepers, he knew that if they hit anything, it would be on his shoulders.

A wave of water crashed over the bow as the ship surged ahead, diving into the next trough. Donnelly watched the water wash over the sides and mentally noted that everything on the deck previous to the wave hitting them appeared to still be there. Off to his left, he watched as *HMCS Ottawa*, having caught up to his ship, handled the same trough, exposing her bow as she climbed up and over the next wave.

Reaching down to his left, he punched the intercom button labelled SONAR.

"Sonar, bridge. Anything?"

"Nothing, sir," came from the speaker mounted on the console to his right. "Not at this speed. We still have *Victoria* on Lazcom but we're having trouble holding lock on her."

"Could the sea state be causing that?" *Vancouver* was riding the waves like a roller coaster and surely that had to be having an effect on the communications system.

"No, sir."

"Okay, keep a close ear on the sonar, just in case."

About one hundred feet behind and a deck below, the leading seaman at Sonar Station One stifled a laugh. The only thing he'd pick up in this mess would be if a torpedo hit the ship—maybe.

Donnelly looked out the bridge windows. The earlier message from *Victoria* had alarmed him, and he had no doubts that the Chinese captain might very well try to sink the Canadian boat. The Lazcom acting up was not good. Hopefully that would sort itself out quickly or they would have no way to keep tabs on the Canadian submarine.

Reaching for the intercom, Donnelly pushed the button that would connect him with the communications console and had them prepare a satellite link to MARPAC. Quickly typing a short message regarding the Chinese submarine's actions and the problems with the Lazcom into his Blackberry, he sent it to the comms officer's in-ship email address. He would encode the message before sending it on to Admiral Leger at Esquimalt.

* * *

Prime Minister's Office, Ottawa, Ontario

Fifteen minutes later, a hard copy of the message was sitting on the Prime Minister's desk.

"Shit! They're looking to get rid of the witnesses!"

"It would appear so Prime Minister," Caroline agreed. "They won't get my boat though. Rene will not allow anything to scratch *Victoria*, let alone sink her. He's still livid about the dent."

"Okay, but I don't want to take any chances. Let's see if we can take this thing down a few notches." Pressing the intercom button on his phone, he waited for an acknowledgement from his secretary.

"Yes Prime Minister."

"Sandy, get me the Chinese Ambassador on the phone. He's probably not in his office this early in the morning, so you may have to check with the director's office at CSIS. He will know where to find him."

"Yes, sir. Right away."

Two minutes later, the intercom buzzed.

"Prime Minister, I have Ambassador Jyu on the line. He is in his office."

That answered the question of whether or not the ambassador was in the loop as to what is going on. Waiting a few moments to allow the ambassador to stew, the Prime Minister finally picked up the phone.

"Mr. Jyu, how are you? I hope I did not awaken you."

"I am well, Mr. Prime Minister, and no, I am working early," he replied, trying to sound nonchalant and failing. "May I ask how you are this morning, sir?"

"Not so great, Ambassador. It appears that one of my submarines is being harassed by one of yours. I would appreciate it, Ambassador, if you would see to it that the captain of your warship is ordered to cease and desist immediately."

The line was silent. Standing by his desk in the Chinese consulate building just north of Ottawa's Byward Market, Jyu had to grasp the receiver harder to keep from dropping it due to the sweat lining the palm of his hand. His mind raced. A Canadian submarine? He had been briefed about the on-going Pacific operation and had received an update that the Russian submarine had been eradicated, but nothing else and certainly nothing about the Canadians becoming involved. The call just after dawn from the Canadian Prime Minister had surprised him. Quickly regaining his composure, he spoke into the phone.

"I will look into this right away, Mr. Prime Minister. I am sure our warship means no harm," he added, assuming the Canadians could not yet know of the Russian submarine's sinking.

"I appreciate that Mr. Jyu. I am sure it is just a case of two submarines bumping into each other. Just a simple coincidence," he added, turning the screws further.

"Oh yes, Mr. Prime Minister. I am sure of that as well. I will contact Beijing immediately and will let you know as soon as I have a response."

"Thank you," the Prime Minister replied. After hanging up, he added, "You lying bastard."

Caroline looked over at him, hiding the shock at hearing him speak so bluntly. They went back a long time together and she assumed it was the exhaustion they all felt finally starting to get to him.

"Hey." he noted, catching her look. "Sorry, but this is really pissing me off. Thank God you have that new communications device so Rene can keep in touch with our warships out there."

* * *

HMCS Victoria, Pacific Ocean, West of Seattle, Washington

"Lazcom is down, sir. I've tried everything."

"Keep at it Yokov, we need it working right now!" Commander Bourgeois ordered.

Rene regretted raising his voice but he was deeply concerned. They had gone from being part of a hunter killer group with two frigates, to suddenly finding themselves very much alone with no way to communicate anything to the warships above. Meanwhile, another submarine was stalking them from behind. Looking at the young man examining an access panel on the side of the sonar console he smiled and added, "You fix this petty officer, and you'll never pay for a pizza again this year."

"You got it, sir!" Yokov responded with a smile, before turning to one of the leading seaman next to him and growling, "I said Robertson! This is a Phillips you sod!"

Rene subconsciously checked their depth and heading. He would have preferred to have Yokov on the 'phones but he knew the Lazcom better than anyone else aboard and they desperately needed the device working again.

* * *

Beijing, China

In Beijing, a late afternoon morning breeze from the east had pushed most of the pollution away from the city, allowing the Chinese President to enjoy the rare sight of bright sunshine streaming into his office. He was relaxed now. The mission against the Americans had failed but he found an odd sense of relief in that. The mission had been far too risky and now he would have to start working to convince the uncle of the operation's architect, Admiral Dai, that his nephew was too unpredictable, a 'loose cannon' as the Americans would call him. With a relative holding a great deal of influence in the Central Politburo of the Communist Party of China however, even the President would have difficulty removing the naval officer, unless … No, he thought; the days of people conveniently 'disappearing' had to end. His own choice to lead the navy had been the current Political Commissar of the Navy who agreed with him on the future direction that China and her leaders should take. Perhaps now would be a good time to forward his recommendation again.

The President let out a long sigh. Too many with power in the country today were afraid to loosen their ties to the old ways. China's economy was set to explode, becoming the world's largest, but to do so successfully meant the workers would have to be treated and paid much better. Worker's rights was the original goal of the Communist movement, he had continually argued to all who would listen, but sadly, to no avail.

Looking out the window again, he could see the clouds of pollution beginning to return. What a sad …

A knock on his door broke his train of thought.

"Yes?"

China's Foreign Minister walked into the room and stood before his desk. A look of fear clouded the man's face as he appeared to be searching for the right words to say.

"What is it?"

"My President, I have just spoken with our ambassador to Canada."

The President felt a chill crawl down his spine. Had they discovered what had happened in their north?

"And?"

"My President," he started before pausing again, seeming to work up the courage to continue.

"What?!"

"My President, the Canadian Prime Minister has demanded that we order our submarine to stop harassing theirs. I am told he was quite angry."

A wave of relief flooded the President's mind over the message not having anything to do with the Canadian north, and just as quickly, the panic returned as he realized what might have happened. Had his men sunk the wrong submarine?

"When did you receive this message?" The President quickly regained his composure.

"Five minutes ago, my President," the minister replied. "As soon as the call was finished, I came right over."

"Good. Good."

It was very early in the morning in Canada, the President realized. If the Prime Minister himself had called the ambassador, the Canadians were obviously gravely concerned at what was going on, but it also meant that their submarine could not possibly have been sunk as his own phone would have rung then. All of which left him pondering just what was going on in the Pacific?

"Should I contact the navy, my President?"

"No, this is not important. I will deal with it myself," the Chinese leader replied. "You may go, and thank you for bringing this message to me right away."

"Thank YOU, my President," the minister gushed unashamedly before turning on his heel and leaving the room.

Looking out the window once again, the President considered his options. He knew the captain of the Chinese submarine and his family, and was not concerned that the officer would do anything as stupid as attacking the Canadians. Perhaps the Canadian submarine had come upon the Chinese boat on its way back to China. The President allowed himself a relaxed smile; Kuo would have found it impossible to pass up the opportunity to practice his attack manoeuvres on the other warship as a way of showing off his prowess. Hopefully he had already broken contact and was on his way home.

* * *

HMCS Vancouver, Pacific Ocean, West of Seattle, Washington

"Nothing, sir," replied the leading seaman at *HMCS Vancouver's* Lazcom panel to his captain's query. "It's not us—we're communicating fine with *Ottawa.*"

"And you are sure it was an intermittent breakup? We didn't just lose her all at once?" Donnelly asked.

"No, sir. We were in the middle of a chat and lost her—then she was back—and then I lost her for good," the sonar operator noted. "Yokov commented on the problem just before we were cut off so I don't believe it's a result of their situation."

"Okay, keep an eye on it in case they connect again."

Commander Chris Donnelly headed for his cabin where he sat down and drafted another message to Esquimalt indicating the current situation and their inability to re-establish contact with *HMCS Victoria.* He knew that information would not be well received. Taking the folded note up to the bridge, he passed it over to his executive officer and asked him to take it down to comms to be sent right away.

"Oh, and Chad? Ask for a receipt. I need to know they received it."

"Will do, sir."

Slumping down in his chair, Chris looked out the windows at the roiling ocean which was showing no sign of abating as wave after wave of green water washed over the ship's bow sending the frigate up over a crest before allowing her to come crashing down the other side.

* * *

HMCS Victoria, Pacific Ocean, West of Seattle, Washington

Three thousand yards away from *Vancouver,* and a few hundred feet below the surface, *HMCS Victoria* cruised along smoothly, untouched by the heavy wave action on the surface.

"Okay Yokov, get back on the phones. It doesn't look as though the Lazcom is going to be working for us today."

"Aye, sir."

With his best sonar operator back in control of *Vic's* sonar systems, Rene at least felt secure that they would not lose track of the other boat.

"Clear baffles," the petty officer ordered, adjusting his seat. It was one of the few times someone other than the watch or commanding officer could order a course change, although technically it wasn't as the submarine would turn through a full 360 degrees until it was back on the same course as before. Listening carefully, Yokov focused on the sounds picked up by the sensitive microphones mounted to the boat's hull and strung out along the towed array.

"Baffle check complete," he whispered so loud that he might as well have spoken the order out loud. "He's still hanging back there."

"How far?"

"About fifteen ... TORPEDOS! Starboard bow! Range fifteen hundred yards! No aspect change!"

Rene jumped up smashing his head into a light fixture.

"Damn! Launch countermeasures! Helm, come left 30 degrees! Down thirty to five hundred feet! Smartly!"

The sailor at the helm repeated the orders while Master Seaman Corey Parker who had been monitoring the engineering panel opened a first aid kit, grabbing one of the padded bandages for Commander Bourgeois who managed to cut his head open at least once a month.

"Hold still, sir. It's pretty bad," Parker announced, wiping the blood running down the side of Rene's face. The commander ignored him as he grabbed the attack scope mount to balance himself as Victoria's deck tilted down and to the left.

"Sonar! Aspect!"

"Changed ... following ... reaching the decoys now. Sounds like two fish but I can't be sure."

Behind them, one of the YU-4 torpedoes abruptly twisted to the right as it detected Victoria's decoys, actually hitting one of them which knocked its gyroscope off balance. The torpedo's computer, sensing that it had no way to track anything further, disarmed the warhead and shut the motor down, causing it to sink into the depths where it would implode at six thousand feet.

The second torpedo swam through the decoy's bubble field just as the guidance wire broke off, and no longer connected to the Chinese submarine, its sonar immediately went active.

"Active sonar! Torpedo!" Yokov announced. "YU-4 Chinese! Distance eight hundred yards ... bearing one eight zero."

Helm, left twenty! Reciprocal course! Down twenty to eight hundred feet. Engineering, as we pass seven hundred, shut everything down!"

Listening to be sure the young man at the helm repeated the order correctly, Rene mentally crossed his fingers. The ploy might work. Hopefully, the change in aspect by his boat, followed by the depth change and sudden drop in speed would confuse the torpedo's guidance system enough for it to miss.

Yokov slowly removed his headphones, holding one ear cup in place over his left ear so he could still follow the torpedo's sound but would not be deafened in both ears by an explosion. There was nothing more he could do now and he looked around the control room, imagining which bulkhead would suddenly implode followed by a crushing wall of water. The crew was silent; the only sound being made by the helmsman as he manoeuvred the boat and noting 700 on the digital display in front of him, turned the throttle knob to zero.

Everyone felt the deceleration as *Victoria's* huge screw stopped turning and the submarine began to drift. At the sonar console, Yokov listened as the torpedo seemed to slow behind them and then go silent. He was about to let out the breath he had been holding for the past thirty seconds when the high pitched pinging resumed directly behind them.

"Torpedo directly astern!"

Rene looked up at the overhead which had scarred his head for two years now and said a silent prayer that it would continue to do so. Just as he finished his plea, the Chinese YU-4 torpedo's warhead exploded.

* * *

HMCS Vancouver, Pacific Ocean, West of Seattle, Washington

The explosion was easily picked up by the sonar operators aboard *HMCS Vancouver* in spite of the heavy seas tossing the frigate about like a bathtub toy.

"SHIT!" Leading Seaman Don Murphy exclaimed, the sound of the explosion still ringing in his ears. "Bridge! Explosion! I couldn't get much of a range or bearing, but it was to the northeast."

Donnelly jumped from his seat and headed aft to the Operations Centre, ordering action stations sounded as he ducked through the opening off the bridge. Catching himself, he called over to the XO to order up extra crew to watch for debris on the surface and to radio over to *HMCS Ottawa* on VHF in case they missed the explosion. Seconds later, he was crouched next to the sonar operator at station one.

"What have you got, Murph?"

"One explosion. I can't say how far away because of the sea state. I thought I picked up active sonar; high frequency like a torpedo just before the blast," the leading seaman noted, "but everything is still washed out right now."

"Any breakup sounds?" Chris asked, not wanting to know the answer.

"No, sir. Nothing. But, I doubt we'd pick them up in this mess."

"Okay, keep at it Murph. Shout if you pick up anything else."

Commander Donnelly stood and walked slowly to the communications console while forming in his mind the information he would send to Esquimalt. Feeling the eyes of the sailors in the space watching him, he calmly pulled a notepad from his breast pocket and jotted down a brief message.

"Send this now, priority one."

"Aye, sir," a petty officer replied, reaching for the note and taking only fifteen seconds to type the message on his keyboard and transmit it.

* * *

MARPAC, CFB Esquimalt, British Columbia

Five minutes later, Leger's aide rushed into the admiral's office, nearly knocking O'Hanlon over in his hurry. He didn't say anything, just handing a printout over to the admiral.

"One explosion—probably torpedo—no breakup sounds. Will send when we have more," Leger read aloud. Looking up, he thanked his aide and ordered him to stand by the comms room in case anything else came in.

"Shit," Admiral O'Hanlon muttered, his mind racing. If it was a torpedo, it had to be the Chinese attacking *Victoria*, but if there was only one explosion …

"One explosion," Leger repeated, thinking out loud. "Rene would not have fired first, but his tubes would have been ready to fire. Why didn't he get a shot off?"

A blanket of silence hung over the room like a thick fog. Nobody wanted to speak next as it seemed obvious to both admirals what had likely happened. *Victoria*, caught unaware, had probably only had enough time to try and evade the torpedo before she was hit.

Sitting quietly, General Kristoff Nikolev absentmindedly clasped his fingers together. Staring at his hands, he could only imagine what had happened aboard the Canadian submarine and wondered, as he had so many years ago, how any navy managed to find men who would go to sea in them. Remembering a particular voyage long ago aboard one of the Soviet boats, he pictured the crew who had delivered him and his men to Canada and how that submarine had almost been sunk by the Americans. Back then, no one would have ever learned what had happened to them, and the names of the crew would have been quietly etched into a monument while their fate remained a mystery forever.

Reaching for the phone on his desk, Leger punched three buttons and was instantly connected with the Minister of Defence's cell phone.

"Caroline Wheeler," the minister answered, noting the Esquimalt Base ID and feeling a sudden chill envelope her body.

"Minister, *Vancouver* has detected an underwater explosion," Admiral Leger began. "Only one, and there were no other sounds but they are still dealing with some heavy weather out there."

The 'one explosion' was not lost on the minister who realized that someone had probably managed a lucky hit with the first shot and sunk their target.

"Have they been able to contact our boat?"

"No, Minister, but they are still trying and have begun a search for wreckage. I will let you know the moment I have anything else, but I have to go right now."

"Yes, of course admiral." Caroline paused, collecting her thoughts. "I will inform the Prime Minister right away. Admiral, you know my thoughts are with your men."

"Yes, Caroline," he replied. "Minister, we don't know for sure ..."

"I know, Ray. Listen; is Admiral Carroll still with you?"

"Yes, ma'am. Right here in the room."

"Can you put me on speaker, please?"

Admiral Leger tapped the 'SpkrPhone' button and placed the receiver in its cradle.

"You're on speaker, Minister."

"Admiral Carroll, could we ask for one of your DSRVs to help locate our boat if the worst has happened?"

"I will alert them the minute we hang up, ma'am," the retired CNO of the US Navy assured her. "You will have whatever you need."

Admiral Carroll had met Caroline in Halifax after *Corner Brook's* mission to France and although he had come up through the 'old boy' navy, this woman had immediately earned his respect with her no-nonsense attitude; more so when he had learned of her exploits flying a Royal Canadian Air Force Hercules over Iraq during the war there.

"Thank you, admiral. I'll clear here and let you guys get back to work, and Ray," She added, "anything at all, call me."

"Yes, Minister."

Leger pressed the disconnect button and stood.

"Let's get over to the communication's centre. We can't do much from here." Looking over at Kristoff, he added, "Well General Nikolev, I guess we're about to remove the last of the security limitations that were in place between our countries before today."

"Thank you, admiral. If there is anything the Russian Navy can do, I will contact them right away."

"We appreciate that, General." Admiral Leger appreciated the offer but he could not shake the feeling that it was too late. As they began to file out of the office, Admiral Carroll hung back.

"Brent?"

"Oh, God ..." O'Hanlon turned to face his friend. "I'm sorry. In all the ..."

"Can you contact Cookie somehow?"

The men froze, all of them looking at George Carroll standing in the middle of the room. His eyes were filled with a combination of shock and sadness. He had been as startled as the rest of them at the news but as he had finished speaking with the Minister of Defence it had struck him that he had to tell Heather something in case the navy's rumour mill picked up the story.

Leger pulled out his cell phone and punched Cookie's number. It rang five times before going to voicemail.

"Damn! Let me try aga ..." He was interrupted by a shrill beep from the phone.

"Admiral? Did you just call? Sorry, we were just checking out the Canex and ..."

"Cookie! Get the girls over to the comms building. I'll meet you there."

"Yes, sir. What's up?"

"There's been a development. Don't say anything to the girls. Not a word, and don't stop to chat with anyone."

"Yes, sir," the petty officer replied, trying to feign a smile which Heather saw right through. "We'll meet you there."

"Something's wrong," she said. "Let's go."

* * *

CP-140 Aurora 'Triple One', South of Vancouver, British Columbia

Fifteen minutes later at Canadian Forces Base Comox, a unique buzzing sound emitted from BlackBerrys belonging to members of the two ready alert flight crews, and shortly afterwards, a pair of CP-140 Aurora aircraft from 407 Long Range Patrol Squadron, carrying a full weapons load as well as a few extra observers who clambered aboard at the last minute, taxied to the main runway where they received immediate permission to take off.

Other aircraft in the busy Vancouver air traffic control zone had been quickly routed away from a corridor stretching from the base, through the control zone and out over the Pacific to the south west. A commercial pilot, originally angered at the delay, was surprised by the sight out her left window of two Auroras clawing their way into the clear blue skies.

"Something's up somewhere," the Air Canada first officer noted to her co-pilot.

The pre-flight crew briefing by Comox's 19 Wing commanding officer had been short and to the point. "Ladies and gentleman, your mission is SAR and possibly hunt and destroy. You will be brought up to speed in the air. One of our boats is missing," he noted. "Get going!"

The men and women had rushed from the room to their aircraft, arriving in time to see the armament teams checking over torpedoes hanging from their mounts inside the aircraft's bomb bays. Both flight crews noted the live Mk-46's, causing one sensor operator to stop in his tracks and exclaim, "Shit!" before continuing on his way to the ladder leading up into the aircraft.

Now, as the aircraft levelled off at twelve thousand feet, the radio operator of Aurora 140111, call sign 'Triple One' pressed the intercom button on his keyboard.

"Ah, sir? We're cleared for weapons arm."

"Roger, clear for weapons arm."

Looking over to the pilot on his left, the aircraft commander shook his head.

"Damn it Carl! What in hell have those bubble heads gotten themselves into this time?"

* * *

HMCS Vancouver, Pacific Ocean, West of Seattle, Washington

"Sir, from *Ottawa*, they're locked and loaded."

Commander Chris Donnelly sat in his chair on *HMCS Vancouver's* bridge and shook his head, replicating the Aurora officer's action far to the north east. "Thank you, leading seaman," he responded. "Chad?"

Vancouver's executive officer had just come onto the bridge from the control room where the ships sonar team were trying to find any sign of *HMCS Victoria*.

"Nothing, sir. We tried a few active pings but no joy. That might be partly because of the sea state however. It's wreaking havoc on our 'tail'. The *Halifax* class frigate's CANTASS towed array which would normally settle down in the ship's wake was being whipped around by the heavy seas, and even if it had picked up anything, it is doubtful the operators would have been able to tell where it was coming from let alone what it was with all the acoustic interference from the tumultuous sea conditions.

"Okay, XO, the Met guy says there are only another couple hours of this weather and then things should start to calm down."

"I'll get back and see what we can find. I'm sure *Vic's* fine."

"Yeah, she better be."

Donnelly had thought through the repercussions that would occur if *HMCS Victoria* was in fact sunk. He referred to the possible loss of the submarine, rather than its crew, as a way of dealing with the horrible thought that he would never see a lot of his friends again.

"Chad?"

"Sir?"

"Find that Chinese boat too."

"Yes, sir."

Vancouver and *Ottawa* were sailing two thousand yards apart in a large circle while the ship's sonar operators strained to hear anything that might indicate the presence of the missing Canadian submarine. They were all beginning to feel that it was pretty hopeless. Submarines were deadly weapons, but once anything hit one of them, it was pretty much 'game over'.

Staring out at the waves washing over the ship's bow, Chris noticed that they were indeed smaller than the ones from an hour earlier and the sky had begun to brighten somewhat. As he looked up at the clouds, a small speck of blue interrupted the overcast and from it, a long, narrow ray of sunshine reached for the ocean's surface. The streak of light seemed to widen a bit and then as though someone had turned off a light switch, it disappeared and was gone.

A flood of disappointment washed over Chris. It was as though a sign had been given that their search was futile. He shoved the thought aside and sat up in his chair as the intercom buzzed alongside him.

"Bridge, comms. We have contact with a pair of Auroras. Triple One plus one is two hundred miles out and inbound to take part in the search."

"Thank you," Chris replied. "Let them know that we have Cyclones operating up to seven hundred feet and they can have the space above that."

That was a relief. Maybe the Aurora's MADs will pick up something. Either way, the more eyes out here, the better the chances are that someone will at least spot something floating on the surface. Once *Victoria's* hull had imploded ... he corrected the thought ... IF *Victoria's* hull had imploded, anything buoyant would have been free to float to the surface. He imagined for a second what it must have been like aboard the submarine, and quickly pushed that thought away.

* * *

Prime Minister's Office, Ottawa, Ontario

In the Canadian capital, the sun was shining brightly and the temperature had climbed throughout the afternoon to a balmy thirty-four degrees. Ottawa's sidewalks were crowded with tourists and the ever popular Byward Market was overflowing with people; some shopping and others just there for the social aspect.

Canada's Prime Minister was busily tearing through a small pile of paperwork that required his signature, while at the same time trying to work on a speech for a gathering of the local party faithful later in the week. He liked to write his own speeches, allowing his advisors to edit them if necessary, but only after they explained why whatever changes they wanted should be made. He believed that if he was always upfront about his plans and more so, his beliefs, he would avoid the deadly pitfall of anyone accusing him of saying something in contradiction to an earlier comment.

Leaving the speech for a moment to sign a pile of 8 x 10 glossies that would be sent to the party's major contributors, he stopped to look at the image smiling back at him in the photo. "We're going to have to update this," he said to the empty office. "There are a lot more gray hairs on this head now."

The Prime Minister chuckled to himself and dropped the pile of images into their packing box before picking it up. Crossing the office and placing the box on the small table to the right of his desk, he was momentarily startled when a sharp rap came from the door just as he walked past it. Opening the door, he saw his Minister of National Defence standing there and one look at her face told him that he was about to acquire a few more gray hairs.

"Bad news?"

"Yes, Prime Minister. Very bad."

"Come in, Caroline," he said, standing aside and waving at one of the chairs in front of his desk. "Sit, and I'll get you a coffee."

Caroline sat down and tried to form in her mind how she would break the news. She took the cup of coffee and cupped her hands around it, savouring the comfort the warm porcelain afforded her. Instead of sitting behind his desk, The Prime Minister sat in the other chair usually reserved for guests, and sensing that something bad had happened, took a slow drink of coffee, giving his minister a few moments to collect her thoughts.

"What happened?" he finally asked.

"We may have lost *Victoria*, sir."

The Prime Minister stared into space for a moment, imagining what kind of horrors the crew may have gone through, while at the same time, his mind worked at light speed contemplating all of the events this loss would set in motion. Focusing again, he looked over at his defence minister and could see a tear beginning to well up in one of her eyes. She quickly ducked her head and made as though she was moving her hair back while secretly dabbing the wetness away.

"Oh God, Caroline." It felt as though a red-hot poker had been shoved through his heart. "What happened?

She shared what little information they had so far and the Prime Minister could tell from the tone in her voice that the tear in her eye did not emanate from sadness, not yet anyway, but rather from anger. The briefing finished, she took a long drink of coffee. She would need a lot of caffeine over the coming days, she realized, as there would be little time to sleep until this whole episode was resolved.

"I checked with the US Navy on the way over and they already have their DSRV on the way to San Diego," she explained. "A submarine is ready to embark with it as soon as it's off the plane."

"Assuming *Victoria* is damaged and on the bottom, how long would they be able to hold out?"

"The area we believe them to be in is not exactly flat," she replied. "They might be above their crush depth, on a ledge or undersea mountain, but most of the seafloor around there is well below that."

"We'd better start preparing for the worst, Caroline. It won't take long for the press to figure out that something serious is up, and they are already champing at the bit as it is over the Arctic story. How long before we'll know anything definitive?"

"If we don't hear anything from them within the next six to seven hours, we can probably assume the worst."

"I'll call the other Party leaders and let them know. We'll need to meet and come up with a solid response for China."

He looked up at the ceiling, contemplating how the situation could escalate further. Obviously not to all-out war with the massive Asian country, but the Canadian people would surely want their pound of flesh over this.

"I'm heading back to my office for a meeting with the CDS. If you need me for anything, Prime Minister, please call and needless to say," she added, "I will call you if we hear anything."

"Yes," he replied, lost in thought, reaching for the door. Then stopping, he looked at her and noted almost as an afterthought, "This Chinese submarine … can we sink it?"

* * *

HMCS Vancouver, Pacific Ocean, West of Seattle, Washington

Aboard *HMCS Vancouver*, Commander Chris Donnelly absentmindedly gazed out the bridge windows half hoping to see *Victoria* surface alongside as she had done so many times before when the two warships had exercised together. The waves were down to less than five feet now, and the clouds appeared to finally be breaking up, allowing the occasional ray of late afternoon sunshine to reach the ship.

Chris noticed how quiet the bridge was; no one wanting to risk conversation that might lead to discussing *Vic's* chances. He didn't blame them. Most of *Vancouver's* crew had mates aboard the submarine. He did as well. Rene was … is his favourite poker victim. He'd miss those games. There was no point in trying to deny it any further. They had not heard anything from the Canadian boat for far too long. Chris still held a message in his hand that had arrived earlier, advising him that the *USS Michigan* was making preparations to head their way with the DSRV aboard.

When first deployed by the US Navy, the Deep Sea Rescue Vehicles had been a bit of a joke amongst submariners. No one thought for a moment that anybody would ever be rescued from a sunken submarine. Then *Kursk* had gone down and it had been discovered later that some of her crew might have been rescued had the Russians reacted sooner, and suddenly, the concept of surviving a submarine disaster seemed to be a remote possibility, assuming of course it happened somewhere above the boat's crush depth.

"Sir, message from Esquimalt."

"Thank you," Chris replied, taking the note and unfolding it. He read it twice before folding it back up. Interesting, he thought. Someone in Ottawa was pissed. Moving to his chair, he jabbed the intercom button. "XO to the bridge!"

Moments later, one of the secured hatches leading to the Command Centre clanged open as the executive officer stepped onto the bridge.

"In the mood for Chinese tonight, XO?"

Donnelly handed the message from Esquimalt over to Chad.

"Looks like it, sir. Damn," replied *Vancouver's* XO, stunned at the brief message ordering them to locate and sink the Chinese boat. "Could be hard to catch her at this point though."

"Yes, but you know, an old salt giving a lecture back in Kingston once told me something that's stuck in my head ever since."

"What was that?"

"He said, 'When it comes to killin' subs, once you think you know what the other guy is going to do, ignore that idea and come up with another one.'"

"Sage advice."

"Yeah, I hope so," Chris smiled. "Helm, make your heading zero eight five. Maintain this speed."

The helmsmen repeated the course, giving his captain a questioning glance.

"East?" Chad enquired.

"Why not?" *Vancouver's* commanding officer replied with a smile. "I'd head west, towards home, if I were in his shoes, so he must be heading east."

As *HMCS Vancouver's* bow swung about, Chris sent a message to *HMCS Ottawa* to continue searching their sector. He did not expect them to find anything, but they had to try, as the only thing worse than *Victoria's* sinking would be for the submarine to disappear without a trace. That would be more than the families back home could bear.

He had read how the families of the *USS Scorpion's* crew had held out hope until the horrible truth had finally been confirmed long after the submarine had sank, and he did not want to return to Esquimalt without conclusive evidence of the Canadian submarine's fate, no matter what that fate was.

Shaking the thought, Commander Donnelly headed for the Ops Room where he nearly ran into the ships NCIOP coming up the passageway.

"I was just coming up to have a word with you, commander," Chief Petty Officer Gerald Deveau announced as he stepped aside to let Chris enter the space.

"How's the team today?" Donnelly asked, making his way to the ship's sonar console.

"We're pumped, sir. I heard a rumour that we're going after the Chinese boat."

"News travels fast around here, chief. Yeah, we've got to find her and take her out," Chris confirmed. "Your guys up for it?"

Commander Donnelly had asked the question in a light hearted way, but he was also feeling out his NCIOP to make sure there would be no issues with sinking a submarine containing a lot of men.

"Hell yes, sir. We don't want to hit the dock without being able to tell the peeps back home that we avenged ol' *Vic.*"

"That's what I needed to hear, chief. You have your orders. We find them; we sink them; we go home. No more; no less."

"Aye, sir. No more; no less."

* * *

MARPAC, CFB Esquimalt, British Columbia

Cookie pulled up to the gate of the navy base at Esquimalt and was surprised when he was given only a cursory glance by the guard who recognized the admiral's SUV, and waved them through the gate. He soon found out why. As they passed the communications building entrance, another MP, standing on the curb, directed him to stop the vehicle and asked them all to go right in, explaining that he would look after parking the SUV. Cookie nodded thanks as he passed over the keys, and felt Yelizaveta give his hand an anxious squeeze.

Stepping out of the vehicle, Heather stood still for a moment, looking up at the entrance. A wave of dread washed over her as she began to climb the steps and for a moment she felt as though she might faint but managed to shake off the feeling. Looking up, she saw her father opening the door and seeing the pain in his eyes, Heather broke down; her body wracked by sobs as she dropped to her knees. Yelizaveta rushed over and sat with her, holding her hands as Admiral Carroll rushed down the steps and wrapped his arms around his daughter.

"We don't know anything yet for sure, honey," he whispered, trying to console his daughter.

"Damn him!" Heather yelled through the tears, jumping to her feet. "Why didn't he come home? What the hell was he thinking? The stupid idiot …"

"I know, Heather. I know."

"Didn't you try to stop him? Didn't ANYBODY try to stop him?"

"No, honey. We thought it was best for him ..."

"To get killed? Is that what was best for him?" Her shouting drew the attention of everyone around the front of the building.

"Come inside, honey. We are ..."

She looked up at him and suddenly looked away, brushing the tears from her cheeks and swollen eyes. Taking a deep breath and slowly releasing it, she turned back to her father. A subtle, sense of peace had broken through the angst that had gripped her only moments earlier. It was the same feeling she had felt when they had first notified her of Darren's disappearance from the Arctic. Reaching out, she took her father's hand.

"It's okay, daddy. Darren is alright."

* * *

HMCS Victoria, Pacific Ocean, West of Seattle, Washington

He couldn't remember being brought into the room this time. His arms were tied to the chair and his legs were secured in a way that left them spread open. Somehow, Darren realized that he was naked. He could sense the cold concrete floor beneath his battered feet, but for some reason, he could not move his head to look down. Not that it would have mattered in the pitch blackness that enveloped him. That was odd, he thought. There had always been a light on and they had always left his …

Slowly, the door in front of him opened with a loud creaking sound—much louder than before. Ugly Russian stood there facing him, his huge body silhouetted by a bright light behind him. The torturer's imposing bulk was not what caught the submariner's eye however. Something clutched in the man's right hand, something shiny, was all Cole could focus on. As his eyes adjusted to the light from outside the room, he saw that the device was covered in bloody shreds of flesh. Panic gripped him and he was finally able to look down. The floor beneath the chair was covered in blood; his blood.

"NOOOOO!!!"

"COLE!"

"NO!!!" the submariner yelled again, trying to reach down to stop the blood. For some reason, his arms were no longer tied but they would not move. Why won't they move?

"COLE! Snap out of it!"

Snap out of it? Couldn't they see that he was dying? Couldn't they … Suddenly Ugly Russian had disappeared and now just the light from the hallway shone in his eyes, only the light kept moving and he was having trouble focusing on it.

"Welcome back to the world of the living, chief," quipped Lieutenant Kirk MacIntosh from across the weapons space.

The light shining into his eyes finally went away, replaced by the face of the boat's medical officer, slowly swimming into focus. Darren looked up at him and tried to sit up but a wave of nausea caused him to slump back to the deck.

"Not so fast, Cole. You took a pretty hard hit there but you'll be okay," *HMCS Victoria's* medical officer noted while carefully wiping blood away from around the bandage he had applied to the petty officer's forehead.

"I'm not sure about the tube hatch you ran into though," said Kirk, pointing at one of the hatches which hung open. "Looks like your head must be the harder of the two."

"What happened?"

"We took a close hit amidships. *Vic's* got a few leaks but by some miracle she held together. We're sitting on the bottom at the moment," the lieutenant explained. "I swear that if we get home, I'm going to kiss the first Limey I run into."

"Was anybody …"

"No," the medical officer cut him off. "The captain is going to have the mother of all scars to outrank his older ones, but other than a few bad cuts and bruises, we're okay. You're in the worst shape."

"How long was I out?" Cole tried to move again and this time managed to bring himself to a sitting position while noting the pile of bloody bandages around him on the deck. No wonder he'd dreamt that he was bleeding to death.

"About seven hours, Kirk replied as he worked on the broken torpedo tube door. "Doc said not to move you where your noggin took such a crack," he smiled.

"Thanks for patching me up, doc."

"You're welcome, Cole. Now lay back down and Kirk, try not to trip over him," he joked. "We're at ultra-quiet. We think the Chinese boat assumes he got us."

"Can we move?"

"Don't know," answered Kirk. "We don't dare try for a while. The boat took a pretty heavy hit and we might sound like a dump truck when we start up."

"Ah …" A sudden dizzy spell hit Darren and he closed his eyes trying to make his head stop spinning.

* * *

Type 041 SSK, PLA Navy, West of Seattle, Washington

To the east of where the crew of *HMCS Victoria* was licking their wounds, the Chinese *Yuan* class SSK was slowly picking up speed. The submarine's captain was trying to distance his boat from the surface ships and aircraft which had been hunting him relentlessly, and he was certain that heading east towards the United States would throw them off his tail. The lack of any contacts from astern for the past twenty minutes seemed to confirm his thoughts.

"Bring us around to port, sub lieutenant," Kuo ordered. "We must check behind us again."

As the boat slowly circled to the left, the sonar operators listened carefully while staring at the display screens. Ten minutes later, with nothing being detected on their tail, the submarine was back on its easterly heading.

"We have escaped them," the Chinese captain announced proudly. "Men, you have not only managed to destroy one of the most advanced American submarines, but we have also successfully escaped from a large anti-submarine force. Although nothing will ever be spoken of this, you will be heroes in the eyes of the People's Navy and our government."

Everyone in the control room smiled, although some of them were hoping for a more practical reward from their government. Being a hero did not feed a man's family. One of the naval non-commissioned officers had been heard explaining how a destroyer crew had received a handsome reward last year for their part in chasing a South Korean frigate out of Chinese territorial waters and all the way back to its own base.

Kuo looked around the space. He was proud of his command, and even more proud of his men. They had performed admirably and with one less *Virginia* class submarine in the American fleet, it would be that much sooner to the time when the Pacific Ocean would became China's realm. This had also been an excellent demonstration of the SSK's capabilities. Kuo remembered well the earlier classes of China's submarines, mostly worn out Soviet types, and his many friends who had died sailing in them.

Glancing at the digital clock on the forward bulkhead, he noted the time, planning to stay on this course for another two hours. That should ensure his escape, and afterwards, they would begin a long, slow turn to the north, and finally west; towards home.

Having risen quickly through the ranks, at 44, Kuo was one of China's youngest warship captains. His rise had been mostly due to the intensity he had applied to his studies, but also to the uncanny ability he possessed when it came to selecting the best men for his crew. Part of that success was also due in no small part to influence from a great uncle who had fought with the Chinese Communists against Chiang Kai-shek during World War II, and who was now a senior member of the government.

He looked at the clock again and smiled. By this time tomorrow they would be well on their way home to the large but private celebration which would be waiting for them.

* * *

HMCS Vancouver, Pacific Ocean, West of Seattle, Washington

Commander Donnelly slowly surveyed the expanse of water surrounding his command. The ocean's surface that had been a raging torrent just hours earlier was now almost calm, and perfect for hunting submarines. Well, almost perfect, he reflected. Another of the ocean's anomalies was causing *Vancouver's* sonar operators grief at the moment. A rarely seen, closely bunched group of thermal layers had formed in the area, the perfect hiding place for a sub trying to evade detection.

Chris had earlier considered calling one of the CP-140 Auroras over to scour the shallower depths with its MAD, while he let *HMCS Vancouver's* 'tail' search the deeper layers, but flying at low level, his quarries' passive sonar might detect the aircraft's engines and he did not want the Chinese boat's captain to know that he was still being hunted. Vancouver's CO was pretty sure that by now his adversary was feeling confident that he had given them the slip. Of course if they did not soon find him, he would be proven right. Every minute made the potential search area where the boat could be hiding larger.

Fighting the urge to buzz sonar and ask again if they had anything, he continued to scan the waves. Chief Petty Officer Deveau, the ship's

NCIOP had been unable to hide his annoyance the last time Chris had appeared behind him looking over his shoulder.

"I will let you know the moment we detect something, sir," he had promised Commander Donnelly, unable to hind the exasperation in his voice.

* * *

Prime Minister's Office, Ottawa, Ontario

In Ottawa, a solemn Minister of Defence had returned to the PMO where she sat quietly while he completed a phone call. As the Prime Minister hung up the phone, he noted the concern etched onto his minister's face and without saying anything, poured two cups of coffee from the pot that had become a permanent fixture in his office since the situation had begun. Handing one of the steaming mugs over to Caroline, he sat back down and nodded to her, expecting the worst.

"Admiral Leger said to give them a few more hours," she began, stopping to take a sip of the hot liquid. "He said he wasn't ready to write them off yet."

"Can't say I blame him. I'm not looking forward to announcing this loss to the country any more than he is," the Prime Minister noted, sadness ringing through his words. "No, I'm not looking forward to that at all."

He vividly remembered walking into a room at 5th Canadian Division Support Base Gagetown last week where he had spent time with the families of the soldiers killed up north. The wives and girlfriends of the men had all seemed so young. A half dozen children had sat quietly in the room, one of them holding an infant, and it had taken all the strength he could muster not to turn around and run away—away from the room and away from the responsibility that bore down on his shoulders.

Dismissing his security detachment, he had spent a couple of hours alone with the families of men he had never met, trying to convey how important they and their job had been to Canada. He'd sat on the floor talking with the children who had no idea who he was, and the prospect of repeating that scene with the families of forty-eight more men and women was more painful than he could imagine and he pushed the image from his mind, returning his thoughts to the present.

"There is one bit of good news, Prime Minister. Our CSIS agent has returned with the US Marine who gave up Cole to the Chinese and they also reported that they have captured his contacts in British Columbia. They are being interrogated now and CSIS will let us know what they find out," Caroline noted, not burdening him with the information about Admiral Dai. There would be time for that later. "We will question the prisoner further but it seems doubtful he'll have anything more to tell us."

"What will happen to him?"

"That depends on how this ends," she replied. "We can charge him as an accessory to the deaths up north and any others resulting from this incident. Either way, he'll be kept at Edmonton and left to rot if I have any say in the matter."

The Prime Minister smiled for the first time today before adding, "You, and me too."

* * *

HMCS Victoria, Pacific Ocean, West of Seattle, Washington

"Battery is at sixty-five percent, sir."

"Thanks, Parker." Commander Rene Bourgeois added the information to all the other details running around inside his head at the moment. *HMCS Victoria's* crew was quietly cleaning up the mess from the shaking the submarine had taken from the torpedo's near miss. The damage was serious but not fatal—yet. Rene and his engineering officer had carefully examined what they could of the inner hull and although a few trickles of water had leaked from around one pipe flange, there did not appear to be any damage to the boat's pressure hull.

Their main concern now was what would happen when they tried to move. As with most modern submarines, *Victoria* had a single propeller attached to a shaft which exited the hull where it tapered to a point at the submarine's stern. The shaft could have been slightly bent, which at best meant they might squeal loud enough to be heard all the way to Australia when they applied power to it, and at worst, the packing around the shaft might give way sending a high-pressure torrent of water into the submarine.

Aside from that, he pondered, if the Chinese boat was still out there, any noise they made would be the end of *Victoria*. He looked

275

again at the bulkhead closest to where the torpedo had exploded, almost expecting it to give way at any moment. Someone had been watching over them. Those Brits make good boats after all. That fish should have easily blown in the side of his submarine.

The reason the pressure hull had survived the blast actually had less to do with the submarine's British builders and more to do with the crew who had repaired a dent found by the Canadians after *Victoria's* arrival in Halifax. The pizza-pan sized dent had been one more embarrassment to the Royal Canadian Navy after they had acquired *Victoria* and her three sisters. Discovered by the press, it was media fodder for a couple of weeks as it appeared this would add yet another delay to the submarine becoming fully operational.

The repair crew tasked with fixing the dent had applied the most modern, high strength technology to the patched section and upon finishing, one welder had joked that the repaired area of the hull was twice as strong as the rest of the boat. He was right, but that was not the only thing that had saved the boat that day.

The Chinese YU-4 torpedo's sonar computer had misjudged the distance to *Victoria* and had exploded the warhead prematurely, but the blast had still sent a strong shock wave through the boat's hull. A combination of luck and good workmanship had saved *Victoria* ... for now.

"Okay, Mark. Let's see if the lady can move," Rene announced. "Sound action stations." It was a wasted command. Most of the crew had not moved from their positions since the blast and were silently dreading this moment.

"Blow just enough ballast to get us off the bottom. Helm, rudder amidships. Ahead slow, VERY slow," *Victoria's* captain ordered. "Be prepared to shut down the moment I give the word."

"Rudder amidships. Ahead slow, VERY slow," the leading seaman repeated. There was a new order for the books, he thought.

Behind them, a comparatively small amount of electricity flowed into the fifty-four hundred SHP electric motor attached to the submarine's shaft. For a moment, nothing happened and then the submarine moved ahead.

"All stop!"

"All stop, aye."

"Sonar?"

"Nothing, sir."

Rene smiled.

"Helm, ahead slow this time. Same course. Be prepared to stop immediately though."

"Ahead slow. Same course, ready to slam on the brakes, aye. Sorry, sir."

"That's okay, Crane."

Rene was relieved. Humour from his crew was the first sign that things were returning to normal. Again there was a slight nudge as the submarine began to move. Glancing over his shoulder to the sonar console, he saw one of the operators signalling with a huge grin and his thumb in the air.

"Helm, hold this speed and course."

"Holding speed and course," Crane echoed. "Helm responding normally."

"Good, that means no rudder damage. Sonar?"

"Normal signature, sir," Yokov replied. "We're still good here."

"Helm, up 10. Take us up twelve feet and then back to this depth."

The deck tilted up slightly for a few seconds before levelling out, and then tilting back down until they reached the original depth.

"She's responding fine, sir," Crane noted.

Rene looked up at the overhead and breathed a quick prayer of thanks. Looking down at the chart table, he noted their location and grabbing a pencil drew a line pointing north east, writing 'Home' at the end of it before circling the word.

"Mark, take us home," he ordered. "Let's keep this depth and speed for another thirty minutes and if we don't hear anything out there, we'll know that we're clear of the other boat.

"Home it is, sir," Lieutenant Killiam replied. "Helm, come left ten to zero four zero. Maintain depth and speed."

As *Victoria's* rudder moved, the submarine, no longer taking on water, and with a five degree list to port, came about until her bow was pointing back to British Columbia and home.

* * *

MARPAC, CFB Esquimalt, British Columbia

As *Victoria* began the slow trip home to Esquimalt, Admiral Raymond Leger sat behind his desk looking over the latest pile of reports. In spite of the potential disaster unfolding around him, the regular day to day activities of a modern navy continued and some of those activities required his immediate attention.

Dropping the report he had been reading and leaning back in his chair, Leger, once again pondered the announcement he would have to make if no word was heard from *HMCS Victoria* within the next few hours. Contingency plans were already in place to gather the families of the submarine's crew into the base gymnasium where they would be given the news along with what was known so far. There was always the risk that someone would turn on their cell phone and call the media in the middle of the meeting but that was a risk he would have to take.

The Prime Minister and Minister of Defence were already on their way to the west coast along with the Chief of the Defence Staff who would be sharing the announcement with him. Not that their presence would make it any easier, Ray thought. He pictured some of the families he knew personally and imagined the impact of their submariners not returning home again. There would be those who coped better than others but the submarine community was a tight one and the stronger ones would seek out and help the rest. He closed his eyes for a moment and tried to rub some of the exhaustion out of them, knowing that he would have to be the strongest. I'll just close my eyes for a few moments, he thought.

The buzz of the telephone's intercom jarred him awake. He had fallen asleep for the first time in … he had no idea anymore.

"Sir, they're here."

"Send them in," Ray replied, standing. As he came around his desk, the door in front of him opened and the wives of Commander Rene Bourgeois and Lieutenant Mark Killiam entered his office.

"Please ladies, sit down," he began, closing the door. "I'm afraid I have bad news and I wanted to make sure you were informed about it first."

* * *

Type 041 SSK, PLA Navy, West of Seattle, Washington

"Surface contact."

Kuo's head shot around.

"Can you identify it?"

"Not yet, sir. It is weak, but the track is two six three degrees and I am detecting no change in bearing," the young officer explained.

"He's following us. It must be a warship."

Kuo was surprised. They were below a pair of thermal layers and it would be impossible for a surface ship to have heard them.

"Helm, come left to zero seven zero. This depth."

The helmsman repeated the order and typed the new course into his keyboard. The computer sent a message to the submarine's helm controls which in turn moved the huge rudder ten degrees to the left, automatically holding it there until the computer sensed they were almost on the new course and compensating perfectly so the rudder was amidships as the boat reached the new heading.

"Zero seven zero, sir. Same depth and speed," the petty officer manning the helm noted.

"Sonar?" Kuo looked expectantly at the officer dwarfed by a huge pair of headphones.

"The direction is ... no, he is coming about."

The captain looked at him, almost expecting the man to smile and say it was a joke.

"Contact is now astern once more. Bearing is not changing."

* * *

CH-148 Cyclone, Vamp Zero One (Vancouver)

"A bit low."

"Yeah, got that. Bringing her back up to one hundred feet."

The CH-148 Cyclone hovered just above the wave tops, an occasional splash reaching up and soaking the bottom of the helicopter's dull gray fuselage, while the aircraft's dipping sonar head was nearly seventeen hundred feet below the surface; almost to the limit of the cable's length. The pilot glanced over the instrument panel as he frequently did during flight, stopping frequently to read the strain gage which showed the amount of stress carried by the sonar's cable/communications line.

"Cable stress within parameters," Captain Amanda Stone announced through the intercom from the CH-148 commander's seat. To her right, Lieutenant Vic Kowalski punched one, zero, zero into the flight control computer's keyboard and felt a slight downward pressure as the helicopter climbed to the new altitude where it stopped, held there by the automatic flight controls.

"Holding at one hundred feet," Vic announced.

"Still have him, TAC?"

"Sure do, sir," Master Corporal Doug Trent replied from the dark recesses behind the pilot's seat.

The Chinese submarine's captain would not have been wrong in assuming that no one would be able to track him with the complex thermal layers protecting his boat. That however, had changed with the Cyclone's introduction to service with the Royal Canadian Navy. The CH-148's, L-3 HELRAS sonar was the most technologically advanced in the world and that, along with the helicopter's rotor design which allowed it to hover close to the water's surface at a minimal noise level, meant the Canadian sensor operators were now able to passively listen at depths previously only reached by active sonar.

"*Vancouver* sends they have the information, and have forwarded it to MARPAC," Trent added, confirming that the Lazcom link between the helicopter and the frigate was still locked.

On *HMCS Vancouver's* bridge, Commander Donnelly was pacing. "Sonar, anything besides what's coming in from Vamp Zero One?" He knew better than to ask again, but damn it, he had to do something. His hunch to head east after the sub, had paid off, but the cat and mouse game was driving him crazy and he couldn't really do anything until *HMCS Ottawa* caught up to them. To ensure *Vancouver's* Cyclone would be able to stay out and search as long as possible, the helicopter was not carrying any weapons and now *Ottawa* was steaming for their location at flank speed so her Cyclone could be sent in for the kill once they were in flying range.

It had been a gamble, but sure enough, ten minutes after the Cyclone would have had to return to the ship had she been carrying torpedoes, her crew had found the Chinese boat. For almost half an hour now, they had been tracking the elusive submarine, fighting the feeling of utter frustration at not being able to do anything.

"Worst part is that *Ottawa's* bird is going to get the 'kill'," Amanda had commented when the message had come in that their sister ship's Cyclone was on the way. "We'll just be a footnote in the report."

* * *

RCAF CC-150 Polaris Enroute to Esquimalt

"Excuse me Prime Minister, it's the President."

The Royal Canadian Air Force captain standing next to the communication console aboard the CC-150 Polaris acted as though the wireless phone headset he held was red hot as he handed it over. Placing the unit over his head, the Prime Minister tried to sound cheerful as he greeted the President of the United States.

"Good morning, Frank!"

"Good morning to you David. I was just curious; are you declaring war on China?" The President was trying to inject a little levity into what he knew was a bad situation for his friend. "If you are, we probably should know about it down here."

"Not yet, but I'll let you know." He couldn't help but chuckle.

"I know you're in the air, David, but I just wanted to let you know that if there is anything we can do …"

"Thanks, I appreciate that."

"My navy guys tell me they think you have the Chinese submarine."

"It looks that way."

"So …"

"I don't know," the Prime Minister intercepted the question, not wanting to get into a conversation about the Chinese boat's future.

"I understand. Again, if you need anything …"

"Thank you, Frank, and hey, I really appreciate the call."

Pressing the disconnect button, the Prime Minister handed the headset back to the officer who appeared in the aisle. Turning to his Minister of Defence, he smiled.

"That was good of him."

"Yes," Caroline responded. "Hopefully we won't need his help."

As the President hung up the phone, he reflected on the conversation with the Canadian leader. Turning to his Secretary of State, who had joined him in the Oval Office and had been listening in on the call, he smiled.

"You know, Charles, the media up there is always on the Prime Minister's case about how he kisses my ass. Hell, they should be on some of our calls," he noted in exasperation. "The man doesn't talk to me before he does anything, and half the time doesn't even let me know about it afterwards."

* * *

HMCS Vancouver, Pacific Ocean, West of Seattle, Washington

HMCS Vancouver's crewmen ducked as *Ottawa's* Cyclone slammed onto the frigate's flight deck for a hot fueling before heading into the hunt. Running towards the helicopter and ducking below the spinning main rotor, they quickly connected the fuel hose to the aircraft in order to get it back into the air as soon as possible.

Mk-46 torpedoes hung from two of the Cyclone's hard points and through the cockpit's Perspex, the refueling crew could make out the men inside furiously checking over the submarine killer's systems.

"Fueling complete! All clear!"

The order had come from the loudspeaker mounted on *Vancouver's* hangar and sent the deck crew scurrying for cover again as the helicopter's rotors sped up and the machine lifted from the deck.

"That went smoothly," Chris noted to his XO from the frigate's bridge, watching the Cyclone quickly disappear ahead of the ship. "Hopefully getting that boat will too."

* * *

Type 041 SSK, PLA Navy, West of Seattle, Washington

"Silence," the Chinese submarine's captain admonished the crew, as he had every five minutes since they had detected the ship trailing them. Zhong Xiao Kuo stood in the middle of the control room, his eyes moving from one crewmen to the next, daring anyone to make a sound. The submarine lay dead in the water with all but essential systems shut down. The only sound aside from the crew's breathing came from the depth control system, and even it seemed to be operating at a quieter level than usual, as though it too feared the captain's wrath.

"I think it is gone, sir," the officer sitting at the sonar console announced in a harsh whisper.

"Are you certain?"

"I feel confident, sir," he replied nervously, fearing that he might be wrong, but fearing the result of not saying what he thought even more. Kuo saw the nervousness in the man's countenance and appreciated that he was taking a chance voicing his speculation.

"Thank you, lieutenant. Your expertise is appreciated," the commander replied before adding, "We will remain at silent stations for a few minutes longer to be sure the Americans have not detected us."

Kuo was hatching a plan for this nuisance of a ship that had been following them. He had already sunk one of the American's mighty *Virginia* class submarines and in his mind, he was imagining the hero's welcome he would receive for destroying what was probably one of their *Arleigh Burke* class destroyers as well.

The warship had been following them for some time and there was no possibility they could have known it was not the Russian submarine they were tracking. Kuo smiled. Yes, he thought. The Russians would be taking all of the blame for anything he did here, for now. Later on, in quiet circles, the Americans would learn that it had in fact been China who had embarrassed them this day, and the balance of power in the Pacific would change forever.

"Helm, ahead slow. Reverse course."

The helmsman repeated the order while turning to look towards his captain, his eyes questioning that he had heard it correctly. Kuo smiled at him and nodded.

* * *

HMCS Vancouver, Pacific Ocean, West of Seattle, Washington

"Bridge, Comms. Vamp Zero One reports lost contact."

"Damn!" Commander Donnelly exclaimed, instantly regretting the outburst.

Vamp Zero One's sensor operator was desperately trying to find the Chinese boat again. In the Cyclone's cockpit, Lieutenant Amanda Stone checked the aircraft's gauges, paying particular attention to the remaining fuel on board. They needed to reacquire the submarine quickly before *Ottawa's* bird arrived with its torpedoes.

"Relax Doug," she tried to calm the frustrated airman. "You'll get him again."

Hunched over his console, Master Corporal Doug Trent listened intently but he could not hear anything other than a few biologicals and the display in front of him contained none of the vertical lines which would have indicated a steady sound source.

"Vamp Zero One, Capital Zero Three is on your six about fifteen hundred yards."

"Roger, on my six at fifteen. We've lost contact. If you guys want to dip one thousand yards on my three o'clock, that would be great," Amanda ordered over the guard channel. As first on the scene, she had control of the search. "Try that for ten and if no joy, switch to my six. I will stay on the original track."

"Sounds good, Capital Zero Three."

Half an hour later, they had still not managed to detect the Chinese boat and Lieutenant Stone was concerned that it had slipped away for good.

"*Vancouver*, Vamp Zero One. We still have no contact. Returning for hot fuel."

"Vamp Zero One, roger."

Commander Chris Donnelly looked over to his NCIOP who was speaking with the sonar team. "Chief, I'm thinking we'd better send in the Auroras and do some active hunting."

"I concur, sir," he replied. "If we don't reacquire him soon, we aren't going to."

"Make it so, chief," Chris ordered. "Let Zero Three know to start pinging. Maybe they'll find him before the big guys do."

* * *

HMCS Victoria, Pacific Ocean, West of Seattle, Washington

"Active sonar, sir. Ours, I think. Sounds like dipping, but it's too far off to say for sure."

Commander Rene Bourgeois turned to look at *HMCS Victoria's* sonar operator.

"Helm, up ten; take us to periscope depth."

"Up ten to periscope, aye."

It was time to try and get a message out before the whole navy was sent out to search for them. Rene assumed Esquimalt must have suspected the worst but at the same time, he wanted to make sure that he was well clear of the Chinese boat before making any noise. As the deck slowly tilt up, he felt the welcomed extra weight in the soles of his feet that a submarine heading for the surface causes.

A minute later, *HMCS Victoria* was cruising silently sixty feet below the surface. Satisfied that he had included all the pertinent information while keeping the message as short as possible, Rene handed the note over to his communications officer who sat down at one of the sonar consoles to encrypt it.

"All set," Leading Seaman Sam Stewart announced, ready to hit the transmit button as soon as the Comms Mast cleared the surface.

"Raise Comms and Induction," *Victoria's* commanding officer ordered. "Engineering, I can only give you fifteen minutes on the snorkel," he added.

"That'll almost do, sir," Master Seaman Corey Parker noted from his wall of lights, displays and gauges which told him how all the boat's systems, including the battery, or as he called it, 'his babies' was doing. It really wouldn't do, he knew, but at least it would keep the submarine's battery from going on the critical list. This charge would bring it to just over sixty percent, he expected. Hardly the eighty percent he felt comfortable at, but then again, considering the current circumstances, he would be satisfied with anything over ten at this point.

As soon as he noted the indicator light showing the comms mast had cleared the surface, Stewart mashed the transmit button. "Message sent, sir," he announced.

"Thank you, Sam," Rene replied.

The moment the GMT clock mounted on the bulkhead indicated they had been snorkelling for fifteen minutes; Rene ordered the diesels shut down.

"Helm, down ten, make depth two zero zero feet."

"Down ten—two zero zero feet, aye."

"Sir!"

"What is it, Stewart?"

"I'm still not seeing a receipt for our message."

"Belay the dive! Does the antennae check out?"

Rene suddenly had an image of his wife sitting in the admiral's office, being told that her husband was dead. In the effort to escape the Chinese boat, little thought had been given by anyone aboard the Canadian submarine that the rest of the world might have presumed them lost.

"No faults showing, sir."

"Are you picking up anything?"

"No, sir. I'd say we're off the air."

Victoria's captain was not happy with that news. The prospect of surfacing the boat to work on the comms mast impressed him even less, but on the other hand, they had to find some way to let someone else know they were still alive.

"Helm, up ..."

"Active sonar! One nine four degrees." Yokov's voice held an edge Rene recognized. "Numerous frequencies, sir. Dipping first and ... buoys now."

"Auroras?" Rene remembered reading that the Cyclones would not be equipped with the 53 Series of sensors yet. Understandable with the dipping sonar they carried. That thing could pick up an oyster fart five thousand miles away, or so one of the Cyclone guys had told him. Rene's expression showed the exasperation he felt. "Helm, down ten to two five zero feet. Rudder left three zero to heading one nine four degrees. Maintain speed."

As the master seaman sitting at the helm repeated the orders, he smiled. Ol' *Vic* had once taken a hit from an unarmed American Mk-48, and now a Chinese fish had nailed the boat when her back was turned. With her bow coming around to point towards the action, he thought, we'll finally show them what this lady can do when she's pissed off.

* * *

CFB Comox, British Columbia

Two hours later, as a dark grey Royal Canadian Air Force CC-150 Polaris carrying the Prime Minister and his party taxied up to the terminal at CFB Comox, Admiral Leger took a deep breath and came to attention noting the Prime Minister wasn't arriving in the 'official' Polaris. To his right, Brent and General Nikolev did the same, while Cookie, Yelizaveta, Heather and George Carroll stood quietly behind them. With the accommodation stairway rolled up to the aircraft, the hatch swung open and the Prime Minister appeared in the opening. He stopped for a moment to allow his eyes time to adjust to the bright setting sun, and forgoing the usual wave and smile, quickly descended the stairs, noting the two admirals and an officer wearing a strange uniform, all standing at attention waiting below. Keeping a respectable distance, the Minister of National Defence and the Chief of the Defence Staff followed the Canadian leader down the steps.

That must be Heather, the Prime Minister thought, noticing a young woman standing behind the officers. He remembered her name from the report on *HMCS Corner Brook's* foray to the Med. If only, he contemplated, this operation had ended as well as that one had. Stepping down onto the tarmac, he greeted Admiral Leger first.

"Ray, good to see you again."

"Thank you Prime Minister. You of course know Brent."

"Of course." The two men shook hands warmly. They had been friends long before Canada's leader had entered politics, back when Brent was still a commander.

"It is good to see you again, Prime Minister" said Brent. "I would like to introduce you to General of the Russian Army, Kristoff Nikolev."

"I am honoured to meet you, sir." Kristoff held out a huge hand.

"The honour is mine, General Nikolev. We owe your country a debt of gratitude for your help in rescuing our sailor …"

The words were not out of his mouth when a sob interrupted him. Turning to the young woman standing behind the general, the Prime Minister took both her hands in his.

"You must be Heather," he spoke in a low, soft voice. "I am so sorry. We're doing everything we can to find them."

"Thank you … he's not dead you know."

"I know. There's still hope."

"Not hope. He's not dead."

Admiral Carroll held her, exchanging a look with the Prime Minister who nodded understanding while reaching out to shake hands. Having a daughter about Heather's age, he understood the admiral's feelings and words were not necessary.

As the Chief of the Defence staff conferred with the Canadian admirals, they all moved towards a pair of SUVs waiting to whisk them down the highway to Esquimalt. The CDS looked up at the clear sky, dreading what was to come in the following days. As he climbed into the back seat of the first vehicle, a petty officer affixed the official flags of rank and position to the fenders. Buckling his seat belt, he looked over to Admiral Leger. "What happened, Ray?"

"I wish I knew. There was nothing left out of the report, general. The best we can tell, they wanted to clean up the witnesses," he explained. "We are pretty sure the Chinese captain did not realize it was a Canadian boat, but we can't say for sure. I guess we're hoping that will come through channels once they return to China and are questioned by their government."

"Damn. Any chance our boat has just gone quiet?"

"We don't think so, and if she was disabled, they would have released the SEPIRB. *Vancouver* has not picked up anything from that, but the Auroras are keeping a close watch on the frequency they use, just in case."

"Okay, how are we doing with the families?"

"They are being notified and should be together by the time we return to the base," Ray replied. "I've already spoken with the CO and XO's wives and they are prepared."

"How did they take it?"

"They'll do what they have to do for the crew's wives and then when this is all over, they will take their turn to grieve." He lowered his head a moment. "My wife is getting ready for when that happens."

"Hell of a way to live," he remarked. "Brent?"

"Nothing to add, sir. I'm glad you're here though."

"Yeah, me too."

"Oh, one more thing," Ray interjected. "The media have been saints on this. They have an idea that something big is going on and that it's not good, but they are holding their tongues until we give the word."

"That's a relief," the CDS sighed. "All we need now is for this to hit the news before the families are told." He paused for a moment as if pondering something and then looked back at Brent.

"Heather seems so sure that her husband is still alive, O'Hanlon. I hope she'll be okay."

"I don't know, sir," Brent replied looking out the window on his left. "But she was right about him when they had him in Russia, and we had almost given up hope then."

* * *

HMCS Victoria, Pacific Ocean, West of Seattle, Washington

"Tube loaded!" Chief Darren Cole slapped the heavy metal door.

"Great!" *HMCS Victoria's* weapons officer replied.

Pressing the intercom button, Lieutenant MacIntosh informed the control room that four tubes were loaded with Mk-48 ADCAPs and ready to fire. A fifth tube remained empty because of possible damage from the near miss, while the last one was still flooded from the explosion and all attempts to pump it dry had failed. All that stood between the men in the torpedo spaces and immediate death was that tube's inner door.

"How's your head, Cole?"

"Fine, sir. I just needed that rest."

"Good. Looks like you may get what you came for after all."

"You know, now that I've had time to think about it ..."

"Yeah, I know what you mean," Kirk nodded. "Coming so close to dying makes it that much harder to kill someone else, in the same boat so to speak."

"Really bad pun, sir."

* * *

Type 041 SSK, PLA Navy, West of Seattle, Washington

"Active sonar, captain," announced the Chinese sonar officer. "Well behind us."

"Good," Kuo replied. "They do not realize we have slipped away. Do you still have the surface contact?"

"I do sir. I cannot classify it as an American *Arleigh Burke* class destroyer though."

"You will once we are closer. Then we will show the Americans that they no longer control the Pacific Ocean!"

"Yes my captain."

Although he would have never dared say anything to dispute his commanding officer, the sonar operator did not understand how the sounds he heard, and could now see displayed as lines on his sonar screen, were going to transform into the American destroyer class's signature. Perhaps it was one of their new Zumwalt class destroyers. He had no idea what they might sound like, but, he thought, they looked strange.

* * *

MARPAC, CFB Esquimalt, British Columbia

The Prime Minister of Canada walked slowly towards the large building that housed the base gymnasium at CFB Esquimalt. To his left, Admirals O'Hanlon and Leger kept pace with him while on his right, the Chief of the Defence Staff and Minister of National Defence followed a few paces behind. All of their faces reflected the grim task ahead.

Inside the gym, the families and close friends of *HMCS Victoria's* crew sat in chairs that had been quickly set up, or simply stood patiently along the walls. Some of them already guessed that something had gone horribly wrong as rumours had begun to float around the base housing of several politicians and high ranking officers arriving at the base.

A few people, having heard the Prime Minister was on his way, worried the most, having seen the earlier news footage released of his meeting with the families of the soldiers from Gagetown who had been killed.

Glancing around the room, those who hadn't figured it out, quickly realized something must have happened concerning *HMCS Victoria*, as all the people in the room were connected with her crew in some way. The wife of Petty Officer 2nd Class Alexander Yokov stood in a corner holding their three month old son. The baby was crying and although she had brought along his favourite toy, he ignored it and continued to cry as if aware that something terrible had happened to his father. Hugging him and cooing did not seem to quiet the child and finally

Marie Bourgeois came over and offered to hold the infant. Handing the baby over, Eva Yokov was amazed at how the older woman was able to quiet her son down and in no time he was asleep in her arms.

"It gets easier once you've had a few," Marie smiled, handing young Ivan back to his mother.

"Thank you so much. He did not have his nap today so he's …" At that moment, Eva looked up and saw the tears in Marie's eyes.

"What is it? Has something …"

She was interrupted by a squeal of feedback from the speakers fastened to the corners of the gymnasium walls. The sound reverberated throughout the space before finally ending with a voice. Looking towards a makeshift platform that had been hurriedly assembled at the far end of the space, and seeing a group of people walk up to it, Eva and Marie sat down on a couple of the folding chairs. They both recognized the Chief of the Defence Staff and Marie recognized Admiral Brent O'Hanlon standing next to him, along with Admiral Leger. He must have flown in from the east coast, she thought, fighting the angst building up inside of her.

An air force lieutenant, looking decidedly uncomfortable, was standing at the microphone. "Excuse me, ladies and gentlemen," he asked softly. "Could I have your attention please?" The room feel silent for a moment as he stepped aside and Admiral Ray Leger walked up to the mike, pausing for a moment to look around at the faces staring up at him. The people sitting near the front saw his jaw quiver for a moment and their hearts sank.

"Friends, I have disturbing news to report to you at this time …"

The admiral explained how contact with the submarine had been lost and although they were not yet certain of its fate, there was a possibility that the boat and crew may have perished. He did not go into details about the situation, but most of the family members guessed that it had probably been a result of the training mission *HMCS Victoria* had been taking part in.

A few people sobbed, and at the back of the room, a baby cried out. The timing was fortunate as it brought everyone back to the reality that, in spite of their possible losses, life would have to go on.

Admiral Leger looked out over the gathering of families and assured them that they would be informed the minute he heard anything. "Yes," he had replied to the first and expected question, "there is still hope."

He detected the relief in the room and followed his reply with a warning that they should have detected the emergency beacon from the submarine by now as it would have been released if at all possible had things aboard *Victoria* reached a critical stage. He hated himself for dashing their hopes, but on the other hand, he could not have them leaving with the expectation that everything would be okay.

"Sir," a young lad sitting in the front row timidly raised his hand. Ray noted that he was probably six or seven years old.

"Yes, son?"

"Are they heroes?"

The room fell silent. Admiral Leger looked down at the boy, and stepping around the microphone, hopped down from the stage. Walking over and resting on one knee to bring himself level with the child, he quietly asked, "What's your name, son?"

"Danny MacIntosh, sir."

"Ah, you must be Kirk's son."

"Yes, sir!" The boy beamed.

"Well," Ray began, "tell you what. You take good care of your mom here and I'll make sure I let you know the moment we hear anything. You have to promise me that you'll be strong though, no matter what happens"

"I will, sir," little Danny replied, a serious look on his face.

"Thank you, son and one more thing … I know that your dad would have been very brave, no matter what happened."

The boy smiled and his mother put her arm around his shoulder. She exchanged glances with the admiral and Ray saw the unspoken plea in them. Returning to the microphone, he looked out over the families of his men and assured them that everything possible was being done to locate the submarine.

"The Unites States Navy is giving us their full assistance and they are rushing their deep sea rescue submersible into the area," he noted. "That is all we know at the moment but please stay close by and we will keep you informed as we know more. If any of you need anything at all, please call my office immediately. We have alerted the media to bury this story for the time being as we realize that you will need to notify the rest of your families. I ask that you be discreet about sharing this with anyone outside of the base until we inform you otherwise, in respect for those family members who may not be reached for a while, and for the safety of those involved with the ongoing operation."

With that, the three men stepped from the stage, and leaving the building, headed for Ray's office, where the Prime Minister and Minister of Defence waited for them. The Prime Minister had felt it would be better to leave the initial briefing of the families to the naval officers. The really hard part for him, he knew, would come soon enough.

One of the US Navy assets also making its way to the area where *HMCS Victoria* was last reported was an oceanographic ship carrying remotely operated submersibles which would be able to locate the wreckage of the Canadian submarine at any depth, assuming they could narrow down the search area. Ray had not divulged that information during the briefing. He did not want to plant the image of a submarine strewn across the ocean floor in the minds of the families; photos he had seen of *Scorpion* and *Thresher* had flashed through his mind. The one fear the officers all held, but did not dare verbalize even amongst themselves, was the submarine never being found and the fate of her crew remaining a mystery forever.

* * *

HMCS Vancouver, Pacific Ocean, West of Seattle, Washington

A short distance ahead of the Chinese boat, *HMCS Vancouver* had slowed to ten knots, while *HMCS Ottawa* pulled off to the north in an effort to broaden their search area. In *Vancouver's* operation room, the tension in the air was palatable. The sonar team was desperately listening for any sign of the submarine which they assumed might be trying to escape the massive active sonar search by the Cyclones and Auroras to the east. At the same time, they were watching for any sign of their own submarine's emergency locator beacon.

One of the sonar operators removed his headset for a moment and ran his hand backwards through his hair before rubbing his eyes. He had been on duty an hour past his usual watch, but he knew he was one of the team's best set of ears, and after the realization of *Victoria's* loss had settle in, he was determined to help find the Chinese submarine. Sliding the headset back over his ears, he listened again but all he heard were the natural sounds of the ocean. Adjusting the tone, he leaned back in his chair before suddenly sitting up ramrod straight.

"TORPEDO!" he screamed. "Bearing zero six three! No aspect change!"

In reaction to the torpedo warning, *HMCS Vancouver's* operations room fell dead silent for about half a second, and then a flurry of commands flew around the space, but it was too late. A huge explosion lifted the frigate's hull almost clear of the water before it crashed down again. Amidst the warning horns and shouted commands, Commander Chris Donnelly tried to pull himself up off of the deck but something was wrong. He tried again but his left leg did not seem to be working. Looking down, he could see blood soaking through the pant leg just below his left knee and dripping onto the deck. Oh hell, he thought.

"CAPTAIN!"

Chris turned his head towards the yell and was about to say something when the space suddenly went dark and he slumped down, unconscious. His last thought was of the videos he had seen over and over again showing how a torpedo explodes below a ship, breaking its back.

The same flaw that had spared *HMCS Victoria* earlier however, now allowed *HMCS Vancouver* to live, as the torpedo had exploded a second before passing directly below her hull. The massive explosion lifted and shook the ship violently, but did not break her keel. All power was lost as the ship's turbines ground to a halt and numerous breaks in electrical conduits throughout the hull exploded in a shower of sparks. Fire alarms rang out, joining the cacophony of flooding alarms and shouts from crewmembers trying to make their way through passages filled with smoke and debris.

The warship lay dead in the water. Dark plumes of smoke escaped from her exhaust vents as some of the crew worked to restore power. Others donned respirators and lugged hoses through the darkened passageways to beat down the fires raging inside two of *Vancouver's* spaces.

A hole below *Vancouver's* waterline had been plugged and shored up twice, but seeing there was no way to secure the inrushing water, the XO had quickly ordered the space evacuated and sealed. As a petty officer securely dogged the hatch, he said a silent prayer that it would hold back the sea.

A short distance away, the crew of *HMCS Ottawa* scrutinized the scene. They had stared in disbelief after a warning had reached them from *Vancouver* an instant before the ship had disappeared beneath a huge geyser of water. Expecting to see her back broken and their sister ship slowly sinking, a huge cheer had gone up when the damaged warship had come into view, obviously crippled, but equally obvious, in one piece.

"Helm, left twenty!" *Ottawa's* captain ordered. "Come to zero one zero! Ahead slow!"

Knowing *Vancouver* would need assistance fast, he ordered the Cyclones back from their search in case anyone needed to be airlifted to his ship, and after confirming they were on the way, he headed for *Ottawa's* operations room. His first priority was to find out where the torpedo had come from, although he suspected that it had been fired from the Chinese submarine which had probably backtracked and crept up on them. With *Vancouver* now dead in the water, the damaged frigate would be an easy target. He briefly wondered at her survival. Most operators realized there was little chance of a ship the size of a frigate or destroyer surviving a modern torpedo and he was concerned at the amount of smoke pouring from the ship, and what damage had been done to *Vancouver's* hull below the waterline.

Lieutenant Commander Nelson Parsons looked over to *Ottawa's* NCIOP who was speaking to three different people at once and gestured him over.

"Do we have him?"

"No, sir. Nothing," he replied, obviously exasperated. "We're trying everything."

"Okay, keep at it. Comms, message MARPAC, '*Vancouver* damaged in torpedo attack – will follow up with more info shortly'."

"Aye, sir."

"Let me know when they respond. I'll be on the bridge."

As he reached the bridge, Nelson grabbed his binoculars and gave *HMCS Vancouver* a long, hard look. She appeared to be listing slightly to port but the angle did not seem to be getting any worse and more importantly, the amount of smoke pouring from openings in the ship was lessoning. That was good. Fire was the number one enemy of any vessel. *Vancouver's* main mast showed the most visible damage. Buckled slightly by the incredible force which had nearly rolled the ship over, it leaned over to starboard by about ten degrees. The recently installed Smart-S Mk2 antennae had broken off its mast and fallen into the ocean. With all the ship's radar antennas now unserviceable or missing, she was blind, and assuming her sonar sensors had been ripped apart by the underwater explosion, deaf as well.

"The engineers are going to have to check that mast out," Nelson remarked to his XO, standing at his right elbow also surveying the other ship. "It shouldn't have come apart like that."

"Definitely not," he agreed. "She must have taken one hell of a hit."

"Sirs," we have *Vancouver*. A master seaman joined them, holding a VHF portable radio towards Nelson.

"Thanks, son," *Ottawa's* captain acknowledged. "*Vancouver*, this is *Ottawa*. How are you guys doing over there?"

"Pretty banged up, sir." *Ottawa's* captain recognized Chad's voice. "Commander Donnelly is unconscious. He suffered a serious leg injury and a bad gash to his head but the medical officer said he'll be fine once he comes to. Casualties are pretty heavy. No deaths that I am aware of. We took on some water but the larger holes are secured and our portable pumps are starting to get ahead of the smaller leaks. The fires are out but we have no main power."

"Can you confirm where the shot came from?"

"It was a quick read but zero six three is what we have," he replied. "Has to be the Chinese boat and he had to be close. There was only a few seconds from warning to impact."

"Okay, we're going down that track to see what we can find. I just sent a message off to Esquimalt. Oh, and Chad? Can you get me a list of casualties and I'll send that off to them right away as well?"

* * *

Type 041 SSK, PLA Navy, West of Seattle, Washington

"You must hear it!" Kuo screamed at his sonar operator.

"No, captain. I did hear the explosion but not the sound of a ship breaking up."

The young Chinese officer was stressed out and tired of the abuse this man kept throwing at him and the other crewmembers. They were the best in the Chinese Navy but this tyrant only wanted to hear what he expected to hear. Reality seemed lost on him, the man thought. Of course he could only afford the luxury of thinking these thoughts and would have never dared voice them aloud to anyone.

Kuo was furious. The American ship had to be sunk! The torpedo had run perfectly and the explosion had come exactly when it was supposed to. He desperately wanted to go up to periscope depth and confirm that the ship had been reduced to flotsam but did not dare. There were still other ships up there and the only thing more important to him than confirming that he had sunk this one was making it back to China alive so he could bask in the glory of the mission's success.

* * *

MARPAC, CFB Esquimalt, British Columbia

"Hell! Have they gone nuts!?"

The Prime Minister's outburst had come as he paced the floor of Admiral Leger's office and everyone avoided the path he was using.

"Ray, has your man got Beijing yet?"

The message from *HMCS Ottawa* had galvanized the Canadian leader into action. Caroline, the admirals and CDS had barely managed to get a word in as the Prime Minister had gone on a tirade over the situation. He was just about to sound off again when there was a quiet tap on the door, followed by a petty officer poking his head into the opening.

"Er, sirs. China is on line three."

"Thank you, petty officer, that will be all," Brent replied, being the closest to the door. Earlier he had decided that if the Prime Minister started throwing things, he was ducking out and taking cover.

Grabbing the phone and nearly demolishing the button marked '3', the Prime Minister bellowed into the phone, "Mister President, if you are declaring war on us, I would appreciate your making it official right now!"

The Chinese President was stunned. Having just met this man the previous month, he recognized the voice, but not the anger. This was no time for protocol. Waving the interpreter beside him out of the room and taking the headset from him, he paused as the other man reluctantly left. Placing the headset upon his own head, he adjusted the microphone.

"Mister Prime Minister, I am sorry, but I do not understand," he began in broken English. "Has something else happened?"

"Your damn submarine just took a shot at one of my frigates and nearly sank it!"

The President felt his pulse quicken and in spite of the air conditioning, beads of sweat broke out on his forehead. He realized that this was the nightmare all the world's leaders had dreaded during the cold war, but at least now, there was little likelihood that this event would escalate into a global nuclear war. Still, Canada had powerful allies.

"No …," he started. None of the thoughts that flashed through his mind seemed to be the right thing to say.

"Can't you call him back?"

"No, the mission he is on is under total communications lockdown," the Chinese leader replied. "We had no idea, sir. I am so sorry. Were many of your men injured?"

The question calmed the Prime Minister down. He didn't know the answer as that information had not yet reached Esquimalt. He imagined another meeting with an even larger group of families than *HMCS Victoria's*, which he still had to deal with. When he replied, his voice was calm as he tried to relax, sitting on Admiral Leger's desk.

"I don't know yet. They've lost communications and the other ship we have there is hunting your submarine." He paused. "Mister President, if we find it, we are going to sink it."

"I understand."

The Chinese leader's response had come immediately. He obvious had assumed as much. The Prime Minister thought he'd detected a note of … Was he hoping they would sink it?

"I am sincerely sorry Mister Prime Minister. I am going to talk to my admirals and see if there is anything we can do. Perhaps something they have not yet thought of."

"Thank you, I appreciate that."

The Prime Minister hung up the phone and looked around the room. His Chief of the Defence Staff, trying to bring the tension down a few points, noted that the call had, 'Gone well.'

"Yeah," the Prime Minister acknowledged. "I believe him. I don't think he has a clue as to what is going on, but I think he IS trying to do something about it."

"CSIS has dug around a bit and the admiral who pulled this off has some high connections in their government, so the Chinese President is probably not going to have a lot of luck," Caroline noted. "I think as far as stopping their boat is concerned, that is going to be up to us."

"We'd better get him quick," Admiral O'Hanlon interjected, "before he sinks half our navy."

* * *

HMCS Vancouver, Pacific Ocean, West of Seattle, Washington

Having regaining consciousness while being carried out on deck, where his head and leg were bandaged up, Chris now stood on the bow, looking back over his ship. Leaning heavily on the crutch he had used to make his way forward, at the protest of his medical officer, he started limping aft, stopping to rest against the gun mount before looking up at the bridge. *HMCS Vancouver* looked oddly naked without her main radar antennae. There were about a dozen serious injuries, but the good news was that no one had been killed, although almost the entire crew was suffering from some sort of cuts or bruises. He looked down at the blood soaked bandages on his leg. Unfortunately, he was one of the dozen, and although the ship's medical officer had literally screamed at him when he had asked for the crutch, Chris knew he needed to be seen by his crew now more than ever. "Besides," he had consoled the lieutenant, "you're always telling me to get out and walk around more."

Now, like the rest of them, he wondered where the Chinese submarine was. They were a sitting duck and he had already been informed that both turbines were unserviceable and could not be repaired. The backup diesel might get them moving but first they had to filter the fuel oil as the tanks had been ruptured and they didn't dare run it in case contaminants destroyed their only remaining source of power.

Overhead, the ship's and *Ottawa's* Cyclones were holding steady off the starboard bow with their dipping sonars in the ocean. He knew they were pounding away with active sonar to make certain the Chinese knew they were there, and hopefully scare them away from making another attack.

The Auroras, having expended all their sonobuoys were flying a higher pattern and waiting for any word of a contact. If the boat was detected, they would drop a full weapons load on it. One of the aircraft commanders had radioed to *Vancouver* over the VHF portable and assured Chad that the Chinese skipper might evade one or two, or maybe even three of their torpedoes, but either way, today he was going to die.

* * *

Type 041 SSK, PLA Navy, West of Seattle, Washington

"Contact, sir!"

Kuo swung around towards the sonar console.

"Surface ship bearing two eight three. Three thousand yards," the petty officer continued.

"Did he detect us?"

"I do not think so. He is not active right now. He appears to be listening and only the helicopters are active now," the petty officer replied, making an effort to sound sure of himself, although he could not imagine how this ship had just suffered a torpedo hit. There were no sounds of damage control taking place. The lieutenant who had been on duty earlier had been relieved and was now under arrest in the food storage area. He did not want to join him.

"Good. We will wait. Let me know when you think he is close enough. He will not escape us this time!"

"Yes, sir," the young rating replied. He was not about to make the same mistake his senior officer had done by questioning the captain.

* * *

HMCS Ottawa, Pacific Ocean, West of Seattle, Washington

"He has to be along this track," *HMCS Ottawa's* commanding officer assured his NCIOP.

"They are so damn quiet though, sir."

"Yeah, give it another few minutes passive and then let's bang at the water again. Anything from the choppers?"

"Nothing yet, sir," he replied. "They thought they had something but confirmed it as a biological."

"Okay. Good work, Bart."

Commander Nelson Parsons returned to the bridge. Hunting these new SSKs was like walking around a gymnasium blindfolded and trying to find a basketball sitting on the floor. You might find it, but more likely you would trip over it and get hurt. It must have been pure dumb luck that the bastard had detected and sunk *Victoria*.

He thought again of his friends who had been aboard the Canadian boat. When he got back to Esquimalt, he'd have to make sure he got in touch with Rene's ... Nelson tried to shove the thought away. He had to remain focused on the mission at hand, and besides, he wanted to tell Rene's wife that he had caught up with her husband's killer and taken the bastard out.

* * *

Type 041 SSK, PLA Navy, West of Seattle, Washington

A short time later aboard the *Yuan* class SSK, the sonar operator looked over to his captain and reported the ship in range.

"Are you sure?"

"Yes, my captain. Range is now eleven hundred yards."

"Torpedo officer! Range the target and fire two torpedoes. I do not want anything going wrong this time!"

"Yes, my captain!" the weapons officer replied without hesitation. A fanatic like his captain, he smiled as he imagined the American ship breaking in two, disgorging its crew into the ocean where the sharks would take care of any survivors. He made one final check of the bearing before reaching for the firing button.

* * *

HMCS Ottawa, Pacific Ocean, West of Seattle, Washington

Buried inside *HMCS Ottawa's* Control Room, a leading seaman stared in disbelief for a split second at the display in front of him before yelling out.

TWO TORPEDOES! Bearing zero seven nine!"

Commander Nelson Parsons felt a wave of nausea wash over his body as he turned to the helmsman who stared at him with eyes like saucers as his mouth hung open.

"Helm! Hard left make ..." The speaker above his head cut his command short.

"BRIDGE! Sonar! Mk-48s! They're Mk-48s!"

* * *

HMCS Victoria, Pacific Ocean, West of Seattle, Washington

"Control, torpedo room, both fish show connect and running."

"Take that you bastards," Darren whispered while *Victoria's* crew collectively held their breath.

* * *

Type 041 SSK, PLA Navy, West of Seattle, Washington

"Sir! I ..."

It was the only sound made within the *Yuan* class SSK in the second it took for both Mk-48 ADCAPs to tear into the Chinese submarine's hull. In the next half second, everyone in the control room and the space aft died instantly as the combined force of over one thousand pounds of high explosive tore through the enclosed area, blowing out their watertight hatches and causing the pressure hull to bulge out momentarily. In the next tenth of a second, the ocean did the rest, crushing the hull of the Chinese submarine in its powerful grip before releasing it to fall in pieces to the bottom.

* * *

HMCS Victoria, Pacific Ocean, West of Seattle, Washington

"Sir," Yokov announced from *HMCS Victoria's* sonar console. "She's gone. Not much breaking up sound. Just one deep whomp!"

"Sounds good to me petty officer," Rene replied. "Helm, get us upstairs, and fast, before someone up there decides to takes a shot at us."

"Upstairs fast, aye sir!" The master seaman at the helm echoed as he punched and turned the controls that sent *Victoria* shooting to the surface. Seconds later, the damaged submarine appeared in the middle of a geyser of water and acoustic tiles before settling down a few thousand feet from *HMCS Ottawa*. The frigate's commander ordered all engines stopped, as the Canadian submarine slowly approached.

A few minutes later, Commander Rene Bourgeois was standing on the bridge atop the submarine's sail looking over at the frigate slowly drifting closer. A yell from the warship's bridge through a megaphone carried easily across the short distance.

"Excuse me, you wouldn't have seen a Canadian submarine around here," Commander Parsons asked, unable to keep his laughter from interrupting the query. "We seem to be missing one."

"Sure," Rene hollered back through cupped hands. "Make fun of the guys who just saved your sorry ass! Damn skimmers aren't worth ..."

The rest was drowned out by *Ottawa's* crew pouring out on deck, cheering wildly.

* * *

MARPAC, CFB Esquimalt, British Columbia

In Admiral Ray Leger's office, the Prime Minister and Minister of Defence had been trying to plan out the next few days with the navy brass and CDS. General Kristoff Nikolev's position would now be Russia's official representative for the upcoming memorial service. The room was thick with emotion as the men quietly went about planning what they expected to be Canada's darkest day in decades.

"We all agree that the service must be held here?" the Prime Minister confirmed. "I want this to be about the navy; not a place for politicians to showboat."

Well, he thought, except for one. But this 'showboating' would be a heartfelt message directed at the men and women returning home. A maintenance airman at Comox had come up with an 'out of the box' solution as to how the Canadian leader would be able to give a message to the crews without the press being part of it.

"Yes, Prime Minister," Caroline replied. "I feel ..."

The door slamming open followed by a wild eyed petty officer caused them all to jump.

"It's *VICTORIA*! She's alive! She's fucking alive AND she killed the fucking Chinese boat!!!" His face sunk as he surveyed the room and realized what he had said.

"Fucking petty officers and their language!" Brent snorted, laughing at the man's shocked expression. "Can't teach 'em nothin' when it comes to manners!"

* * *

Entrance to the Strait of Juan de Fuca

Four days later, a small naval flotilla slowly sailed into the strait separating British Columbia and the State of Washington, on its way to Esquimalt Harbor. At the head of the row of warships, the low, dark shape of a submarine moved quietly through the water. Her special duty contingent lined up smartly along her casing fought to remain upright in the stiff breeze blowing in off the ocean, while at the same time, balancing themselves to compensate for *HMCS Victoria's* slight list.

She was followed by a pair of DND tugs carefully guiding *HMCS Vancouver*. The frigate's list had been corrected through counter flooding and her crew, smartly manning the rails, were a little embarrassed at the condition of their ship. Mostly however, they were just glad to be home.

HMCS Ottawa followed behind. Commander Nelson Parsons, sitting in his chair on the ship's bridge, was finally beginning to relax for the first time in days. "You know," he looked over to the master seaman at the ship's helm. "We may be a small navy, but today, the world knows we are a NAVY!"

His moment of pride was interrupted by a sailor showing up at his elbow.

"Sir? We just received a message from MARPAC to pipe one of the aviation frequencies through the address system."

"What? Sure. Go ahead." Probably Leger wanting to send a 'well done' to the crews, he thought, although why he would do it through an air traffic control frequency was beyond him.

A few moments later, a burst of static was followed by the voice of Canada's Prime Minister addressing the crews of all the ships in the small flotilla.

"Men and women of the Royal Canadian Navy, you have made us all proud on this day. I just wanted to give you my personal congratulations on a job well done and thank you for making me, and every other citizen of this great country, damn proud."

"SIR! Look at that!"

Parsons' eyes followed the sailor's finger to where she was pointing out to the starboard side of the ship. An RCAF Polaris was boring in straight for them at an impossibly low altitude.

"What the hell …"

The words had barely escaped his lips when the aircraft banked over hard and approached the ships from astern, slightly to starboard and only a few hundred feet above the water. Emblazoned down the length of the port fuselage, someone had painted 'Bravo Zulu' in huge white letters that stood out brightly against the aircraft's dull grey paint scheme. Banking over hard as the aircraft passed them, it came around and approached from well ahead of the ships this time, and all the men and women stared in awe at the words that had been hastily painted down the starboard side of the aircraft, 'We're proud of U'. Whoever had painted the message had run out of fuselage, so 'U' had been used instead of 'You'.

Lowering his binoculars, Commander Parsons smiled, having recognized the figure waving from the cockpit. The Prime Minister of Canada's face shone with the grin of a young boy who had just pulled off the world's greatest prank.

'Well I'll be damned," was all Nelson could manage.

A few minutes later, relaxing in a couple of the regular passenger seats aboard the CC-150 Polaris, the Prime Minister and Minister of National Defence quietly sipped their coffee as the plane headed back to CFB Comox. The adrenaline was slowly draining from their bodies and the thoughts of what could have transpired had finally hit them full bore, leaving both in quiet contemplation.

"Would you like to meet and address the crews this afternoon, Prime Minister?" Caroline asked, breaking the silence.

"No. No, today is their time. The crews ... the families ... the navy," he replied, quickly wiping away a tear. "We'll meet with them tomorrow."

"Yes, Prime Minister."

* * *

MARPAC, CFB Esquimalt, British Columbia

As a flypast overhead of Cyclones and Auroras shook the air, a gangway was dropped to *HMCS Victoria's* deck at A Jetty, causing a few more of her anechoic tiles to fall into the water. There were now more bare spots showing on her hull than tiles, and Rene had been shocked to see a huge section of the sail stove in from the torpedoes' blast.

Admirals Ray Leger and Brent O'Hanlon stepped smartly down the gangway to where Commander Rene Bourgeois stood at attention on *Victoria's* deck.

"Damn it, Rene!" Ray exclaimed, saluting the flag and surveying the submarine's dented sail, a look of pure anger on his face. "I hope you realize this will be coming out of your pay!" Then the admiral's face broke into a huge grin as he hugged the submarine's captain, causing the crew to cheer wildly. Any chance at decorum disintegrated at that point as a rush of men up the gangway to waiting family members nearly resulted in some of them going over the side.

After pleasantries had been exchanged along with another huge bear hug for Ray from O'Hanlon, the admirals made their way over to C Jetty where the two frigates were slowly making their way alongside. The crush of families almost prevented them from reaching the two ship's captains and Leger received more than a few kisses from wives relieved that their husbands had returned home safely.

Amongst the last to leave *Victoria* with the rest of the petty officers, Chief Darren Cole reached the end of the gangway to see Heather standing on the pier waiting for him. He stopped for a moment, remembering that other time, so long ago it seemed now, when *HMCS Corner Brook* had returned to Halifax, and she had been there waiting for him.

Walking up the brow towards her, he stopped a few feet away. "Heather ..."

She rushed over and hugged him so hard he couldn't breathe, and all the events that had taken place over the past month suddenly came crashing down as he collapsed within her arms. She felt him sob, and then his arms holding her tighter, and she knew he would be okay.

A few feet away, Cookie, Yelizaveta and Stu stood quietly, lost in their own memories of the past two weeks.

"Well, guys," Stu remarked, breaking the awkward silence, "It's good to be going back home in one piece for a change."

"And you'd better get going, ensign," O'Hanlon quipped, joining the trio. "There's a US Navy Herc up at Comox waiting to take you home. Something about a graduating class refusing to receive their Tridents until you got back. Those SEALs had more discipline back when ..." Catching himself, he stopped and simply smiled at Stu.

"What? They're letting you train those kids now?" Darren laughed, still holding Heather tightly to his side as they joined the small group. Giving the SEAL a quick hug, he took Stu's hand and added, "Keep in touch buddy."

The five friends embraced in a group hug, oblivious to the reunions and tears of joy being shed all around them up and down the pier.

* * *

Beijing, China

From behind his desk, China's political leader stared at the screen of the television hanging on the wall to his left. All the world's news channels were broadcasting the scene from the Royal Canadian Navy's west coast base, as talking heads fell over themselves spewing accolades for the country's military forces, covering everything from Vimy Ridge in World War I to a rumoured secret operation in France a couple of years earlier.

The man looked down. There would of course be a full denial from China of what happened. Later on, Canada would suddenly find trade with his country becoming much more open and profitable. In time, news of this event would probably trickle through his own huge population and the change that was slowly enveloping the country he loved would quicken its pace. Already there were talks of unions, and workers demanding better wages.

The cycle, he pondered, had come full circle. Once again China would be the economic power of the entire world. Europe, was already descending into a financial abyss from which it would take a century or longer to crawl from. North America, falling all over its leftist special interest groups, would not be far behind. With the success ahead for his country however, came the same fatal trap that had doomed them before, and would surely doom them again.

"We will become that which we hated the most," he said, turning from the television to his favourite view from the window.

* * *

MARPAC, CFB Esquimalt, British Columbia

A little after 2:00am the next morning, while Admiral Ray Leger was going through endless debriefs with his captains in the same gymnasium he had earlier addressed *HMCS Victoria's* families, Admiral Brent O'Hanlon and Russian Army Kristoff Nikolev were sitting in Ray's office. O'Hanlon in Ray's chair, which he had rolled around to the front of the desk across from Nikolev who was sitting comfortably cross-legged on the floor. They had been toasting the success of the recent mission and had just emptied one of two bottles of fifteen year old Glenfiddich Scotch that Admiral Leger kept in his cabinet for special occasions. Brent had placed the second bottle safely back in the cabinet to ensure they did not finish it off before Ray made it back to the office. A few things had been knocked over by the two men during their celebrating and some paperwork had fallen to the floor where it now lay in an unorganized pile.

"You know Kris," Brent began shakily, "if it weren't for you guys, Cole would be dead. You know that, don't you?"

"Well in that case," Kristoff replied, his voice slurring the words, "it is good thing you were not good sonar operator or maybe I would be dead and Cole would be too!"

"That is true old friend!" Brent replied as they shared a hearty laugh over the incident that had occurred decades earlier.

"Brent, there is something I mean to ask ..." Kristoff suddenly looked serious and all signs of his inebriation seemed to disappear.

"What is it, Kris?"

"Yelizaveta seems taken by this Cookie. He is a good man?"

"Kris," O'Hanlon began, leaning over and placing his hands on the Russian's shoulders. "You and I should be half the man he is. Besides, they have more in common than Liza realizes my old friend."

Brent went on to disclose a few of the non-classified operations he and Petty Officer Barnes had been on together during his command of one of the old 'O' boats. He could tell Kristoff was impressed. The general suddenly leapt to his feet and headed for the cabinet to grab the remaining bottle of Scotch.

"We must drink to their future!" he exclaimed, opening the bottle.

"No Kris! That's the …"

At that moment, the door swung open and Admiral Ray Leger gazed around in disbelief at his office, and then at the two officers, their uniforms dishevelled, jacket buttons undone.

"What the hell …"

"Ray!" Brent hollered! "We were just about to share a toast to you!"

The three men laughed and Brent stood up with his drink arm outstretched before falling to the floor alongside the Russian. Ray took the glass and poured his old friend a drink, correctly assuming that this was the last bottle of his expensive Scotch.

"You know another thing my old friend." Kristoff became serious again.

"Yes?" Brent replied, wondering why the room was suddenly spinning and just when he had lost the ability to hold his liquor.

"This Chinese admiral who planned this … Dai?" Kristoff began.

"What about him?"

"In old days in Russia … we would have taken care of him."

"Ahh," Brent replied. "I know Kris, but those days are long past."

* * *

Yulin Naval Base, China

Six months later, in his spacious office at the Yulin Naval Base in China, Admiral Quong Dai looked up and smiled as an aide entered his office followed by an attractive young woman. She wore a simple but fashionable black dress that hugged her body's natural curves. Her hands and lower arms were covered by expensive black silk gloves.

Quong had once again been enjoying life in the past few months after his plan to embarrass the Americans had failed miserably. His hide had thankfully been saved by the Canadian Navy removing any witnesses when they sank the Chinese boat that had taken part in the operation.

Fortunately, as always, his family connections had protected him and in a short time, things had returned to normal. The President had been warned by those who really held power in China, not to interfere with Dai's advancement through the PLA Navy. The leader of China's reward for obedience, would be to remain in power, for now.

"Admiral Dai," his aide announced smiling. "I would like to introduce you to your new personal assistant, Lien Shih."

The aide smiled discreetly. He and his compatriots knew what that position entailed, and although it had little to do with the PLA Navy, it was definitely 'personal'.

"Admiral." The striking young woman bowed respectfully.

Undressing the woman with his eyes, the admiral nodded. "I hope you will find working together to be interesting," he announced, smiling mischievously.

"Thank you, admiral," the woman replied, giving him an equally sly smile in return. "I am certain I will."

"You are dismissed," the admiral announced to his aide. "I am not to be interrupted for two hours."

"Of course, sir." The aide shut the door behind him as he left the office. Outside, he instructed the security officer at his desk that he was not to enter the room under any circumstances. They shared a joke about how the admiral obviously preferred his personal assistants to be young, as they walked down the corridor to the building's exit, knowing their services would not be needed for some time.

Looking up at the woman standing before him, the admiral started to rise and then sank back into his chair as she smiled and motioned for him to remain seated.

"You look tense my admiral. I think a massage will be a nice start for you," she purred, coming around the desk behind him, while seductively unbuttoning the top buttons of her blouse.

"Yes. That would be a nice start," the officer smiled, inhaling her scent as she stood behind his chair and began to massage his shoulders.

"I want to show you something I learned," she whispered softly into his ear as her hands slid to his chest.

"Oh yes, please."

"In Canada."

The admiral's face instantly became a mask of shock and fear. With one swift, practiced movement, Agent Lee grabbed his head and jerked it to one side, breaking the old man's neck before he could utter a sound, and looking into his eyes as he died.

The End